D1503077

PACKING
MRS. PHIPPS

PACKING MRS. PHIPPS

A Jo Jacuzzo Mystery

ANNE SEALE

alyson books
los angeles

ALL CHARACTERS IN THIS BOOK ARE FICTITIOUS. ANY RESEMBLANCE TO REAL INDIVIDUALS—EITHER LIVING OR DEAD—IS STRICTLY COINCIDENTAL.

© 2004 BY ANNE SEALE. ALL RIGHTS RESERVED.

MANUFACTURED IN THE UNITED STATES OF AMERICA.

THIS TRADE PAPERBACK ORIGINAL IS PUBLISHED BY ALYSON PUBLICATIONS,
P.O. BOX 4371, LOS ANGELES, CALIFORNIA 90078-4371.
DISTRIBUTION IN THE UNITED KINGDOM BY TURNAROUND PUBLISHER SERVICES LTD.,
UNIT 3, OLYMPIA TRADING ESTATE, COBURG ROAD, WOOD GREEN,
LONDON N22 6TZ ENGLAND.

ISBN: 0-7394-5421-8

CREDITS
• COVER PHOTOGRAPHY BY JASON DEWEY.
• COVER DESIGN BY MATT SAMS.

for KTG and Raff

1

If I had known Charity was going to die on me, I'd have eaten someplace else. Not that I had many choices in Parsee, Georgia.

I didn't have any choice at all, when you came right down to it. The Parsee Home-Cook Diner was the only restaurant within walking distance of Rip's Garage, where my Toyota pickup had just been towed.

Since it was almost noon, Rip strongly suggested I go have a bite while he finished a tire rotation he was in the middle of. I figured he didn't like people hanging around while he worked, especially female people. I thought about giving him an argument, but I was pretty hungry.

I fetched my backpack from the cab and trudged down the road in the hot Southern sun, grumbling all the way. Why couldn't this have happened back in Buffalo, where my cousin was an auto mechanic? He gave special rates to family, which would have been great since I didn't have a steady job.

I used to have a steady job. For six years, give or take a month, I worked at the Box Elder Nursing Home as a certified nurse's assistant. I liked the patients and my coworkers, but the wages were pitiful and there were too many bosses. So last summer I registered with an agency that provides care to people in their own homes. The salary wasn't much different, but no one was looking over my shoulder saying, "Hmm…"

The best part about it was being able to work with one client at a time. I got to really know the person, form a relationship. It was kind of like serial monogamy, much more fulfilling than the assembly line over at the nursing home.

If I'd stuck with Box Elder, though, I'd still have a job. Things disappeared there, sure, but with so many employees, they rarely settled on a suspect. Since I was the only employee in the Ralph Goddard household at the time of the theft, it was easy to settle on a suspect. Me.

I'd been with the Goddards since November. They lived in one of those big ranch houses up in Niagara County where the lawns eat better than some kids in this country do. Mr. Goddard had suffered a serious stroke, and his whole left side was paralyzed. Mrs. Goddard was a tiny woman, unequal to the task of caring for her husband, so their daughter called the Can-Care Agency, and they gave me the assignment. They often assigned the men to me. I was wiry but strong.

I worked at the Goddards' place from 7 to 3, Monday through Friday. My duties were to bathe and dress Mr. Goddard, take him to the john, and try to coax him into exercising. I fixed the noon meal for him and his wife and did the dishes and laundry while he napped or watched TV. Sometimes Mrs. Goddard read to him from seed catalogs or the newspaper. They were avid gardeners. For Christmas I bought them a potted azalea, and we were looking forward to when the weather would be warm enough to plant it outside.

The only problem with the job was the Goddards' devoted daughter, Dora Farr. She came over every day on her lunch hour and showed up again shortly before I left. She made supper for her parents and stayed until they were down for the night. She took care of them on weekends too. I knew it was hard on her, and I tried to do as much as I could to lighten her load, but did she appreciate it? No. She gave me nothing but grief. She was always telling me I didn't know how to cook; I folded laundry wrong; I put the toilet paper roll on backwards. She even told me I didn't know how to make a bed. I'd taken a *course* in bed-making, for cripes sake.

One day she walked in as I was serving her parents lunch. "What's that?" she demanded, pointing her nose like a beagle fixed on a bug.

"Tuna-noodle casserole," I told her.

She marched over to the desk for the care plan. Poking it in my face, she pointed to the line where she'd written "tuna" in a long list of foods Mr. Goddard didn't care for. Meanwhile, Mr. Goddard was gobbling up the casserole like it was going out of style. I'm surprised Mrs. Farr didn't reach over and snatch the fork out of his mouth.

Truth is, she was technically right. I should have checked the care plan before serving him tuna. Now, if he had been *allergic* to it, I would have known—I memorized allergies even before I met a client. But I'd found a can of tuna in their cupboard and I served it—mea culpa, Mrs. Farr.

Mrs. Goddard apologized to me after her daughter had left and Mr. Goddard was down for a nap. "I knew Ralph didn't care for tuna," she said. "I should have reminded you."

"That's okay," I said. "He ate it."

"He ate it at the nursing home too. Sometimes our tastes change as we age. I read that somewhere."

"How did he like Box Elder?" I asked. He'd been there for a couple of weeks while they evaluated his potential for rehab.

"He hated it. If I wasn't there, he wouldn't eat at all. I don't know what he's going to do when Dora tells him he's going back."

"He's going back to Box Elder?" It was the first I'd heard of it.

"Dora put him on the waiting list. She says it's too much for her to take care of him, and we can't afford to hire a second aide."

"The nursing home isn't cheap either."

"I know, but once he's settled in she's going to sell our house and use the proceeds to pay for it."

"What's she going to do with *you*?"

"I'm going to go live with her and Jim in their condo."

"You are?" I screeched. I said it again, trying not to make it sound like capital punishment. "You are? How do you feel about that?"

"Well, it won't be like having my own home. I'll miss my garden. And I suppose if I get sick or something, I'll end up in the nursing home too."

"Does Mrs. Farr have power of attorney for you and your husband?"

"Yes. There was so much paperwork with the medical bills and all, I couldn't handle it—Ralph used to take care of all that. Giving Dora power of attorney seemed right at the time—but between the two of us, Jo, I'm sorry now. It's scary, not being in charge of your own money. We've lost control of our lives." Her bottom lip quivered, and her eyes filled with tears.

"Have you told your daughter how you feel?" I asked.

"Yes, but you know Dora."

"Why don't you call your lawyer?" I said. "Maybe you could void the power of attorney." I was treading on thin ice, saying this. If Mrs. Farr got wind of it, I'd be out of a job for sure.

"I don't think that would work, Jo. He's Dora's lawyer too. I'm sure he'll do what *she* wants."

"There are other lawyers."

"I couldn't do that. There must be another way."

"How about calling the Adult Protection Program?" I asked her. "They deal with all kinds of abuse, including financial. I can get you the number if you like."

"Oh dear, no. I definitely couldn't do *that*. Excuse me, Jo, I think I'll lie down for a while." She grabbed a box of tissues from the counter and hurried from the room.

As I loaded the dishwasher, I silently railed against people who made decisions for their elders without taking into consideration what *they* wanted. And if the elders dared give their opinions, they were ignored. I'd seen it all too often.

It wasn't that I was against nursing homes. They filled a need, and some people thrived there. And as nursing homes go, Box Elder was one of the better ones. But when push came to shove, the people who lived there were at the mercy of their families, the staff, and the bottom line.

One of the patients once told me that after giving up her house and belongings and residing in a double room with a series of strangers for the rest of her life, she figured she'd be able to skip purgatory altogether.

Some days, Mrs. Farr's husband, Jim, who was retired, would come by for a few hours. I figured his wife had sent him to spy on me, but the truth was he wasn't bad to have around. He'd chat with his father-in-law—which wasn't easy since Mr. Goddard was hard to understand—or he'd watch a movie with him. Sometimes they'd play chess, which Mr. Goddard loved. I thought maybe I'd learn how to play so I could give him a game when Mr. Farr wasn't there. Before I got around to it, though, everything fell apart.

It happened on a snowy Saturday in late March, my day

off. It seems Mrs. Farr was taking care of her parents as usual and went to get something from a safe in their bedroom closet. The safe was empty, so she called the cops.

They came to get me at home. I was outside, shoveling snow. They didn't even give me a chance to go in and tell Mom I was leaving; they just hauled me off. I found out later that one of the policemen waited until I was gone, then went inside the house and presented Mom with a search warrant. When I heard that, I was sorry I hadn't tidied up my room. There'd been dust all over. Mom must have been mortified.

At the station, two officers faced me across a table and asked a bunch of questions. Since I hadn't committed the crime, I was calm, cool, and collected, right? Wrong. It felt like the time I was going through the turnstile at the library and the alarm went off. It was the librarian's fault for not desensitizing the book, but I still felt guilty, not to mention embarrassed.

After listening to me stammer for a couple of hours, the officers must have decided either that I was innocent or that I wasn't going to tell them if I wasn't. Anyway, they let me call Mom to come get me. I apologized to her for the whole mess, and when I got home I went up to lie on my bed and mull it over. Every day I'd seen that safe sitting on the Goddards' closet floor when I'd gone in there fetching and putting away clothes. I hadn't paid much attention to it, though—it was none of my business.

In the course of questioning, the policemen had let on that what had been stolen were negotiable securities, jewelry, and quite a bit of cash. If I was going to steal something, it wouldn't be negotiable securities—I wasn't even sure what negotiable securities were. It wouldn't be jewelry either, since I never wore any but my sports watch. And I would never, never touch anybody's cash. If I'd been the stealing kind, I would've taken the coin collection the Goddards kept in a file cabinet in their study. Mr. Goddard asked me to get it out for him once in a while. When he found out I was interested, he showed me the whole collection. He had a 1916-D Mercury dime. I'd been wanting one of those for a long time.

It occurred to me I should have asked the cops if the coin collection was missing too, but I decided it was better to let well enough alone.

By Monday morning the Goddards had quit the Can-Care Agency and the Can-Care Agency had quit me, so to speak, citing their insurance company as bad guy.

During the next couple of days, I had an anxiety attack every time the phone rang—I was afraid it was the police wanting me to come down for another go-around. I kept telling myself there wasn't any way they could prove I was guilty, since I wasn't. But I wasn't born yesterday, either. I watched TV, I read the newspapers. Sometimes innocent people served several years or even died in prison before they were cleared by DNA evidence or another person's confession. As one of the attorneys on *Law and Order* said, it's not a perfect system.

The first thing on my agenda was to get another job, and I figured that might be a problem. Getting canned by the Can-Care Agency wouldn't look good on my résumé.

"Go back to Box Elder," Mom told me.

"I don't want to go back to Box Elder." I said. "Anyway, I called. They said they don't have any openings, which is a crock of you-know-what—they *always* have openings. So that means the news about me must have got around, and probably no other facility or agency in the area will hire me either."

"Their loss," said Rose, who lived with Mom and me.

Actually, it was me that lived with Mom and Rose. They'd met at work about 15 years ago and, to their mutual surprise, fallen madly in love. Rose moved in a few months later, after they'd gotten up the nerve to tell me about their situation. The house was now in both their names, and they split the mortgage and utility bills. I bought most of the groceries and did all the yard work. Also, when anything needed fixing, they paid for the parts and I performed the labor—which was considerable in a frame house built in 1940.

This arrangement allowed me to enjoy a middle-class life on starvation wages. I had a nice computer and a shelf full of games, my own TV and DVD player, and I was able to support the love of my life, a completely paid-for '97 Toyota pickup. In addition, I had a thousand and change stashed in the bank toward my future, which was a lucky thing because my future wasn't looking too good at the moment.

I called all the facilities and agencies within commuting distance and got a few appointments for job interviews. Since I hadn't been convicted, I didn't have to list my brush with the law on their employment forms. However, some loose lip at the Box Elder Nursing Home or Can-Care Agency—both of which I had to list as work experience to justify my salary requirement— must have been sharing some juicy bits of information, because I only got two calls back. Unfortunately they were both from places I would never work—I'd decided that when I was there for the interviews. The patients sitting in the hallway chairs looked more glum than I did.

Each day I was without a job my spirits spiraled further downward, until I was wallowing in a puddle of self-pity. I stayed in my room, sprawled on my bed watching game shows and sad movies. When I got sick of that, I played computer games, but only the ones I was sure I could win. I popped down to the kitchen every morning to raid the refrigerator after Mom and

Rose went off to their jobs at Mary Talbert High School. Rose taught Spanish, and Mom was the principal's secretary. They'd been there forever. For me, high school had been the pits—I couldn't get away with anything.

One morning when I'd been jobless for three weeks or so, I emerged from my room at 9:30 and almost tripped over the *Buffalo News* folded open to the classifieds. I took it with me to the kitchen and put it aside while I ate leftover chicken wings and drank my daily cup of coffee. Then I slid the paper in front of me and spent the rest of the morning rejecting each ad in turn. *Dental hygienist:* couldn't do. *Financial adviser:* couldn't do. *Bartender:* wouldn't do—my father was a mean drunk, probably still is. *Bookkeeper:* couldn't do. *Hairstylist:* couldn't do, wouldn't do. The only job that intrigued me was *Maintenance person,* but the ads demanded a working knowledge of something called HVAC. Whatever happened to plain old *janitor*? I went back to bed.

When my mother came home, she cooked up a batch of tapioca pudding, the definitive comfort dish in our family. She brought a bowl up to my room and sat on the edge of my bed. I could see there was something on her mind. I ate slowly, rolling the warm gluey balls around my mouth to squeeze out the last bit of flavor.

She tried to wait until I was done, but she couldn't. "So, Jo," she said.

I knew I was in for a deep discussion. She'd said "So, Jo" when explaining what Kotex was for and before telling me that Daddy had left us, among other depressing things. (Having Daddy leave was depressing only because we didn't leave him first.)

"So, Mom," I said in resignation.

"You need a job."

Duh. "Look, I went through the newspaper you left outside my door, but I didn't see a thing. The problem is, there isn't anything I'm trained to do except what I'm trained to do. And with my reputation as a successful thief, I'll never get another job doing it."

"Of course you will, honey. In the meantime, Rose and I think you should sue somebody, but we're not sure who, so that's neither here nor there."

"I don't want to sue anybody." That wasn't true. I'd considered it. It was the American way. At the moment, however, all I wanted to do was put this sorry mess behind me. "So what *is* here or there, Mom?"

"I've found a job for you. It's only temporary, but by the time you get back they'll have caught the real culprit and you can get on with your life. *Then* you can sue somebody."

"By the time I get back from where?"

"Florida."

My line of defense, always mobilized when talking with Mom, eased back a bit. It had been a warm winter, which probably meant it was going to be a lousy spring. I wouldn't mind getting out of Buffalo for a while. "Doing what?"

"Do you remember Mrs. Phipps?"

I should have known Mom wouldn't have said "So, Jo" if she was bringing me *good* news. Gerald Phipps was Mom's boss, the high school principal. Mrs. Phipps was his mother.

I remembered Elinor Phipps very well. When I was 13, my mother got me a job cutting her lawn once a week. Every Saturday morning, Mrs. Phipps followed me around her half-acre watching for spots I'd missed, pointing out trees and bushes as if I were blind, yelling at me when I got too close to her flower beds. That fall was the only time in my life I was glad to see school start.

"Uh-uh. I'm not working for Mrs. Phipps again. I'll starve first." I shoveled in the last of the pudding.

"Gerald says he'll pay you a thousand dollars plus all your expenses."

It was sure better than the seven dollars I'd gotten for mowing her lawn. Against my better judgment, I asked, "What would I have to do?"

"Mrs. Phipps has a winter home in Florida, near Tampa. Every spring she drives up here to stay with Gerald for the summer. She's getting old, though, and a little vague."

I figured vague might be an improvement. "I'll bet he wants me to bring her back to Buffalo," I said. "There's no way I'm driving all that way with Mrs. Phipps in the car." *Unless she's in the trunk,* I added silently.

"You won't have to drive her. All you have to do is get yourself to Florida, help her pack and close up her house, and put her on a plane. After that, you can do anything you want before coming back. You could visit Universal Studios."

Forget Universal Studios. I'd go to the beach. A picture came into focus—me, Jo Jacuzzo, lying on a towel in the warm sun, lulled by the sound of gentle waves lapping at a shoreline of white powder sand. Then I remembered the warnings I'd heard about getting too much sun and added a beach umbrella to the picture.

I tried to wipe the rapture off my face, but it was too late. As a clincher, Mom added, "Gerald told me he would be so relieved to know his mother is being taken care of by someone he can trust."

Trust? I'd been feeling very untrustworthy lately, even though I'd done nothing to earn it. If Gerald Phipps still trusted me, I owed him the benefit of that trust. The thousand dollars had nothing to do with it. "Okay," I told her.

"Great," said Mom. "On the way, I want you to drop off a case of Weber's Horseradish Mustard to your great-uncle Dom in Cincinnati. And you can do a little work on his house while you're there."

"Mom, I don't think Cincinnati is on the way to Tampa."

"That's okay. I got you a TripTik."

I'd been had.

2

Before leaving town, I did my taxes, which was depressing enough even before I found out I wasn't getting anything back. It occurred to me that if I didn't find a job, my income this year might be so low I wouldn't even have to file. The thought didn't cheer me up.

Mr. Phipps gave me a check for $300 for anticipated traveling expenses. I bought traveler's checks with it and took another $300 out of my savings account for fun in the sun. It all went into a zippered pocket in my backpack, except for $80 in 20s that I put in my wallet.

I spread all my clothes on the bed and selected the ones that were in the best condition. Then I realized they were in the best condition because I hated them, so I put them back and ended up with the things I wore all the time—two pairs of Levi's, a pair of cutoffs, seven T-shirts in various shades of red, two tank tops, a Bills sweatshirt, and seven pair each Jockey for Her underwear and white crew socks. I took out an outfit to wear on the first day, then rolled up the rest and stuck them in my backpack.

Early Friday morning, April 12, I set off for Tampa, Florida, via Cincinnati, Ohio, singing at the top of my voice, "Baby's on the town again" with a tape of my favorite band of all time, the sadly defunct Ranch Romance.

Lying next to me on the seat were the backpack and two plastic bags. One of the bags contained a half-dozen PowerBars to keep my energy up, and the other was full of maps and tour books Mom got from Triple A. I hadn't brought the TripTik with me on principle—I'd stuck it on the closet shelf under the sweaters Great-aunt Concetta knitted for me every Christmas and I wouldn't wear to wash the dog, if we had a dog, which we didn't because Rose was allergic.

I had plenty of time to get there. Mrs. Phipps wasn't expecting me to appear on her doorstep until the following weekend. I figured I'd spend a day or two in Cincinnati working at Uncle Dom's house and still have time to dawdle. When I hit good weather, I intended to take the back roads and see more of the south than the manicured edges of the interstates.

Another thing I wanted to do on the way was have a look at the beach at Destin, a town on the Florida panhandle. One of the nurses at Box Elder had gone there on her honeymoon and couldn't say enough good things about it. I was planning to stay a few days if I could find a cheap-enough motel.

The first mishap of my trip came when I was south of Buffalo, only a few miles from home. It was rush hour, and the lines at the tollbooths for Interstate 90 were long. I pulled behind a dump truck over at the left. Immediately the truck's backup lights came on, and he started moving toward me. I laid on my horn and he braked, but it was too late—a bar on the truck hit the front of my pickup and cracked my grill.

The driver got out and was all apologies. He said he'd spotted a shorter line and didn't see me behind him. While he called the police on his cell phone, I stood in back of my wounded Toyota and waved my arms wildly so other vehicles wouldn't get in line behind us. For my trouble, I received every insulting gesture I'd ever seen and a few I hadn't.

A New York State trooper eventually arrived. He had us pull over to the side of the road, which took a lot of traffic-directing on his part. Funny, I didn't see one driver flip *him* the bird. He took down our names and license numbers, and each of us gave our version of the accident while he drew up some little diagrams. Then he wrote the dump truck driver a ticket.

The Toyota seemed to be running okay, so I continued on my way, but I wasn't singing anymore.

It was early evening when I finally got to Cincinnati, and then I had to find Uncle Dom's house—I hadn't been there since I was 10. Mom had written the directions on the back of a supermarket tape with a dull pencil, and I could hardly see them. Every time I made a turn, I had to pull over and decipher my next move. Also, her tiny map ran off the bottom of the tape and continued on the other side above THANK YOU FOR SHOPPING AT TOPS.

When I finally got to his house, Uncle Dom wasn't there, so I retraced my path to a McDonald's to use the bathroom and get a burger. Then I returned and sat on Uncle Dom's stoop in the dark, discussing him with the neighborhood kids. They told me he had a girlfriend who lived in the Dahlia Apartments and he spent most of his time over there. *Wait till I tell Mom!*

They also said he was a prime suspect in several local cat disappearances.

The best bit, however, was that he pushed an evangelist off his porch last year and had to do community service. That's my family, heathenish to a fault.

Uncle Dom finally came home at 8:30. "I didn't think you'd

be here yet," he said. He looked a great deal older than I remembered from his last visit to Buffalo. He still had a lot of hair, but it was snowy-white. His teeth were snowy-white too. Either he'd gotten dentures or he'd been using those little strips.

After we went inside to the kitchen, I asked about his girl-friend, but he denied having one. Then he handed me a cottage cheese carton full of lasagna and a wax-paper-wrapped cannoli he'd brought home with him.

As I ate, he said, "Where's my mustard?"

"Behind the seat of the truck. I'll get it when I'm done."

"I don't know what's wrong with the state of Ohio, they can't make a decent mustard," he said. "By the way, you can't smoke in the house."

"I don't smoke," I said.

"Me neither. I gave it up six months ago. Why's your hair so short? You look like a boy."

"I like it this way. It's comfortable."

"No wonder you're not married. How old are you now?"

"Twenty-seven."

"No kidding?" he said. "I remember when you were crapping your pants." Thanks for sharing, Uncle Dom.

We went to bed early so we could get all the work done on the house tomorrow and I could be on my merry way. I didn't sleep much, though. His foldout sofa had a horizontal bar under the thin mattress that hit me right in the shoulder blades. Also, the sofa—the whole room, in fact—smelled like six-month-old cigarette smoke.

The only thing Uncle Dom had in the house for breakfast was All-Bran, so I had to make a morning run for a McMuffin. When I got back, he had the ladder extended against the house. Turned out what he wanted me to do was the second-story work. He didn't trust his knees to climb anymore, he said. Last year he'd almost fallen.

The first thing I did was climb on the roof, make sure the shingles were nice and tight, and lop off any tree branches that were threatening them. Next I cleaned decaying leaves and other slimy stuff out of the rain gutters. Then Uncle Dom brought out a bottle of Windex and a six-pack of paper towels and had me clean the exteriors of the upstairs windows. This job was complicated by the fact that there were zillions of birdhouses tacked next to and hanging in front of every one of them, which may have explained the cat disappearances. My final and yuckiest job was to go around and clean out the birdhouses.

By the time I finished it was almost dark, and I was filthy and exhausted. When I got out of the shower, a woman with teased gray hair and a couple of chins was in the kitchen fixing dinner. Uncle Dom introduced her as Mrs. Cucchi from Meals on Wheels. I'd never heard of anybody from Meals on Wheels who cooked in your kitchen and stayed to eat, but I didn't make waves. Her pot roast was out of this world.

That night I slept like a baby, horizontal bar and all.

I meant to take off early Sunday morning, but it didn't work out that way. I didn't wake up until after 9, and that was only because Meals on Wheels was banging around the kitchen, cooking up a big breakfast of eggs, sausage, and home fries. After I ate, I remembered my manners and offered to do the dishes. I thought they'd say, "No, don't bother, Jo. You just be on your way." Instead they reached for their jackets and left, telling me to lock the door after myself.

I finally hit the road at 10:30. Driving wasn't as much fun as it had been on Friday because I was achy from Saturday's climbing and reaching. By the time I hit Chattanooga, I was ready to stop. I found a nondescript motel just off the highway that advertised HBO. After downing a fried chicken dinner at the attached restaurant, I watched three bad movies, one right after the other. I'd seen two of them before.

The next morning, I crossed into the state of Georgia. The day was sunny and warm. I told myself it was time to get off the interstate and have a look at the hinterlands. First chance I got, I exited and cruised down a series of country roads, using the compass to keep me in a general southerly direction. I amused myself by singing songs from *Annie*. When I was in the third grade, it was our school musical. Our teacher, Mrs. Shoemaker, was bound and determined that her class was going to get all the best parts, so we spent a couple of hours a day rehearsing the songs. We probably should have been learning the times tables—I still have to count on my fingers for anything past eight times eight. I didn't get a part in *Annie* either.

In the middle of "It's the Hard-Knock Life," I noticed I had an accompaniment, a clanking noise. I pulled over and took a gander under the hood—I knew my way around an engine. Everything looked fine, so I got in and took off, figuring I'd have it looked at in the next town. Immediately the clanking grew louder.

I pulled over and raised the hood again. The belts were intact. I checked the oil and the radiator. No problem there. Unfortunately, except for filling the window-washing-fluid reservoir, that was as far around an engine as I knew my way. I slammed the hood and got back in.

In case it had been a temporary condition, I turned the key; a few strands of black smoke drifted up around the hood. It didn't look good.

I was sorry I hadn't taken Rose up on her offer to lend me the cell phone she carried in case some failing student decided to get even. I'd told her no thanks, because if she'd got beaten up or worse while I was off traveling with her phone, I'd have felt terrible.

Anyway, if I'd had a phone and called Triple A, they'd have asked where I was, and I'd have had to say, "I'm on some two-lane road in Georgia that runs roughly north and south. There's a crop of something green in the fields on both sides as far as I can see. And I think the last town I went through started with D." They'd probably have canceled Mom's membership on the spot.

Several cars went by before it occurred to me that I should be flagging them down. Several more ignored my flagging, and finally an ancient Thunderbird convertible pulled over. The driver had tucked her gray hair under a silky scarf, but she could have saved herself the trouble. She pushed a shock of it out of her face and said, "Out of gas?"

"No, I think it's my engine or something. Do you have a cell phone? By the way, where am I?"

"You're between Dimock and Parsee. My house is just a few miles up. Why don't you come use the phone and have a piece of pie while you wait."

I'd have been a fool to turn it down. I pulled my backpack from the Toyota, locked up, and got in the Thunderbird. As the woman drove, she chatted away about cars and car trouble and somehow worked in her grandchildren. She thrust her hand in the purse on the seat between us, drew out a billfold, and handed it to me. "The first photo is little Emily," she said, "and the next ones are the boys, but they're a lot bigger now."

Don't give me your billfold, I wanted to tell her. *You don't know me—I might be a thief. Just ask the Goddards.*

The pie turned out to be rhubarb, not one of my favorites, so I told her just a small slice. Triple A took Mom's card number without argument and promised to send a tow truck to get me so I could guide it to the Toyota. After an hour and a half, during which I learned way too much about Emily and the boys, all that actually happened.

Bobby the tow-truck driver poked around the Toyota's engine for a few minutes and said it didn't look like a quick fix.

"New York?" he said as he attached great chains to its underside. "Did you see them buildings hit?"

"No, thank goodness. I live in Buffalo."

'Huh," he said, obviously unimpressed.

"It's the second-largest city in the state," I told him.

"You don't say. Now, do you want to go north to Dimock or south to Parsee?"

"What would you recommend?" I asked.

"Well, Parsee's a little farther, but there's a place there called Rip's Garage, and Rip's the best mechanic around. If I had a broken-down vehicle, that's where I'd want to take it."

I asked if there was a Toyota dealer in either town.

"Down here we buy American," Bobby said, and ended the conversation by switching on an earsplitting motor that slowly dragged the Toyota up the ramp to his truck bed. When peace was restored, I told him Parsee would be fine. It was in the right direction, at least. If there was one thing I hated, it was backtracking.

Rip's Garage was a one-bay affair, and the one bay was full. Rip came out as my truck was being lowered to the ground. He was the dirtiest man I'd ever seen. His clothes were thick with grime and grease, and so was his skin where it wasn't covered— and, for all I knew, even where it was covered. If I was Mrs. Rip, I wouldn't let him in the house.

When all four wheels were on the ground, he raised the Toyota's hood and eyeballed the innards. He said he was about finished with a rotation, so why didn't I go get myself some lunch at the Parsee Home-Cook Diner down the road, and by the time I got back we'd know what we were dealing with. The slice of pie had worn off, so I thanked Bobby, who was sitting in the shade drinking a beer, and took off walking.

3

The diner was one of those retro jobs with little jukeboxes in every booth, the kind of place that had so much chrome, you could watch yourself eat at three different angles.

The dozen or so booths were all occupied, and the only empty stool at the U-shaped counter was between two burly guys. I hate eating at counters, but I took the stool anyway, careful to keep my elbows in as I stowed the backpack between my feet.

When the waitress came, I ordered the meatloaf special because that's what the guy on my left was having and it looked pretty good. While I waited, I drank my ice water and kept an eye on the bank of booths. If one became vacant, I intended to move.

The guy on my right finished his lunch and left. Almost immediately a young woman sat down and took the menu from its place between the ketchup and the napkin holder. She had short blond hair that curled around her ears, and she was wearing lots of eye makeup. She looked like Cameron Diaz but with more curves.

She glanced up from studying the menu and caught me staring. In a gentle drawl she said, "So what's good here?"

I quickly looked away. In certain situations I'm terribly shy. I do fine with people I have to do business with and people I'm related to. But I don't do well with people of my own generation, especially those who look like Cameron Diaz. The waitress came with her water, and she ordered a salad with a lemon wedge and a Diet Coke.

The people in a nearby booth suddenly got up and left. I watched the waitress clear the table, planning to jump over there the minute she was finished. Then I heard my mother say. *Jo, don't you think you should speak to this young woman before you leave? She spoke to you. It's only polite.* I was trying to think of something that would tell her hello and goodbye in the same breath when a middle-aged couple came in and started moving toward my booth.

Forget polite. I was reaching for my backpack when my food arrived.

I moved my eyeballs to the right. My neighbor was checking out my plate. "You could have recommended the meatloaf," she said.

"Well, I've never had it before," I said. "It might not be any good. It might be terrible." I stared at the meatloaf. It didn't look half as tasty as the slice on the next guy's plate.

"Go ahead, eat," she said. "It's going to get cold."

I picked up my fork and took a bite. It wasn't too bad, actually. Not as good as Mom's, but nothing ever is.

"I'm Charity."

I swallowed a badly chewed mouthful. "What?"

"Charity. Charity Redmun. It's my name. What's yours?"

"Jo."

"Nice to meet you, Jo. Is that Jo as in Josephine?"

"It's JoDell, but I like Jo."

"I do too. It's short and sweet. There's no good nickname for Charity. My little brother use to call me Cha-Cha."

"Really?" I wished she'd talk to somebody else.

As if reading my mind, she said, "Excuse me a minute, Jo," and introduced herself to the fellow on her other side. He was more than happy to chat, and his voice was so loud, I couldn't help but hear. He told her his name was Jeff and he lived in Mississippi. He was in Parsee for a few weeks installing a new computer system in the high school. And by the way, he was staying at the Georgia's Best Motel, room 12A, if she felt like stopping by.

She told him she wouldn't be in town that long and turned back to me. "Are you from around here, Jo?"

"No. I live in Buffalo, New York."

"Oh, brrr!"

"The summers are great," I said. From a lifetime of hearing people trash the Buffalo weather, I'd become a wee bit defensive. Okay, it was cold and snowy a lot of the time, but if you didn't have to live there, leave it alone.

"I'm from Charleston, South Carolina," she said. "Have you ever been there?"

"No."

"You should visit sometime. It's a wonderful place, very historic." Her salad finally came and she started eating. I hoped she'd lost interest in me, but no such luck. After a few bites she leaned forward, looked me full in the face, and said, "Have you ever driven a motor home?"

"No."

"I'm driving one for the first time, and I'm scared to death. I don't know what to do."

"If you're scared to drive it, why don't you get rid of it?" I scooped some mashed potatoes into my mouth. Now that we had something to talk about besides me, I relaxed a bit.

"That's what I'm doing, I'm getting rid of it. I'm taking it to my brother in Tucson, but I'm never going to make it. I can't steer it, it's all over the road. I'm so scared."

"What are you going to do?" I asked.

"I don't know. I can't get back on that interstate, I know that much. But if I don't, I won't make it on time. What do *you* think I should do?"

"Tell your brother to come get it." I thought it was a brilliant suggestion. When Charity didn't drawl, "Why didn't I think of that?" I glanced over. She had laid her fork down and was staring at the pepper shaker with tears rolling down her cheeks.

I threw my napkin on the counter. The conversation was giving me indigestion. "Good luck," I told her. I picked up my check and slid a tip under the plate.

"Wait, Jo! I didn't mean to get emotional. Don't go, please. Finish your meal." She blew her nose on a paper napkin. "It's just that I needed to talk to somebody. You looked kind."

"I *am* kind! But I can't help you. I have my own problems. My truck was just towed to the garage down the road. They're checking it now to see what's wrong."

"Oh, I'm so sorry. I hope it's not an expensive repair."

"I hope so too," I said, "especially since I'm between jobs."

Charity brightened. "You're not working?"

"Temporarily. I'll find something soon."

"Jo, would you be interested in driving me and the motor home to Arizona? I'll pay you."

"Why do you think I can drive it if you can't?"

"You just said you drive a truck."

"It's a small pickup," I told her.

"You could try."

"I really can't. I have a commitment."

"Couldn't you postpone it?" she pleaded. "As I said, I'll pay you. How about $500 and a plane ticket?"

"Thanks, but—"

"You'll be back in Parsee by Friday afternoon at the latest."

"Look, Charity, I really can't. I'm sorry."

"That's okay." She slumped. "I'll find somebody. I have to."
She looked like Eeyore surveying his popped balloon.

"I've got an idea," I said. "Why don't you come over to the
garage where my truck's being looked at? Maybe the owner
knows somebody local who'd like to make a few bucks."

"Thank you, Jo. I'll do that. Will you drive the motor home
there for me? I'm just not ready to get behind the wheel again."

"Sure." No harm in that. I wasn't looking forward to the swel-
tering walk back anyway.

She led me to a dirt lot at the side of the building. Several
cars and pickups and two motor homes were parked there in
no organized fashion. One of the motor homes had WELLAWAY
printed on its side. It was the size of an overgrown panel truck
and would've been a cinch to drive. It had New York license
plates, however, so I figured it wasn't Charity's. I was right. She
was heading for the one that was big as a Greyhound bus. The
logo BYVISTA was scripted in burnished gold on its fiberglass
side, next to an airbrushed canyon glowing peachy-cream in
the sunset.

I was even more impressed by what was attached to its rear—
a late-model fire-engine-red tricked-out Ranger Supercab. I was
glad the Toyota wasn't there to see my lascivious grin.

Charity pointed her key ring at the monster RV. It went
be-e-ep, and a set of steps under the door on its broad side silently
slid forward. I followed her up and in.

The inside of the ByVista seemed even bigger than the outside.
Charity took me on a tour, starting with the bedroom in the back.
Incredibly, it had a queen-size bed, two closets, a bank of drawers,
and even a little desk. The adjoining tile bathroom had a glass-
doored shower, a sink in an elegant vanity, and a marine toilet.

Next there was a neat little kitchen with sink, stove, refrigerator, microwave, cupboards, and a stacked washer and dryer. A table and chairs sat across the aisle, in front of a big window.

The living room was next, with a matching sofa and recliner arranged around a large-screen TV. The cockpit was part of the living area too, with its oversize swiveling buckets. Charity gestured at the driver's seat, saying, "Ta-da."

I sat and adjusted levers until I was comfortable. It felt good to know that, if nothing else, I had the seat mastered. I turned my attention to the confusing array of gauges, buttons, and knobs that made up the instrument panel. Other than the usual speedometer, odometer, and such, the only thing I recognized was a built-in citizens band and a radio with a CD player.

Charity handed me a key. I inserted it and turned, and the engine roared into life. I put it in reverse and looked up to check the rearview mirror, but there wasn't one. There were big side mirrors, but the area directly in back of the ByVista, including the entire Ford Ranger, was totally blind. "How do you know what's behind you?" I asked Charity.

"You don't. The newer models have TV cameras in back, but this one doesn't. Anyway, you can't back up right now."

"Why?"

"It's got something to do with the Ranger's hitch. It'll break or something."

I looked at the cars parked in front of me. "So how are we supposed to get out of here?"

"We'll have to unhitch the Ranger."

"You've done that before, right?"

She gave me a sorrowful look.

I turned off the motor and we went outside. Using what little knowledge I had of hitches and my good sense, I got the Ranger disconnected, and Charity drove it out of the way.

Praying to whatever deity might be around, I backed the

motor home into the road. Then I put it in drive and slowly eased forward. I had to go half a mile before I spotted an area alongside the pavement that looked solid and wide enough to hold the heavy vehicle. Charity pulled up behind. With a great deal of difficulty we got the two parts of the hitch lined up, then reversed the process of unhooking.

When we were finished, she asked me to get the keys out of the Ranger. As I did, I noticed the gearshift lever was in park. "Shouldn't it be in neutral for towing?" I asked her.

"Oh, yes. Thanks!" she said.

I took care of it, sincerely hoping she'd be able to find someone to help her out.

As we approached the garage, Rip emerged from the shadows of the interior and watched me pull the ByVista off the road. Charity opened the door, the steps slid forward, and we descended.

"Very nice!" Rip said. I didn't know if he meant the motor home or Charity.

I did the introductions, and Charity went into her spiel about being afraid to drive the ByVista, and did he know anybody she could hire? He said if she'd wait a few minutes, he'd make some calls. Then he turned to me.

"I've located your problem, miss. You blew your engine."

"How'd I do that?" I wailed.

"*You* didn't do it. One of your pistons shattered, and fragments fell into your crankcase and seized the crank. It's your typical equipment failure. You'll need a new engine."

He said it in the same tone he would have used to remark that it looked like rain. I tried to match it, ignoring my internal keening for my shattered piston. "Do you think it happened because that dump truck backed into my grille?"

"A dump truck backed into your grille?" For some reason, Rip thought that was rip-roaring funny. When he finished laughing,

he said, "Nah, I don't think that could have caused it. It would
have had to damage your radiator, and your radiator looks fine.
I think it was just a bum piston."

"What do you think I should do?"

"Well, I don't have a '97 Toyota engine in stock." He laughed
again—life was just a barrel of fun for Rip. "If you want, I can
nose around for a rebuilt one. If that doesn't work I'll have to
order a new one, and that's going to cost you a bundle. You in
a hurry?"

I shrugged. "Sort of."

"Tell you what. There's a couple of nice pickups out back. I'll
trade you even, and you can be on your way." He pointed to an
open doorway at the rear of the shop. "Go take a look while I see
if I can find a driver for this little lady."

The "nice pickups out back" were pitiful. One of them, a
white Dakota, had suffered a serious swipe that had creased its
side and taken out a taillight. The passenger door would never
open again. The other, an old GMC, had a cracked windshield,
and most of its paint was missing.

I started to wonder about Rip's integrity. Even with a blown
engine, my Toyota outdistanced these wrecks by a mile. Bobby
the tow-truck driver had praised Rip highly, but what if Bobby
had an ulterior motive? For instance, what if Bobby lived in
Parsee—he wouldn't have wanted to take me to Dimock and
then have to drive all the way back home, now would he?

Charity wasn't around when I went back in, but the ByVista
was still parked out front. I told Rip no thanks on the trade. I
also told him to start looking for a rebuilt Toyota engine. He
said okay, but it might take several days to find one, and then
he'd have to install it. "Want me to order a new grille for you
too?" he asked.

"No. That's okay," I said. "Is there a motel around here?"

"There's three of them down the road a bit. I'd recommend the Georgia's Best, $32 a night. No pool, but it's real clean."

Great, I was going to spend my vacation in a pool-less motel in Parsee, Georgia. Maybe I could look up Jeff the computer guy, see if he might be interested in a game of gin.

As an afterthought, I asked Rip, "Does that tow-truck driver, Bobby, live around here?"

"Yeah, over on Magnolia. I'll tell him you're looking for him. Watch out, though. He's got a real jealous wife." I waited to see if he was going to bend over laughing. He didn't. I should have backtracked to Dimock.

I went out to begin my trek to the Georgia's Best Motel. Charity was leaning against the side of the motor home drinking from a can of Diet Coke. "Hey, Jo," she called. "Sorry about your truck. How long will it take him to fix it?"

"I don't know. Just a couple of days, hopefully. Did he find somebody to drive you to Arizona?

"He's still trying. So what are you going to do for a couple of days?"

"Wait for it. He gave me directions to a motel."

"You're going to sit around a motel room in this fusty little town when you could be off seeing America with me?"

I didn't say anything, but the possibility didn't seem as outlandish as it had before. I had new expenses.

She sensed my indecision. "Oh, Jo, please come with me. I don't want to travel cross-country with some strange man."

"Why do you have to go?" I asked. "Why don't you let somebody take the motor home to Tucson for you? Then you could go back to Charleston and forget the whole thing."

She ignored my suggestion and moved in for the kill. "What if I were to offer you a thousand dollars?"

A thousand? Here I'd been slaving as a certified nurse's assistant for pennies when I could have been out on the road earning a thousand here, a thousand there. "Did you say I'd be back to Parsee by Friday afternoon?"

"Definitely. I'll buy you a first-class ticket."

Yes! A wide seat and cloth napkin. It was all coming together. By the time I got back to Parsee, Rip would have my pickup fixed and ready to go and I'd have a thousand dollars in my pocket to help pay for it. I'd still be able to get to Tampa next weekend, as expected, to pack up Mrs. Phipps. "I'm in," I said.

I popped my head in Rip's office to tell him he could stop looking for someone to drive the motor home.

"You're kidding," he said. "I just lined up somebody to cover for me here at the garage so I could do it."

"Too bad," I said, trying to sound like I meant it. "I'll call you in a few days to see how you're coming with the Toyota."

"Yeah, yeah." His tone was surly. He picked up the phone and started punching buttons.

I went back out and got in the ByVista. Charity showed me a cupboard where I could stow my things. I swung in the driver's seat, still dented in the shape of my bony rear, fired up the engine, and hit the road with Charity Redmun.

4

Interstate 20 originated in the eastern half of South Carolina and meandered west through the states of Georgia, Alabama, Mississippi, Louisiana, and a great deal of Texas. Before reaching El Paso, it merged with Interstate 10, which had been roughly paralleling it to the south. It was by far the fastest and most direct route for Charity and me to take from Parsee to Tucson.

Turned out there was an entrance to Interstate 20 a few miles south of Rip's Garage. The three motels Rip mentioned were clustered around the interchange. As we approached, I watched the cars and trucks whizzing across the overpass, wishing I'd had a few more hours of driving practice.

"How's the acceleration on this thing?" I asked Charity.

"Not as bad as you'd think," she said. "It's got a big engine."

I took the west on-ramp and climbed, building up speed as quickly as possible. We hit the interstate at just under 50 miles per hour. There was so much length to us, an unfortunate SUV had to dart over and wedge between two semis. Both the SUV and the rear semi laid on their horns. A cold sweat broke out all over my body. I was glad when they disappeared over the horizon.

The ByVista moving fast turned out to be a whole other animal from the ByVista moving slow. For one thing, it was so wide it felt like we were hanging over both sides of our lane. I had to keep my attention glued to the white lines, especially the left one. If I erred, I wanted it to be on the shoulder side.

The wind was a real problem. It was barely stirring the trees at the side of the highway, but to me it felt like a nor'easter. Gusts caught hold of the ByVista's wide sides and tried to throw us into the next lane. And even worse, the 18-wheelers manufactured their own wind. As they passed, we were violently pushed away, then sucked back in their wake. I had to be on my toes every minute.

The invisible Ranger was a cause of worry too. It took me a long time to trust it was going to stay hitched. In my imagination, I saw it breaking free and taking off on its own trip. I sent Charity back to the bedroom a couple of times in the first hour to check on it through the small window between the closets.

I did okay, though. Charity said so too, although I'm sure she would have said whatever it took to keep me in the driver's seat. To help me relax, she chatted the miles away.

She told me it had never occurred to her that she wouldn't be able to drive the ByVista. Her father had driven it with apparent ease, and on occasion her mother had spelled him at the wheel.

"Come to think of it," she said, "Daddy never did ask *me* to drive it. Do you think he knew I'd have a problem?"

"Nah," I said. "Most parents have a hard time being in a vehicle with one of their kids driving. I'm almost 28, and my mom still pumps an imaginary brake."

"That could be it. Or maybe he thought I was too high-strung. He always told me I was high-strung. Do you think I'm high-strung, Jo?" All the time she was saying this, she was fiddling with a long gold chain she was wearing, twisting and coiling it around her fingers. I forced my attention to the road, but my eyes kept stealing back to those nervous fingers. I wanted to grab them, hold them still. Kiss them. *Kiss them? Okay, Jo, rein it in. It's a long walk back to Parsee.*

"I don't know you well enough to say if you're high strung or not," I told her.

Charity accepted that and started telling me about her misadventures in motor-home driving that morning. She'd started out from Charleston, South Carolina, on Interstate 26. At Columbia she missed the transfer to Interstate 20 and ended up on a city street—she didn't remember much about it except having a near-collision with a beer truck. After chewing her out royally, the driver led her to an interstate on-ramp.

Atlanta was a nightmare, she said. She'd forgotten to look at her map ahead of time and didn't know which bypass to use. The one she chose turned out to be in the middle of a repaving project. She'd been forced to maneuver the wide vehicle through a narrow lane for miles with the tires on one side several inches down on the dirt shoulder. She thought sure she was going to rupture one of the holding tanks. And all the while, drivers behind her were honking impatiently.

Soon after that, she exited to get fuel and pulled up on the wrong side of the pump. The station was too small and crowded to turn around in, so she drove down the road looking for a place large enough to allow it. It was 25 miles before she came to a town with an empty church lot. As she turned, a cupboard door that hadn't been well-latched slammed loudly. It scared her so badly she almost ran into the church.

By the time she got back on the interstate, she was totally freaked out, and her eyes kept tearing up from stress. She took the Parsee exit, ready to go the rest of the way on back roads. But she needed to get to Tucson by Friday, and she knew she'd never make it that way. "Thank God I met you, Jo," she said. "Thank God."

"Why do you have to be there by Friday?" I asked.

"Well, I just do. That's when I have to deliver it."

"To your brother, you said?"

"Yes."

"And the motor home belongs to your parents?"

"It did. I recently inherited it. I used to travel in it with them when I was in the country."

"What country?"

"This country," Charity said. "I live in Paris. But I always came back for a couple of weeks in the summer to take a trip with them. I love to travel. We went to Maine last summer and to Niagara Falls and Canada the summer before that."

"No kidding? I go to Niagara Falls all the time. Did you take the Maid of the Mist?"

"No. Actually it was raining the day we were there. We just drove by the falls."

"It doesn't matter if it's raining," I told her. "You get wet from the spray anyway."

"You're right, Jo. Now I wish we had stayed, but we didn't, we continued on. By the time we got to Tobermory and boarded the ferry, it was sunny again."

"You took the ByVista on a car ferry?"

"Sure. Lots of times."

"That'd be something to see," I said. "I don't suppose there's a car ferry between here and Tucson."

"I'm pretty sure there isn't."

"Bummer. So how'd you come to live in Paris?" I was impressed. I'd wanted to visit Europe ever since I almost went there with my senior class in high school. It seems we didn't raise sufficient funds in spite of the fact that I personally washed hundreds of cars and sold grosses of overpriced candy bars. *Whatever happened to all that money we raised?*

"I studied at the Sorbonne and then at the Louvre. I liked it so well, I decided to stay. Now most of my clients are in Europe," she said.

"What do you do?"

"I'm a specialist in European art. I appraise, consult, and broker sales."

"No kidding! You know a lot about art?"

"I do. I make a good living at it, actually. You might say I'm one of the few art history majors who isn't selling real estate." She laughed.

"You and Sister Wendy," I said. Now she really laughed.

I'd been keeping an eye on the instrument panel; when the fuel gauge needle was down to a quarter, I mentioned it to Charity, and she told me to stop at the next gas station, which I did, pulling up to a pump.

"Not here," Charity said. "We need diesel fuel."

"We do? I'm driving a diesel?" I drove over and proudly got in line behind an 18-wheeler.

There was no door next to the ByVista's driver's seat, a basic design flaw in my opinion, so each time we got out we had to exit through the house door. While I was passing through the living area, I was amazed to see Charity removing her purse, a black leather pouch with a shoulder strap, from the microwave.

"Why'd you put it in there?" I asked.

"That's where I keep it."

"Why?"

"It's where my mother kept hers. She said no thief would think to look in there."

"But the microwave's got a window," I said.

"You can't see in unless the light goes on, and the light doesn't go on unless you turn the microwave on."

"What if the thief uses the microwave?"

"Why would he do that?" she asked.

"Somebody broke into my Great-aunt Concetta's house one Sunday while she was at church and ate a dish of leftover ravioli. I assume he didn't eat it cold."

"My goodness. Did he take anything else?"

"Just some pizzelles. Turned out it was a kid from down the street."

"Well, our cupboard's bare. Nobody's going to heat up any food in this microwave unless they bring their own. Anyway, the ByVista has only a couple of good hiding places." She glanced toward the bedroom.

"Is there's a secret compartment in the closet or something?" I winced because the word "closet" reminded me of the Goddard's safe.

"Nope," Charity said, swinging the bag over her shoulder. "The microwave is definitely the safest place."

"You may be right at that," I said. It's a polite version of *Yeah, sure*.

I offered to operate the pump. She got it going with her credit card and went off to the convenience store. It took forever to fill the tank; I actually stuck my head under the vehicle to make sure the fuel wasn't running out a hole. As I was washing as much of the windshield as I could reach, Charity came back loaded down with four bottles of water and a 12-pack of Diet Coke. I ran in to use the facilities, and we were on our way again.

"Maybe I should have checked the oil," I said.

"No need to bother," she told me. "Before I left I had everything looked at, and anyway, Dad always kept everything in good shape, ready to go. They often took off on a moment's notice."

"They traveled a lot?"

"Oh, yes. They'd been all over the country. They were planning to get a new motor home this spring, one with slide-outs.

They were going to drive to Alaska this summer and stay for a couple of months."

"Slide-outs?"

"They're extensions, sort of. They roll out sideways to make the motor home bigger."

"Bigger than this one?"

She giggled. "My sentiments exactly."

"How did your parents die, Charity?" I was curious, because the way she'd been talking, they'd been alive until fairly recently.

She took a breath and slowly exhaled before answering. "It was a terrible tragedy, Jo," she said. "They were murdered a few weeks ago, right in their own home."

"Oh, my God!" I said. I'd expected an automobile accident, a plane crash maybe, but not this.

"A burglar broke in, tied them up, and shot them. One of my mother's friends happened to drive by, heard the shots, and called the police from her car. They made it in time to catch the guy. He's in jail now, awaiting trial." Her voice was trembling, and she was working her chain again

"Oh, Charity, I'm so sorry"

"It's been awful, truly awful. I flew right home, and since then it's been one stressful thing after another. I don't know when I'm going to be able to get back to work."

"Can't your brother help you?"

"I'm afraid not. He's stuck in Tucson." She jumped out of her seat. "You know, talking about work reminded me, I need to make some calls. I hope we're not in a black hole."

"You've got a cell phone?"

"Sure. It's in my purse. If you ever want to use it, just ask."

"Thanks, I will." I needed to let Mom know about my change in plans, but I'd wait until I wasn't driving.

I heard the microwave open and close, and Charity went back

to the bedroom. Soon I heard her talking to somebody in a foreign language, French maybe.

I entertained myself by musing about her brother, who was "stuck" in Tucson. I wondered if he was disabled or something like that. Being in my line of work, I understood disability.

The miles flew by. We crossed into Alabama and the Central time zone, gaining an hour, so I changed the digital clock on the dash. I saw signs for the cities of Birmingham and Tuscaloosa—names I knew from high school history class. Our social studies teacher had been born and raised in Montgomery, and she made it come alive for us: cotton plantations, the Civil War, the fight for civil rights. A billboard invited me to tour an antebellum home. I waved and said, "Next time."

From Alabama, we drove into Mississippi. The clock on the dash said it was 7, but my shoulders knew it was 8. Time to stop.

We picked Lake Stewart RV Park because its billboard had a picture of a boat with billowing sails cutting through sparkling wavelets. Charity rented us a site next to the lakeshore. It was a pull-through, which meant we didn't have to unhook the Ranger, rah-rah.

The lake may have been beautiful out in the middle, but we were parked by a shallow end. There were no sparkling wavelets here, just rotting weeds and green scum that smelled like a sewer. It was a warm night, but we had to keep the windows closed.

Charity told me she thought we should be plugging something in and hooking up a hose or two, but she wasn't sure what or where, since her father always took care of it. I asked if she had any manuals I could study. She brought me an armload of booklets and papers, and I started reading.

First I learned you had to get the motor home level or the

refrigerator would clog up and stop working, so I followed the instructions for the automatic leveler system, which involved manipulating some of the mysterious gadgets in the cockpit.

Next I read if you didn't plug the ByVista's cord into an electrical outlet, the refrigerator would soon deplete the house batteries, and the lights would go out. It was becoming clear to me that an RVer's life is pretty much geared to the whims of his or her refrigerator.

I found a flashlight in a cupboard and braved the lake's stench long enough to identify our utility post and plug the ByVista's thick black electric cord into it. As soon as we had unlimited power, Charity put her cell phone in its charger. Then she figured out how to aim the satellite dish and was soon curled up on the sofa with *Private Benjamin*.

I returned to the manuals and found out that in order to keep your storage tanks happy, you needed to hook your water hose to a faucet and your sewer hose to a sewer, so I went out and took care of that too.

By then I was bushed and thirsty, so I helped myself to a bottle of water from Charity's stash. While I drank, I flipped through the rest of the manuals, skipping those with information I didn't need right at that moment. My brain was full.

When the movie ended, Charity got an armful of bedding from a closet and showed me how to convert the sofa to a bed. I guess I hadn't really expected to share the queen-size bed with her, but somewhere in me there must have been a glimmer of hope, because I sighed out loud.

"Is something the matter?" Charity asked.

"No," I said. "It's just that I slept on my uncle's fold-out sofa the other night and it wasn't very comfortable. But this one may be a lot better."

"I'm sure it is. This is where I slept when I traveled with my folks, and I always slept well." She said good night and went to her bedroom, closing the door.

I made up the sofa bed and spent a while searching for a Charity-size depression. When I found it, I snuggled into it and fell soundly asleep.

In the morning I took a shower in the bathhouse. The place was full of women in various stages of washing up, and the water that came out of the nozzle was barely lukewarm. I was thinking nasty thoughts about the management when the shower next door turned off and my spray suddenly became scalding.

"My goodness, Jo, your back is bright red!" Charity said when I got back to the ByVista and hitched up my shirt. "I've got just the thing for it." She went in the bedroom and came out with a small bottle. "I brought this lotion from Paris," she said, and put some on my back, rubbing it in with a light hand. When it was all rubbed in, she applied some more.

"That feels good," I told her. "But I don't want to use up all your stuff."

"If it really feels good, I don't mind," she said, putting more on and rubbing far beyond the boundaries of the burn. I leaned back against her hands, willing them not to stop, but after a minute she pulled my shirt down and said, "That ought to do it. We'd better get going now."

I got in the driver's seat and leaned back. I didn't know if it was the lotion or Charity's hands, but I'd been healed.

We were headed for the park gate when I spotted a motor home identical to the Wellaway that had been in the lot next to the Parsee Home-Cook Diner the day before. It had a New York license plate, so it could have been the same one.

I figured, like us, they'd been lured by the sailboat-in-the-waves highway sign, but they'd been smarter. They took a site by the entrance, far away from the smelly lake. The spaces up there weren't pull-through like ours—you had to back in. Whoever was driving the Wellaway had done a lousy job of backing. A forked branch was caught in their folded TV antenna.

We got on the highway and continued our journey west. I was still achy from fighting the wind the day before, but luckily it had calmed down and I could relax a little. After a couple of hours behind the wheel I got hungry, and Charity okayed a meal break.

On the other side of Jackson, I pulled into a "travel center," which seemed to be a fancy name for "truck stop" because it advertised a breakfast buffet. Charity picked a table by the window. I ate heartily, not knowing when I'd get my next meal—I'd never gotten any supper at all last night. Fortunately I had found a PowerBar in a pocket of my backpack.

Charity skipped the buffet and ordered orange juice, a scrambled egg, and a slice of toast. She didn't even eat the crust. I offered to filch a slice of bacon for her from the buffet, but she said, "No, thanks."

A nearby rack of pay phones reminded me I still hadn't let Mom know about my change in plans, so I asked Charity, "When we get back to the motor home, could I use your phone? I have to call home."

"You can use it now." She rummaged in her purse and came up with the cell phone. "Do you want some privacy?"

"No, that's all right. What's today, Wednesday? Nobody will be there, anyway." I took the phone from her and dialed. My own voice politely asked me to leave a message. "Hi, Mom and Rose," I told the machine. "It's Jo. I'm doing fine. I had a bit of truck trouble in Georgia, but it's being fixed. I made a new friend too. Her name's Charity and I'm staying with her in her motor home. You should see it, it's even got a washer and dryer. And don't worry, I'll still make it to Tampa by the weekend. Love you."

Charity smiled as I handed the phone back. "A new friend? Thank you. I like that."

My ears got hot. I didn't really consider her a friend—I mean, she was a nice person, sure, but I barely knew her. I'd just said it to make Mom feel better and keep her from sending out the troops to find me. Mom could be a bit overprotective, so when I thought it best I omitted things and skewed details.

Of course I didn't tell Charity that. After breakfast, we fueled up and I squeegeed miles worth of suicidal bugs from the windshield. As we were driving out of the pump area I spotted the Wellaway motor home parked on the other side of the restaurant. It was definitely the same one I'd seen at the RV park this morning—the forked branch was still caught in the TV antenna.

This was getting weird. I'd seen that vehicle three times in less than 24 hours. I tried to remember, did the Goddards' daughter own a motor home? Could Dora be following me, watching to see where I was going to stash the booty? In my mind's eye, I saw her speeding down the interstate after us, her beagle nose poking out of the Wellaway's window, her face evilly gleeful.

I knew it was a silly idea, but I drove over and peered in the windshield just in case. The cab was vacant.

"What was that about?" Charity asked when we were back on the highway.

"I don't know, exactly. I keep seeing that motor home."

"Seeing it where?"

"It was parked at the diner where I met you, and also at the RV park this morning."

"You never saw it before you started traveling with me?"

"No."

"Let me know if you see it again, okay?"

"Why? Do you know who it is?"

"I have no idea." Her leg started doing a nervous dance. Pretty soon she got up and went back to the bedroom.

To amuse myself, I looked through the stack of CDs in a built-in holder in the dash. They were all classical, so I put them back. Despite my mother's love of opera and the great composers, I didn't find them hummable.

Next I turned on the CB and surfed channels. The only voices that came in clear had Southern accents so thick I could only make out half of what they were saying. It seemed to be two guys arguing over what was the best place in Tupelo to eat catfish. Their loving descriptions made me wish I had something to write on in case I ever got to Tupelo. Then two semis zoomed past and the voices faded.

A little while after that, we crossed the Mississippi River. What a thrill! "Charity," I called, "it's the Mississippi River!"

"I've seen it," she called back.

She'd seen it? Well, I'd seen it too, five or six years ago when I'd flown to St. Louis with my buddy Weezie to visit her sister. But the Mississippi River was like a rainbow or a sunset—you should always look.

I was rewarded for looking too. A tug was pushing a grid of covered barges toward us from the south. I did a quick count: five across and eight down—there were 40 big barges lashed tightly together. How was the tug captain able to steer it?

Driving off the bridge, I entered the state of Louisiana. I watched for bayous, but there were only flat fields and trees. I did see an exit for Bee Bayou Road, but it wasn't like seeing one in person. I promised myself that someday I was going to make it to southern Louisiana, where bayous abounded. While I was there, I might stop in New Orleans for Mardi Gras. I wondered if Mrs. Phipps would need packing up again next year.

Within a few hours, Shreveport whizzed by, and we crossed into Texas. "Turkey, Texas," I sang, but not too loud, "the home of Bo-ob Wills." It suddenly occurred to me that here I was, halfway across the continent, and I hadn't seen a highway toll booth since I'd left the state of New York. The interstates in every one of the other states I'd crossed had been totally toll-free. How did they fund their road repairs and fix their bridges? Maybe our governor could call and ask them.

It wasn't very long until my stomach started growling again. Charity was still in the back, so I took the initiative and pulled into a Burger King that had advertised truck parking on a billboard a few miles back. When you're driving a behemoth like the ByVista, you can't go to just any old fast-food place.

As I brought the motor home to a stop, Charity came out of the bedroom. She didn't look any less uptight than when she'd gone in. "I'm going to get a burger," I said. "Want one?"

"Thanks, no. I try not to eat meat." She sat down and scanned the parking lot. "You don't see that motor home here, do you? What was it called?"

"Wellaway. No, I don't see it."

"It's probably only a big coincidence, your seeing it three times, don't you think?"

"Could be. In any case, if they're following us, wouldn't we get here first? We should look for it when we go to leave."

"Following us? Why would they be following us?"

"I have no idea," I said. "You're the one who seemed worried." This woman was sure good at leading me into dead-end conversations. I started for the door.

She jumped up. "Okay, I'll come with you. I'll get a soda and maybe some fries." She fetched her purse from the microwave and followed me out.

When we were settled in a red padded booth with our respective refreshments, I said, "Charity, if you don't eat meat, why did you scold me for not recommending the meatloaf back at the diner in Parsee?"

"I was just trying to make conversation. I needed help, and you looked like someone who might help me," she said.

"No kidding? Would you say I looked trustworthy?"

"Definitely."

Excellent. "Thank you."

"What did you think about me?" she asked.

"I thought you looked like Cameron Diaz," I said.

"I wish. She's half my size."

"You really do look like her. You've got her eyes, and your mouth turns up at the corners like hers, even when you're not smiling. It's very attractive."

"Well, thank you." She smiled, and her shoulders dropped a full inch.

"Is that why you never eat? You think you're fat?" I asked.

"I eat!" She picked up a French fry and took a bite.

"Sorry," I said.

"Okay, I've got a weight problem. What woman doesn't?" She looked at my Double Whopper, king-size fries, and chocolate shake. "Well, you, maybe. If I ate like that, I'd be as huge as my mother was."

"I'm sure your mother was a fine-looking woman, no matter what size she was. And you're fine-looking too. You could eat all you want and you'd still be fine-looking."

"Thanks, Jo. That's nice." She blushed a little as she finished her fries and ate a couple of mine.

When we came out, I looked around for the Wellaway, but it was nowhere to be seen.

5

We were still an hour east of the Dallas–Fort Worth area when my muscles started complaining like road-weary children. I suggested to Charity we find an RV park. She counter-suggested that we go through the cities first in order to avoid the morning rush hour, so that's what we did. When we were south of Dallas, Charity saw a Wal-Mart sign and said, "I know! When we get to the other side of Fort Worth, let's find a Wal-Mart and boondock."

"What's a boondock?" I used to shop at Wal-Mart a lot before they were accused of bad business practices, but I'd never seen anything called a boondock on their shelves. Maybe it was in the camping department.

"It's a verb," she said. "It means to stay somewhere that's not really a campground, usually for free. My parents used to brag about all the places they'd boondocked. Wal-Mart parking lots were their favorites."

"What about the hoses?"

"We'll use the storage tanks. That's what they're for."

"But we won't have any electricity. The refrigerator will quit." Since there wasn't anything in it but water and Diet Coke, it was a moot worry.

"It's a three-way. It runs on propane too."

"Do we have propane?"

"Oh, yes. Dad would never run out of propane. What do you think the stove uses?"

I hadn't thought about it. I hadn't used the stove and didn't plan to, so that was one of the booklets I'd skipped last night.

Charity went back to check the panel that monitored the levels of the tanks. "We have lots of propane," she called, "and the batteries are at full charge. There's water in the fresh water tank, and the waste tanks are empty. We have a generator too, in case we need to recharge the battery. We're in great shape to boondock."

"Are you sure it's okay with Wal-Mart?"

She came forward and sat down. "I'm sure. Everybody does it. Anyway, I'll clear it with the store manager first."

"You're sure it's safe?"

"My parents never had any problem." She paused and looked at me. "Jo, you don't want to boondock, is that it?"

She'd hit it on the head. If we were going to be spending the night in parking lots, that meant I'd be forced to use the ByVista's creepy plastic toilet. So far I'd managed to avoid it by running to the bathroom every time we stopped to get food, fuel, or stay the night.

The motor home toilet reminded me of when I was 10 and Uncle Greg took a bunch of us kids out for a boat ride on Lake Erie. Shortly after we left the pier, he led us down a narrow set of steps and showed us the contraption we were supposed to use if nature called. The instructions for using it were so lengthy, detailed, and riddled with dire warnings of what would happen if we did our pumping in and pumping out in the wrong order, I was petrified. I held it in for three and a half hours, which was especially excruciating with all the lake water sloshing against the hull. It spoiled the boating mystique for me completely.

Another thing I'd avoided using was the motor-home shower. Restoring its pristine tiled loveliness after showering would take longer than the shower itself. That wasn't a problem tonight, though. I could get away without a shower—all I did all day was drive.

What the hell, I finally decided. *If Charity's so keen on this boondocking thing, it won't kill me to use the dumb toilet for one night. I just won't drink much.* "How do we go about finding a Wal-Mart?" I said.

"Take the next exit."

"How do you know there's a Wal-Mart there?"

"They're everywhere. I'll ask at a gas station. They'll know."

When we exited, we found ourselves on a busy street with wall-to-wall mini malls, restaurants, and motels. After several blocks I spotted a Texaco station, but it was on the other side of the street and I was in the wrong lane to turn. I eased over and made a U-turn at the next intersection. Bad mistake. The front tire went up on the far curb, and when it came down again there was an ugly crunch. "I'm sorry!" I said. "Whatever it is, I'll fix it."

I maneuvered the motor home into the gas station. When Charity opened the door, there was a loud grinding noise. She said, "It's the automatic step. I think it's crushed."

"Oh, no. I'm so sorry."

"That's okay. Better that than one of the tanks."

I could have kissed her.

Charity struck up a conversation with a woman who was pumping gas and discovered that the nearest Wal-Mart was back a couple of exits. My dislike of backtracking kicked in, but my aching shoulders told it to kick out again.

When we were finally pulling into the Wal-Mart lot, I saw Charity was right about boondocking—everybody did do it.

Several motor homes and trailers were already there, clustered in a corner.

I took a spot near them and operated the automatic levelers. After that I fetched the refrigerator manual and found out how to switch to propane. Finally I went to have a look at the crushed step. To my relief, it appeared fixable. Charity searched for tools and found some in one of the lower storage compartments. I blessed her dear departed father who'd had the foresight to carry a good-size wrench.

Sitting on the pavement and bracing myself against the ByVista with my feet, I gripped the step with the wrench. After about 20 minutes of intense tugging and grunting, I got it pried out and somewhat back to its original shape. It was sluggish, but at least it was moving again. Now I did need a shower. And my shoulders were screaming. I put the tools away and went in to take some aspirin.

Charity had gone into the store. As I was washing up, she came back with a bagful of magazines. "We have official permission to stay the night," she said with a big grin. "They have a grocery store too. Shall we go give them some business?"

Since I was starving again, I decided to suspend my Wal-Mart boycott for an hour.

A sign near the entrance said the store never closed. Yes! A 24-hour toilet! I felt better about the whole thing. I took a cart and threw in a loaf of bread, a jar of chunky peanut butter, and a glass of grape jelly. Charity bought a bunch of romaine, a bag of carrots, two lemons, more water, and more Diet Coke. Between us, we had the makings of a meal.

After we ate, Charity picked up one of her magazines, so I went out and took a walk around the building. A semi was being unloaded onto a rear dock. I recognized it as one that had buffeted us on the highway a couple of times. Like a sleeping bull, it looked harmless in repose.

I walked the perimeter of the Wal-Mart lot and looked in all the adjacent lots, but the Wellaway wasn't anywhere around.

Charity was running the generator when I got back, watching the late show on TV. When it was over, I ran in the store to use the bathroom and went to bed. I slept very well, considering where we were. At 7 A.M. I woke up with a pulsing bladder. I sprinted across the parking lot, into the store, and past a gray-haired greeter, who hollered "Welcome to Wal-Mart" at my back. Luckily, there was a free stall. Actually at this hour they were all free.

Since there wasn't anything to hitch or unhook, we were soon on our way. I could understand why people liked this boondocking thing.

A few miles out of Fort Worth, I saw my first cactus—other than the little grafted monstrosities they sold in the supermarkets in Buffalo. This one was flat-leafed and bushy—a real *cactus*. And even better, just past Abilene, giant windmills stood tall on a hill. Each had three gleaming blades that sliced the air as lazily as if the strong prairie gusts were babies' breaths. There must have been 80 windmills, or even more.

Charity laughed at my excitement and said she was getting a little bored with admiring the roadside—would I like her to read to me from one of her new magazines? I told her sure, hoping it would be *People* or at least *Newsweek*. It wasn't. It was an article from *Money* about picking mutual funds. Mercifully, she started feeling nauseated after 10 minutes and turned on the radio instead. We were in the middle of nowhere, so the only station that came in was a true country station with cattle futures and Hank Williams tunes. In a commercial, a voice asked, "Have you ever been out in the field and had your hydraulic hose break?"

"Doggone it, yes," I said. "That happened to me last week."

"Me too," laughed Charity.

When we lost the station, I was afraid she'd start in with the mutual funds again, so I asked what her childhood had been like.

"It was happy," she said. "My father was a builder of commercial properties and an investor. We were quite well-to-do. My mother was active in the best social circles, and I attended excellent schools."

"How did you get interested in art?"

"That was my father's doing. He was an avid collector. I grew up with the old masters. As soon as I could read, he started taking me to galleries and buying me art books. For my 16th birthday I got my own Cassatt."

I didn't want to admit I didn't know what that was, so I said, "Is your brother interested in art too?"

"Paul has his own interests. What about you, Jo? Tell me about your family."

I was starting to notice that she clammed up or changed the subject whenever I mentioned her brother. I thought about pressing her but decided she must have her reasons. So I told her about Mom and Rose, leaving out the details of their relationship since I didn't want to deal with any ramifications at the moment. I told her what kind of work I did, leaving out the Goddard fiasco. It occurred to me that I didn't have any business complaining about what Charity had left out.

When I finished, she said she couldn't believe that at age 27 I was still living with my mother. I told her I couldn't believe it either, but it worked for now.

Then I found myself telling her all about my life as an only child with an alcoholic father, how he could be perfectly amiable when he came home from whatever job he had at the moment but changed for the worse as he worked through his first six-pack. I'd go to my room directly after supper but could still hear his yells and the terrifying bumps and moans. Some mornings Mom could hardly walk.

That may have been more about my life than Charity wanted to hear, because as soon as she was politely able she retreated to the bedroom.

It had certainly put me in a funk. I saw the passing landscape through a dark haze of emotions. If it was lovely, you couldn't prove it by me. I drove for hours on tire-rutted roads, stopping only to fuel up and down a couple of hot dogs at a Flying J truck stop in Pecos.

Brooding mountains appeared on the horizon and followed us along. It felt like we'd been in Texas forever.

6

A few miles after Pecos, Interstate 20 merged with Interstate 10 and traffic got heavier. The mountain range that had been paralleling the highway moved in, and we started to climb. Except for the sparse greenery, these mountains weren't much different from the rollers in Pennsylvania, round and gentle, certainly not the craggy giants I'd seen on Western postcards. The road had plenty of curves, however, and my shoulders soon told me they were about done for the day.

I told Charity I thought we should go upscale from Wal-Mart tonight and boondock at a Lord & Taylor. She laughed and said I should start looking for an RV park. By the time I saw a camper icon, the mountains had retreated and the land had become flat again. Following CAMPGROUND signs with hand-drawn arrows, we traveled six miles north, three and a quarter miles east, and two miles north again, and finally arrived at the gate of Ariel's Pond Campground. Seeing the word "Pond" and remembering stinky Lake Stewart, I was ready to head back to the highway, but Charity said to give it a chance.

We went through a gate and stopped in front of a house with a sign on the door that said OFFICE. Charity had her purse out of the microwave before the motor home came to a full stop.

"Why don't you try for a spot near the bathhouse?" I said. "I need a shower."

"Okay." She opened the door and jumped out, not waiting for the maimed step to crawl forward.

I watched her cross the lawn, the hem of her skirt swaying to the bounce of her step. The door marked OFFICE swung open. A ruddy-faced man stepped out, sucked in his gut, and greeted her with a smile.

Since it looked like she might be a while, I pushed out of the driver's seat and crossed to the cupboard to get clean clothes for after my shower, but it was slim pickings. Almost everything I'd packed was on my back or dirty, or both. I'd seen this situation coming, however, and had purchased a miniature box of Tide at the last truck stop. Tonight I was planning to try out the ByVista's washer and dryer.

I helped myself to a fluffy towel from the linen closet and stuffed it into my backpack along with the last change of clothes, my tooth things, and a bar of soap. I'd just returned to the driver's seat when Charity came back waving a piece of cardboard with "Space L-27" and "4/18," the next day's date, written on it in black marker. "Mr. Ariel says the pond is odor-free and the bathrooms are only two rows over from this site, so I took it," she said.

"It's on the water?"

She nodded. "It was $10 extra."

We found L-27. It wasn't a pull-through, so I had to unhitch the Ranger and back in the ByVista, but with Charity's help it was no big deal. We were sandwiched between a Bounder and an Airstream. Curtains rustled in the Airstream as our fellow RVers checked out their new neighbors.

Charity stuck the dated cardboard inside the windshield

while I went out to hook up. I sniffed in the direction of Ariel's Pond. It was actually more the size of a large puddle, but the guy hadn't lied. It didn't smell.

When I went back in to grab my backpack, Charity had the dish pointed and was surfing channels. "No good movies tonight," she said.

"Go look at your $10 pond," I told her. "I'm going to find the showers."

It was dark when I came out of the bathhouse feeling fresh and frisky. I decided to take a walk around the park, maybe indulge in my new hobby of looking for the Wellaway. I found it in a site near the gate. I wondered if they'd parked there so they could see the ByVista leaving in the morning.

The curtains were pulled tight, but shadows were moving on them and I heard a man's voice through an open window. Whose voice? Whose shadows? I couldn't stand the suspense. I went to the door and knocked.

The man who opened it was a stranger, but I knew I'd seen him before. It wasn't until a woman appeared behind him that I remembered where. It had been at the Parsee Home-Cook Diner—they were the middle-aged couple who took the empty booth I was coveting.

"Hello," he said pleasantly. "May I help you?" He was wearing jeans and a plaid shirt like many other RVers I'd seen. His graying hair was thin on top and long around the edges.

"Hi," I said. "I see you have New York plates. I'm from New York too."

"Where in New York?" he asked. He had a slight English accent.

"Oswego." *That was dumb. I'd never even been to Oswego. Why hadn't I taken a moment to write a script before knocking?*

"Really? We live north of Syracuse," he said.

Whoa, a little too close to Oswego. "Actually, I just moved to Oswego. I grew up in Buffalo."

"I see. Well, come on in." He stepped aside. "We're Roy and Lois Parker."

Lois smiled. "I'm so glad to meet you." She had the accent too. Like Roy, she was dressed RV-style, but she wasn't as comfortable in the costume as he was. Her jeans were stiffly new, and her white shirt was crisp and businesslike. I wondered if she was wearing pantyhose underneath it all.

I glanced around. So this was how the other half of the motor home crowd lived. There was a bedroom area, a kitchen area, and a living area, but they were all crammed together. There was no recliner, no large-screen TV. My heart went out to them.

I put my backpack on the hard divan and sat next to it. Roy and Lois took seats in the dinette across the aisle, turning their upper bodies toward me. Two paperbacks lay on the table between them. I strained to see the titles but couldn't.

"I'm Delia Frank," I told them. It was an amalgam of my parents' first names. "I'm on my way to Los Angeles. I'm an actor." It was the only reason I could think of to go to Los Angeles.

"You are?" Roy really seemed to care.

Lois became animated. "Our niece in Toronto wants to be a professional actor. She's still in high school. She was Lady Macbeth last year, and we went up to see her. We were so proud."

I hadn't known we'd have so much in common. "How nice. Are you from Canada?" I asked.

"Originally. We've lived in the states for years and years, though," Roy said.

It all sounded plausible. In an effort to put them off balance, I said, "We first noticed your motor home back in Parsee,

Georgia. We've seen it so many times since then, we started to think you were following us."

They laughed merrily. Roy said, "Why would we want to do that?"

Lois said, "And who's *we*?"

Dang! Think fast, Jo! "My husband and I," I lied. "His name's Luigi." Luigi was my maternal grandpa—I was working up the family tree.

"Is Luigi an actor too?"

My turn to laugh. "Oh no, he's retired. He's a lot older than me." *Good thinking, Jo. That explains why we're traveling across the country, me and Luigi.* "Have you been RVing long?" I asked.

"Oh, yes," Roy said. "We've been at it a long time."

"We were in Florida for the whole winter," added Lois.

"Living in this?" Had I sounded too incredulous?

"We're used to it," Lois said. "It's fine as long as it doesn't rain." More laughter. "What kind of rig do you and Luigi have, Delia?" Roy asked me

"It's a...an Airstream."

"Is it the one down by the pond? We saw it when we took a walk."

Oh, my God, they'd been out patrolling. "No," I said, "we're on the other side."

"Oh. Well, Airstreams are very nice," Lois said.

"We like ours." I tried again to get the spotlight off me. "So where are you headed?" I asked. "Texas sure isn't the shortest way between Florida and New York." *I should know.*

"We're on our way to visit our grandchildren in San Bernardino," Lois said, fetching a framed photo from the counter. As she sat back down, I saw a flash of ankle. Yep, pantyhose, or at least knee-highs.

She handed me the photo. "The one on the left is Shelley and the other one is Shirley. They're twins."

Lois wasn't lying about that last bit. Two identical, identically dressed little blond girls were identically posed in front of a sky-blue screen painted with fluffy clouds.

"Cute," I said and handed it back.

"We can't wait to see them again." Her voice was so full of love, I wondered if I'd been wrong. These people certainly seemed genuine. Perhaps the whole thing was a coincidence after all. We were all RVers, we were all going the same direction. It wasn't a stretch to think we might be stopping at a lot of the same places. But just in case, I wanted to take a look around. "Could I ask you a favor?"

"What is it, love?" Lois asked.

"I have this..." I lowered my voice. "...condition. May I use your bathroom?"

"Why, of course," she said, pointing to a small door at the back. It was next to a double bed that was crammed against the wall so tight, the inside person would have to climb over the outside person to take a 3 A.M. tinkle.

When I was safely latched in, I checked the tiny medicine cabinet. It held tooth-cleaning supplies and an extra bar of soap. In the cupboard below the sink were a couple of towels and washcloths and two bottles of shampoo, different brands. Not much stuff for people who had been RVing "a long time."

Through the thin door, I heard a low conversation going on in the motor home proper, but I couldn't make out any words. I pulled the flush lever and emerged to find them with their noses in their paperbacks. I could see the titles now—his was a Zane Grey; hers was one of those two-inch-thick romances.

Roy didn't look up, but Lois did. "Are you all right, dear?"

"Yes, thank you."

She returned her attention to her book. I was being dismissed. "Maybe I'll see you again," I said slyly as I shouldered my backpack.

Roy stood and shook my hand. "I certainly hope so. We'd love to meet Luigi." He opened the door and stepped aside.

Before leaving, I was tempted to say, "Look, I'm Jo Jacuzzo from Buffalo. Who are you, really?" And they could say, "We're best friends of the Goddards and we have our eye on you, baby," or "We're with the Charleston, South Carolina, police, and we're following suspected serial killer Charity Redmun. We figure she's about to strike again." At least then we'd all know what we were dealing with. And if they really were Roy and Lois Parker from north of Syracuse on their way to San Bernardino to visit their twin granddaughters, they'd simply chalk me up as one of those crazies you meet on the road and go check the bathroom to see if I'd stolen the soap.

It wasn't until I was halfway back to the ByVista that it struck me as odd that Roy and Lois had both opened their books to page one.

When I got back, Charity was sitting in a lawn chair behind the Airstream next door, chatting with a man and a woman. She saw me trying to sneak into the motor home and called me over. I was introduced and told that Harry and Betty were full-timers.

"That means we don't have a house anymore. We sold it." Harry said. "We live in the Airstream."

"Airstreams are very nice," I said. Lois had thought so, anyway.

"We've been in Florida for the winter, and now we're on our way to spend the summer on the Oregon coast," Betty said.

"No kidding?" I said. "I just met some other people who spent the winter in Florida. They have a Wellaway."

Harry and Betty looked at each other. "The whole winter? I don't think so," Harry said.

"Why not?" I asked.

"Wellaways are rental RVs. I think the company's based somewhere in New York State. Nobody would live in them a whole season,"

"Cheaper to buy your own," Betty added.

I wished them well on their travels and went inside to start my laundry. While it sloshed, I puzzled over Roy and Lois, the rented motor home, the paperbacks opened to page one. I had noticed something else too. In the space above the Wellaway's cab, a second bed had been made up, complete with comforter and pillow. Evidently neither Roy nor Lois wanted to sleep on the inside of the wall-bound bed. Of course, another explanation might be that they weren't really married.

All this speculation was making me crazy. I transferred my laundry to the dryer and turned on the TV. I wasn't up to cop shows, so I watched a sitcom about a dysfunctional family until Charity came in.

When I told her I'd visited the Wellaway, she was indignant. "I can't believe you did that. Why didn't you come tell me first?"

"It didn't occur to me."

"It should have! You knew I was concerned. Well, what did you find out?"

I told her everything the Parkers had said and described the Wellaway's interior as best I could. I told her about the two beds too, and the books. "Are you thinking Roy and Lois could have something to do with your parents' death?" I asked.

"Anything's possible," she said. "Jo, do you think we could sneak out of here without those people in the Wellaway seeing us?"

"I don't know. Do you mean now? My laundry isn't dry."

"I mean *now*."

I ran out and started unhooking the cord and hoses. Curtains moved in one of the Airstream's windows. Harry and Betty were wondering what I was doing.

When I went back in, Charity had lowered the dish and otherwise battened down the hatches. I pulled the ByVista out of the site and we quickly hitched up the Ranger, which was harder than ever in the dark. Before long we were inching toward the park exit. Gritting my teeth at the crunch of tires on gravel, I coasted past the final lane before the campground gate, the lane the Wellaway was on. When we got to the gate, it was closed. Charity grabbed the flashlight and ran out to open it. She came right back. "It's padlocked," she said. "I'll have to get Mr. Ariel."

The house was totally dark except for the flickering colors of a TV in one of the windows. After Charity knocked, I saw a progression of lights go on. The door opened, and Mr. Ariel appeared in a plaid flannel bathrobe. They talked for a couple of minutes, and Mr. Ariel stomped across the parking area to the gate. I heard him muttering as he unlocked it. Charity came back in, shutting the door as quietly as possible. "What a grouch!" she said. "I should have asked for a refund."

I looked down the lane to see if the Wellaway might be pulling out, but all was quiet. Mr. Ariel swung the gate open, and we were a mile down the road before I turned on the headlights. After we got on the Interstate, Charity fetched the flashlight and studied the map. She told me that we were about to cross another time line.

It didn't matter—I was already in a time warp. *When Superman returns from his faster-than-light flight around the earth, Jo Jacuzzo will find herself back in her room in Buffalo, New York, talking to her mother about going to Florida and packing up Mrs. Elinor Phipps. And this time she'll say no.*

Charity directed me off the highway into a town, and we drove around looking for a place to hide. We ended up pulling in back of a strip mall.

As soon as I turned off the engine, Charity jumped up and started pacing the room—it was actually more of a circling than a pacing since she couldn't go more than a couple of steps in any direction. "No house lights, Jo," she said, "We don't want to call attention to ourselves. And definitely no generator. Your laundry will have to wait until tomorrow."

I wheeled out of the driver's seat and onto the sofa. "Well, I got my shower at least," I said.

She stopped pacing and turned to me. "Jo, I'm sorry I snapped at you about visiting the Barkers."

"Parkers," I said. "And it's okay."

She dropped right next to me. Now I was *really* glad I'd had my shower. "It's not okay," she said softly. "I had no right to talk to you like that." Her mouth was close to my ear. "You've been nothing but kind and nice to me since the day we met. I'm truly sorry."

The room was dark except for the mall security lights shining through the windows. The warmth of Charity's body on my right arm was way beyond my comfort zone. "You're nice to me too," I said lamely, trying to edge away one buttock at a time.

"I hope so," she whispered as she put her hand on my shoulder and gently kneaded.

A fight erupted in my brain between my good sense and my libido. *The woman's just being friendly. Kapow! What are you talking about? It's perfectly clear she wants me. Biff! You and what other delusional fool? Wham!* I leaped up, knocking her sideways. The security lights reflected in her wide eyes as she pushed herself upright.

"Is something wrong?" she asked.

"No…yes," I said, "I'm thirsty." I crossed to the refrigerator. Grabbing a bottle of water, I tore off the cap and chugged.

When I came up for air, she said, "You know, Jo, I feel bad for making you drive that last bit. You look awfully stiff. I've got some of that lotion left. Why don't you let me give you a relaxing shoulder rub?"

It was a version of a line I'd used once or twice to coax a shy maiden into my nefarious clutches. A couple of my body parts snapped to attention. Slowly and deliberately, I put the empty bottle under the sink. "A *shoulder rub*?" If I were Groucho Marx, I'd have been pumping my eyebrows and tapping my cigar.

She rose and glided toward me. Was she going to kiss me? Had I eaten anything smelly since I brushed my teeth? She walked right past and went into her bedroom. "Come on, Jo, you can lie on my bed," she called. "And take off your shirt."

I followed, shedding my T-shirt as I went, wondering if I was going to get a shoulder rub or a *shoulder rub*.

It was a shoulder rub. I had no idea her hands were so strong. She straddled my waist and kneaded my back, arms, and shoulders like I was a glob of Play-Doh. "Ow, ow, ow," I whined.

"You're so tight!" she said.

Under some circumstances that would have been something I'd love to hear, but this wasn't one of them. I rolled out from under her and, grabbing my T-shirt, dashed to the front. By the time she got to the door, I had my bed half made.

"Feeling any better?" she smiled.

"Yeah, lots," I lied. I'm sure my face was beet-red.

"Okay. Good night, then."

She went back in the bedroom, but this time she left the door open. Was it an invitation? I told myself to stop conjecturing and go to sleep, but it wasn't that easy. As soon as I emptied my brain of Charity thoughts, every dumb and mean thing I'd done since third grade paraded across my brain, followed by a brass band of money worries. Finally I turned on a light and read an article in Charity's *Glamour* about fashion trends in the workplace until I drowsed off. At 3 A.M., when the bottle of water I'd chugged had run its course, I had no choice but to use the ByVista's toilet. I was right; it didn't kill me.

Charity came out of the bedroom before daybreak with the map in her hand and said that if we got going, we could be in Tucson in time for dinner. I told her that sounded great. As I drove, she called an airline and bought a first-class seat on a flight leaving Tucson at 9:10 the next morning. It would take me to Atlanta, and then I'd have to find my own way to Parsee.

She called Rip for me too. He told her he'd found a rebuilt engine for my Toyota and was installing it as they spoke. Things were looking up.

7

I needed all my concentration to get through El Paso. The highway ran right through the middle of the city, and traffic was fierce. Along the way I glimpsed a beautiful stand of palm trees. It took my breath away—I'd never seen a real palm tree before.

One of the many El Paso exits was for Juárez, Mexico. Charity told me we were very close to the Mexican border, and the peaks to our left were probably Mexican mountains. *Las montañas de Mexico*—how exotic! Our neighbors went to Mexico last winter, and all they could talk about was the tiny bananas and huge oranges.

After leaving El Paso, Interstate 10 headed north for a while. Billboards, businesses, and buildings under construction lined the frontage roads throughout much of the 30-some miles to Las Cruces, New Mexico. We skirted Las Cruces, and the highway turned west again and started climbing. For some reason somebody had put a giant sculpture of a roadrunner next to a steep incline. I stared at it when I should have been accelerating and wound up scaling the hill in the snail lane with the big trucks.

I couldn't believe the speed limit here was 75. A soon as the road stopped climbing, everybody who could get their vehicles going that fast did. I was edging the ByVista toward 70 when I saw Charity eyeing the speedometer. I eased it back to 65.

On both sides of the interstate New Mexico was flat with mountains looming in the distance. I would've loved to park the motor home and take Charity and the Ranger four-wheeling. Who knew what we might find?

We stopped for breakfast in Deming. Charity passed on eating—surprise, surprise—so I took some flyers from a rack in the restaurant foyer to keep me company. One of the flyers was full of things for tourists to do and see in the mountains. There were cliff dwellings, a huge copper mine, and a town with the beguiling name of Silver City. I'd have liked to take a little trip up there, have a look around. It was gradually hitting me that here I was in the wild wild West and I wasn't seeing anything!

Charity was in the passenger seat peering out the window when I got back "I've been watching for the Wellaway, but I haven't seen it," she said. "I think we shook it."

"I hope so." I slid into the driver's seat and buckled up.

"How are your shoulders today?'

"Fine. Great." I moved them in wide circles to show her how great they were.

"That's wonderful," she said, and unfolded her map.

I stole sidewise glances at her as I drove, thinking about how ready I'd been to have sex with her last night. I couldn't believe it—she wasn't my type at all. I'd always gone for women who had what I called the "librarian look": rimless glasses, dark hair that was short or pulled back, tailored slacks and blazers.

Charity was nothing like that. Her clothes were soft and full of ruffles and textures. She wore eye makeup in shades of brown and bright coral lipstick. Her hair was blond with platinum highlights, probably from a bottle. As I watched, she absently reached up to arrange a renegade curl, and I felt a severe tingling between my legs. Embarrassed, I forced my attention to the road.

In a few minutes, Charity said she needed to go back and take a nap, did I mind?

I didn't.

The terrain west of Deming continued to be flat with stubby trees and round bushes. I wondered if the bushes would be tumbleweeds someday. "Driftin' along with the tumblin' tumbleweeds," I sang, then stopped because I was singing myself to sleep. As we passed the city of Lordsburg, I turned on the radio and found an oldies station to keep me awake. I kept it low so it wouldn't disturb Charity.

In the middle of "Help Me, Rhonda," a big sign with a Native American sunburst on it welcomed me to Arizona. I couldn't remember ever being so glad to get anywhere.

When the Lordsburg station faded, I messed around with the CB for a while and caught a conversation between two guys who had to be the drivers of two semis coming up behind me. I couldn't believe the dirty and demeaning things they were saying about women in the vehicles around them. After a few minutes, I slowed down so they'd pass. As they did, I put on my guy face so they wouldn't entertain each other with tales of how many places in me they were going to stick it. I guess the subterfuge worked, because all they told each other as they passed was "Goddamn RVs" and "Shouldn't let 'em on the fuckin' road."

I turned the CB off and tried the regular radio again. All that would come in was a crackly station playing mariachi music. Unfortunately I couldn't sing along, but it was pretty and peppy and kept me awake. "ESTEREO EF EM!" shouted the DJ between songs.

Suddenly I noticed the fuel tank was way down past a quarter.

Dang, Jo, why didn't you stop in Lordsburg? It was a relief when I spotted a gas pump icon at the next exit.

When I got to the bottom of the ramp, I didn't see a station anywhere. The road ran south, shimmering in the heat, until it disappeared. To the north, it went 500 feet and ended, like it was waiting for a town to be built. I sat there wondering if I should try to find the promised station or get back on the interstate and take my chances. I finally drove down the shimmering road, promising myself I'd turn back if I didn't see a station within two miles. In exactly one and a half miles a station came into view. It sat on the southeast corner of a deserted crossroads with nothing around it but desert.

The building was small, a frame structure with peeling paint and an open bay that looked like it hadn't been used in years. Stenciled across the top was PINTO GAS AND REPAIR. The only indication they were open was two motorcycles parked in front and a propped door. The interior was a black pit. If I'd had any options, I would have opted to keep going.

I pulled in and panicked because I didn't see a diesel pump. Then I spotted it off to the side by itself. The paint on the pump was faded, and weeds were growing out of cracks in the pavement around it. It wasn't pay-at-the-pump—it had one of those ancient displays where the numbers hiccup into view. I wondered if it even worked. It did.

Maybe it was the isolation and the pounding sun and the dilapidated condition of the place, but I didn't like being there. As soon as the numbers in the window jerked to $20, I shut off the pump. As I replaced the nozzle, the $20 jumped to $20.01.

Since I didn't want to wake Charity, I decided to pay out of my own pocket. Twenty bucks wouldn't break me. I crossed to the gaping door and went in. It was very dark inside. The one small window was over by the register. The bulbs in the widely spaced fixtures couldn't have been more than 60 watts each.

I waited inside the doorway for my eyes to adjust. After a minute I remembered I was still wearing my sunglasses. As I shoved them up on my head, I heard low snickers from the shadows at the end of the counter.

I crossed to the register, where a girl who looked to be about 13 was perched on a stool. Her hair was long and black and so straight it must have been ironed. She was wearing low-slung shorts and a long-sleeved shirt that ended just below her breasts. I wondered why a person would need long sleeves when their whole middle was bare.

She took a drag on a cigarette and said on the out-breath, "Twenty dollars and one cent."

"I shut the pump off at 20," I told her. "The one cent was its own idea."

More snickers.

"Twenty dollars and one cent," she said again, rolling her eyes for effect.

I dug my wallet out of my back pocket and counted the bills. Any which way I did it, they added up to $14. My traveler's checks were tucked away in my backpack in the motor home cupboard. I considered going back for them, but that didn't fit in with my plan of getting out of the place as fast as possible.

I lifted a leather flap in the wallet's dollar compartment and took out my Visa card. It was bright and new-looking. I rarely used it—Mom and me were pay-as-you-go kind of people. As the girl ran the card, I stole a glance in the direction of the snickers. Two young men wearing identical baseball caps were leaning on the end of the counter, staring at me. I quickly looked away, giving my rapt attention to a poster that was tacked on the wall to my left. It was a drawing of a skull wearing an army helmet. Flames and smoke rolled out of its gaping holes. Underneath were two sets of crossed rifles flanking the words FIREDOG MILITIA and a phone number.

The girl cleared her throat. I jumped. "Wanna sign?" she said.

I scribbled my name on the charge slip and picked up my card. As I hurried to the door, I heard a male voice say, "Dumb dyke." The girl giggled. I stopped short and looked directly at the staring guys.

Get out of here, Jo, said my wiser self, but I was too pissed to listen. "What's your problem?" I asked the men.

"Ain't me that's got the problem," one said. He straightened up, resting his hand on the butt of a pistol in a holster on his left hip. The other guy followed suit.

Get out of here, Jo. Now.

The guy who didn't have the problem looked out the doorway and nudged the other with his elbow. I followed his gaze. Charity, wearing black Levi's and a white peasant top, had exited the ByVista and was heading toward us. I ran out and got in her way.

"I'm going in to get a Diet Coke," she told me.

"They don't have any." I ushered her into the motor home, jumped into the driver's seat, and did the best imitation of a peel-out I could manage.

In my last look at the tittering idiots, I'd noticed what made their hats identical. The icon on each was a helmeted skull with smoke rolling out. I had no idea what the Firedog Militia was, but I was sure glad to get out of there.

I told Charity what had happened at the station. When we pulled over at a truck stop to top off, she bought me a Popsicle and lectured me about mouthing off to strange men. It reminded me of Mom, and I was comforted.

8

What you've heard is true: Out west, the sky is very big. There are no tall trees to spoil your view. It takes a cloud forever to get across.

When I was a kid, my friend Kate and I used to lie on our backs in the yard and try to dissolve clouds by imagining a hot spot in the middle of them. We didn't think that up ourselves. Kate's mother read it in a book and probably decided it was a way to keep the kids quiet for a while. She had five, so she was motivated.

The thing was, sometimes it worked—the cloud would vanish before your eyes. Well, yeah, sometimes it wouldn't, but that was usually when I got brassy and picked a bigger cloud than I could handle.

I was thinking about that as I drove through eastern Arizona. Charity was in the bedroom doing whatever it was she did back there. The road was straight, traffic was light, and the clouds were the perfect kind for dissolving. Because I hadn't done it for so long, I chose a wisp that was hanging over the road near the horizon. I didn't give myself good odds, because I was alternating my gaze between the road and the cloud. But dang, in a couple of minutes it started to break apart, and soon it completely disappeared.

Next I selected a small puff that looked vaguely like Richard Nixon's head. It had the nose, anyway.

I am Jo-El from Cyclopia. The death ray of my intermittent eye is closing in on Commander Nix-on-u in Space Craft One. No way is he going to make it across the cosmos and back to the imperial planet of Californicate!

"Is that a police car behind us?" Charity called from the bedroom. I looked in the rearview mirror, and there it was, a shiny black Buick with a flashing light on top. It wasn't a proper light—it was the magnetic kind that volunteer firemen in the suburbs back home slap on their car roofs. No siren either. These Arizona cops were sure sneaky. I pulled over.

A guy wearing a badge approached the driver's window. I slid it open.

"Want to step out, please?" he said.

Step out? Usually they asked for your license and insurance, then wrote you a speeding ticket. Not that I'd know. I wasn't speeding, though, I was sure of that. I'd been using the cruise control.

Charity emerged from the back. "What's going on? It looks like they're messing with the rear of the Ranger."

I swiveled to look at her. "He wants me to step out."

"Why?"

"He didn't say."

"I'd better come too." She grabbed her purse and we exited.

Three men were waiting for us. They were each wearing a badge pinned on a Western-style shirt, two holstered pistols, and a big cowboy hat. I looked around for the candid camera.

"I'm Deputy Conway," said the one who had approached my window. "Please step behind the vehicle." In near-synchronized steps, we all tromped to the rear of the Ranger. He pointed to where the license plate should have been.

"What happened to it?" Charity asked.

"That's what we need you to tell us, ma'am."

"I have no idea. I didn't know it was missing."

I bent to look at where the plate had been attached. All four screws were gone, and there were little scratches around a couple of the holes. I said, "Look, Charity…"

Deputy Conway interrupted. "Excuse me, sir, we need to see your driver's license."

Sir? I wasn't even using my guy face. I took out my wallet and handed him the license. "I wasn't speeding," I said. I wanted to make that clear up front.

He peered at it. "Ah, *Miss* Jacuzzo…"

There were chuckles from the audience, and he played to them, "*Miss* Jacuzzo, you were wavering all over the road. Have you been drinking?"

"Of course not. It's the middle of the morning!" Why had I said that? I never drink. "I never drink," I told him. "Honest!"

He peered at the license again. "Well, no one would blame you if you did. It's your birthday."

Charity looked at me. "It's your birthday?"

"I guess." I hadn't told her on purpose. She was so nice she'd probably buy me a gift or something.

"Jo!" she said accusingly. I looked at the Hats. They were getting a big kick out of this.

"I'm sorry, Miss Jacuzzo," said Deputy Conway, "but we're going to have to take you in for a breath test."

"Can't you do it here?" I asked.

"We don't have the equipment with us. Who owns these vehicles?"

"I do," Charity said.

"May I see some ID?"

Charity dug in her purse and brought out her billfold. She

extracted a driver's license and handed it to him. He inspected it and stacked it neatly with mine in his palm.

"Now, Miss Redmun, may I see the truck's registration and proof of insurance?"

Charity took the Ranger keys from her purse and opened the passenger-side door. Pulling some papers from the glove compartment, she handed them to him.

He compared them to her license and said, "This truck belongs to George Redmun."

"That's my father."

"Does he know you have it?"

She took a deep breath. "My father's deceased, sir. The estate has not yet been settled, but for all intents and purposes this truck is mine."

"And the motor home?"

"Same thing."

"I'm afraid you're going to have to come with us, Miss Redmun. We need to do some checking." He put our driver's licenses and the papers from the Ranger in his shirt pocket.

"Checking of what?" Charity asked.

"Get in the car, please," he said, and took her arm. One of the henchmen opened the back door of the Buick.

Charity broke free. "I can't leave the motor home here. It's not even locked."

"Deputy Ferguson is going to drive it for you and park it in a nice safe place. Keys, please?"

"I'd rather have Jo drive it."

"Not until after the breath test," he said. "Don't worry, Deputy Ferguson is a safe driver. Now, may I have the keys?"

"If you're going to insist that Deputy Ferguson drive it, I'm going to ride with him."

"You're riding with me, ma'am."

Charity stiffened and set her jaw. I figured she was going to give him trouble. For some reason she changed her mind and the fight drained out of her. She sighed and said to me, "Let's get this over with. Give him the keys, Jo."

Deputy Ferguson was a big guy, 6 foot 3 if he was an inch and almost half as wide. He stuck a beefy hand out. I put the ByVista's keys in it, and he headed for the motor home door.

Deputy Conway herded Charity and me into the sedan, then climbed into the front passenger seat. The remaining guy took the wheel and pulled out ahead of the ByVista. I looked back a few times to make sure it was following us. It was, but it was falling way behind. We exited the highway onto a deserted two-lane road. After a few miles we turned right onto a dirt lane, and after a while turned left.

The car we were in was a well-appointed Regal, pretty plush for a police vehicle. The engine was very quiet, and so were all the occupants. I could tell Charity was stressed—she was holding on to her purse so tight her knuckles were white. Her leg was shaking like she had a tic.

The reason for my own silence was practical. I was memorizing turns and making them into rhymes for easy recall. *Shack in sight, hang a right. Horse in pen, left again.* After all, when they were done with us, I was the one who would have to get the ByVista back to the highway.

We finally stopped in front of a stucco structure that looked like an old house. It was the same dirty beige as the gravelly desert that surrounded it. The structure wasn't in very good shape—the porch needed a jacking up, that's for sure.

"This is a police station?" Charity said.

"County substation," Deputy Conway told her, holding the door open. "Go on in."

We entered a large room that needed painting. The windows

were open, but it was extremely hot inside. The only furnishings were a desk with a phone on it, a banged-up metal file cabinet, and a few folding chairs. I didn't see any equipment that looked like it might be used for a breath test.

Charity looked back out the door. "Where's my motor home?"

"It's in a field down the road. Too spongy for it here," Deputy Conway told her.

Spongy? The ground looked like you couldn't dent it with a pickax.

He sat behind the desk, took off his hat, and put it on the desktop. He took our papers from his pocket, spread them out in front of him, and stared at them for a while. Then he picked up the receiver and pounded in a number. Covering the mouthpiece with his hand, he turned to the guy who'd been driving the Buick. "Take the ladies to the next room, will you, Dale?"

Charity and I were ushered into a smaller room that was completely bare of furniture. It might have once been a bedroom, judging from a closet that was missing its door. Dale brought in two folding chairs and went back out, pulling the door shut behind him. I crossed to a window, hoping for a cooling breeze, but no such luck. I looked around for the ByVista. It was nowhere in sight.

Charity joined me. "So what did he say you were doing, Jo? *Wavering?*"

"That's what he said."

"What does that mean?"

"I'm not sure. It was awfully windy." No way was I going to tell her about Nix-on-u and the death ray.

"What do you think happened to the Ranger's plate?" she asked me.

I shrugged. "It doesn't make sense. The screws were missing, but those kinds of screws never fall out." I told her about the scratch marks around the holes. "Somebody must have taken it."

"I wonder if that's what the deputies were doing when I saw them through the bedroom window."

"Why would they do that?"

"Who knows. And now I don't have a license plate. I was planning to drive the Ranger home."

"You still have the front one, don't you?"

"There is no front one, Jo. In South Carolina they don't give us a license plate for the front."

"They don't? There's a front plate on the motor home."

"You must not have looked at it very well. It says GEORGE AND MARTHA REDMUN, CHARLESTON. My parents had it custom-made."

"Your parents' names were George and Martha? As in Washington?"

"Yes." She crossed to the other window and stood staring out.

I followed her. "I need your opinion on something, Charity."

She looked at me. "What?"

"Well, I'm sort of ashamed to tell you this—I don't know what you're going to think of me. But back in Buffalo I had a little brush with the law."

She burst out laughing. I couldn't believe it. She laughed so hard she had to lean against the wall to keep from falling down. Finally she got herself under control and took a great breath. "I'm sorry, Jo. I was wound so tight, I couldn't help it. So you had a brush with the law?" She crossed to a chair and sat holding her stomach like she might lose it again at any moment.

"Never mind," I said.

"Oh, please tell me, Jo. I feel so bad. It's just that… Well, I can't explain."

I felt like forgetting the whole thing, but I really did want her opinion, so I gave her a condensed version of the Goddard incident, ending with, "I was innocent, of course, so they couldn't hold me. But do you think it could be in my record? Do you think this deputy guy might find it?"

"Were you served with any papers?"

"No."

"Did the police tell you not to leave town?"

"No."

"I wouldn't worry then." She got up and crossed back to the window, turning her back on me. Conversation over. I sat down and relieved my boredom by counting the cracked floor tiles and calculating the size of the room. It was 10 by 12.

Finally Deputy Conway opened the door and handed us our licenses and the Ranger papers. "It checks out, ladies. You can go. Oh, and here's a temporary license for your pickup. Affix it to the rear window."

Charity grabbed it, gave him a dirty look, and strode out of the room. I followed. Deputy Ferguson was in the office now, perched on a windowsill. The ByVista was parked out front with the door open and the motor running. So much for the sponge problem.

"Be sure to buckle your seat belts, ladies," Deputy Conway said, all friendly-like.

As we walked to the motor home, I whispered to Charity, "What happened to my breath test?"

She hit my arm. "Shhhh!"

We back the ByVista, and I made a beeline for the driver's seat. Charity took the passenger side. We obediently buckled up. The three men were standing in a line on the porch grinning at us. Deputy Conway waved.

"Let's go, Jo," Charity said.

I pulled out and drove slowly down the narrow road, trying desperately to stay on my half. Silently reciting my rhymes in reverse order and taking the opposite direction at each turn, I got us back to the interstate. As soon as we had climbed the ramp and merged into traffic, Charity threw off her seat belt and ran to the back.

"Are you all right?" I called. If she wasn't, I wouldn't blame her. I felt a little nauseated myself. After a while she returned, slumped down in her seat, and stared out the side window.

"Belt," I said.

"What?"

I pointed to the exposed buckle, and she fastened herself in. Taking a map from the console, she unfolded and studied it. "We're in Cochise County," she said, and replaced the map. Her voice sounded funny, like there was hardly enough breath in her to get the words out.

"Well, Cochise County's going to be sorry they picked on us, I'll bet."

She didn't answer. Her chest was rising and falling much too rapidly. I stole a glance at her face. It was pale.

"Are you hyperventilating, Charity?" I said. "Go breathe in a paper bag."

She got up, and I heard cupboards opening and closing. "We don't have a paper bag," she said. "Will a plastic one work?"

"I guess so."

She came back with a plastic grocery bag. Her color was already better, but I told her to breathe in it a few times anyway. When she stopped, I said, "So what's going on with you?"

"You're better off not knowing," she said.

It drives me crazy when people tell me that. Mom had said it a lot when I was a kid. "Fine," I said, pressing on the gas pedal. "Let's just get to the Tucson airport. Maybe I can fly standby and get out tonight. If not, I'll bunk there until tomorrow morning." We zoomed down the highway.

Charity unbuckled her seat belt, swung out of her seat, and

stamped to the back, slamming the bedroom door as loudly as a quarter-inch-thick door could slam.

I sat there feeling bad. Damn knee-jerk reaction! She had enough trouble in her life without me getting huffy on her. I didn't have time to pile on much guilt, however, because in a few minutes she was back. "Oh, what the hell," she said.

I looked at her in surprise. I hadn't heard her swear before, not that "hell" was all that bad.

"What the hell," she said again. "It'll be a relief to tell you. Maybe you can help me figure out what I'm going to do. But Jo, you can never tell anybody about this. My brother's life is at stake and maybe mine too."

"Your *life* is at stake?" Visions of Wellaways danced in my head. "Charity, what's going on? Tell me!"

"Paul's ransom is gone."

"Ransom? Like in kidnapping?"

"Sort of."

"Where did it go? Where was it? And what do you mean, sort of?"

"My brother got himself deeply in debt with some dangerous people. They were going to kill him. He asked me to pay them back for him."

"And if you don't they'll kill you too?"

"That's what he told me. They'll kill him first, and then they'll come after me."

"How do they know who you are?"

"Paul told them. He had to, he was buying time."

"So this whole trip is about taking money to some loan sharks in Tucson? Haven't you heard of Western Union?"

"I'm not sure Western Union would let me wire four million, Jo."

"Four million dollars?" It came out as a squeal.

"Yes. That's what his debt came to, including the interest.

Four million in cash, and I have to bring it in person."

"Holy shit," I said. "How did you get four million dollars in cash?" I heard Mom's voice, *Now, Jo, is that any of our business?*

"It wasn't difficult, really. I sold some paintings and specified I wanted the payment in small bills."

"You had paintings worth that much?"

"They belonged to my father."

I was out of my league here. We bought our artwork at the mall. "So we've been hauling four million dollars in cash across the country? And you didn't even tell me?" Of course if I'd known, I wouldn't have been able to sleep. I'd have insisted on going into restaurants one at a time or getting take-out. Maybe Charity was right—I was better off not knowing. "Where did you keep it?" I asked.

"Under the bed."

"You're kidding."

"When you lift the panel under the mattress, there's a big storage area. The money was there this morning. I checked."

"So who took it? That guy who drove the motor home? What was his name, Ferguson?"

"Who else could it have been? Maybe they were all in on it. I'll bet they aren't even lawmen. That place back there was a sorry excuse for a county substation."

"Why don't you check it out," I said. "Call the Cochise County Sheriff's Department."

Charity took out her phone. I heard her talk to information and punch in a number.

"Hello. Is Deputy Conway there, please?" she asked. "He's not? How about that tall fellow he works with, I think his name is Ferguson? ...Then how about Dale? ...Well, do you have a number for the county substation on the dirt road not far from the Interstate? ...No, I don't want to speak to anyone else. Thank you." She folded the phone and looked at me, her eyes wide. "They really are policemen. But why would they steal my money?"

"Did you get the number for the substation?"

"The person who answered wouldn't say anything about it, wanted me to talk to the officer in charge,"

"Why didn't you? You could have reported them."

"How do we know the officer in charge wasn't in on it?"

"You're right. The whole bunch of them could be crooked. Well, you're going to have to report them to someone."

"This isn't the time, Jo."

"Why not? And what I'd like to know is how they knew you had so much money with you? And how did they know where it was?"

"They must have searched."

"I don't see signs that anyone searched, do you?"

"What are you saying?"

"I'm not saying anything," I told her. "It's just odd, something to think about."

"What I've got to think about is how I'm going to pay Paul's ransom. Any ideas on that?"

"Not off the top of my head." The top of my head was full of four million dollars. If only I could have had a glimpse of it! I'd never seen that much cash except in the movies, and that was probably stage money.

I forced my mind back to the problem at hand. "When did you talk with Paul about paying the ransom?" I asked her.

"He called me Saturday morning from where he was being held."

"Where was that?"

"He said he wasn't allowed to tell me. Then another fellow got on the phone. He directed me to leave the motor home with the money in it at an intersection in the desert."

"In the desert?"

"Yes, somewhere outside of Tucson," she said. "One of the roads was Nettle and the other was Farley—I wrote down the directions. He told me to park off the road, get out, and lock the door. Then I was supposed to stick the keys on top of a tire and drive away in the Ranger."

"And then what?"

"That's it. When they got the money, they'd let Paul go. What am I going to do, Jo? I'm supposed to have it there by tomorrow afternoon. I was going to drop you off at the airport and take it out there."

"You were going to do that all by yourself? You don't even know how to unhitch the Ranger."

"I do too. I've been watching you. It doesn't matter anymore, though. There's no point in leaving the motor home in the desert without the money, is there?"

"Do the police know about this?" I asked.

"I couldn't tell them. The man said if I went to the authorities or told anybody about it, they'd kill Paul. Think, Jo, if it were your brother, what would you do?"

I measured an imaginary brother against an imaginary four million dollars. It was a tough call, but I decided I'd rather have the money.

I glanced at her. Her shoulders were sagging against the belt. She looked so sad, so vulnerable, so…sexy. I smacked my libido upside the head and said, "I see your problem, but everything's changed now. Why don't we stop at a police station in Tucson and tell them what happened? At the very least they can give you some good advice. Maybe they can stake out the desert tomorrow, follow whoever shows up to get the ByVista, and get Paul back for you. Maybe they'll even get your money back from those bozos back there."

"I can't do that," she whispered.

"Charity, you said it yourself, if the loan sharks don't get their four million, they're going to kill Paul. And then they're going to come after you.

"I can't go to the police, and that's that."

I thought this over for a while, and asked her, "Are you in trouble with the law?"

When she didn't answer, I looked at her. Her eyes were brimming. I groped in my pocket for a tissue and handed it to her.

She wiped her eyes and blew her nose. "Thanks."

"Are you?"

"I can't tell you—this time I really can't. I've told you too much already."

See that motor home flying by? Inside are two renegades who share the special bond of those society dubs "outlaws." Is it Butch and Sundance? Thelma and Louise? No, it's Jo and Charity on the last leg of their ill-fated journey west. Are they about to kiss and leap?

"Jo," she said suddenly, "I've got an idea."

I pulled my mind from the edge of the cliff. "What is it?"

"Maybe I can get in touch with the men who are holding Paul. I can explain what happened and ask for time to get more money together."

"You could raise another four million?" My mind had never been so boggled.

"If I had to. But i t would take some time. Think, Jo, how can I find those people?"

"I don't know if finding them is such a good idea. Loan sharks aren't known for being reasonable."

"It's the only thing I can think to do."

"I don't suppose they gave you a phone number."

"No."

"Does Paul have a cell phone?"

"Yes."

"Try calling."

"I've tried before but it was no use. I guess it couldn't hurt to try again, though." Charity picked up the phone and did the speed-dialing thing. After a few seconds she said, "Well, that's funny."

"What?"

"They say it's not a working number."

"Where does he live?"

"In Tucson. He has an apartment."

"Do you have the address?"

"Yes, but he won't be there."

"We could go talk to the neighbors? Maybe they saw something."

"That's a great idea, Jo." Her shoulders straightened up. "Thank you."

"Don't mention it." *Sweetie.*

9

It wasn't long before we hit the outskirts of Tucson. Scattered industrial complexes gave way to subdivisions and malls, and all at once we were in a city-filled valley ringed by craggy mountains. These were the kind of mountains I'd seen on postcards.

As we exited into Tucson proper, we stopped at a gas station, and Charity went into the mini mart to see if they had a city map. They did. She brought it back to the ByVista and unfolded it on the table.

"We're looking for Wainscot Lane," she said.

My eyes were having a hard time focusing on anything closer than the white line, so Charity found it first. It was in the northeast section of town. We plotted a course.

"Do you think they might let us leave the motor home here?" I asked her. "The Ranger would be a lot easier to maneuver through city streets."

"I'll go ask," she said, and went in the mini mart. When she came back, she said, "It's all arranged. We just need to move it to the back."

After I repositioned and got it leveled, we unhitched the

Ranger. My T-shirt was soaked, so I went back in the ByVista to put on a dry one.

I thought Charity might want to drive for a change, but she tossed me the keys. I got in, started the engine, and eased into traffic. It felt good to drive something smaller than a house. The fact that it was a cool red pickup was icing on the cake.

As we worked our way through the city, I got my first good dose of Arizona architecture. A majority of the structures, both homes and businesses, were one-story and covered with stucco painted white or some shade of beige. I loved the red U-shaped tiles on many of the roofs. And the flowers! It was only the middle of April, but it looked like midsummer, which shouldn't have been surprising since it felt like midsummer too.

We found Wainscot Lane without a hitch. It was a street of matching two-story apartment buildings with narrow concrete driveways between. Paul's building was in the middle of the block. The first empty parking space was a building further. As we walked back, heat radiated from the sidewalk, teasing my sweat glands into action. I splayed my elbows so air could get to my sodden pits.

The door to the foyer of Building Five was firmly locked. An engraved bronze sign above the door read NO SOLICITORS, And four doorbell buttons were neatly grouped at the side of the jamb. Little spaces were provided above them for names, but only the one labeled Apartment 1 had a name on it: Biggers.

"Do you know which apartment is your brother's?" I asked.

"Number 3."

"Ring it," I told her.

"He won't be here."

"Maybe he's got a roommate or a girlfriend."

"I'm sure he doesn't," she said.

"Why don't you want to ring it?"

"Jo, what if this is where they're holding him?"

"That would be a good thing, wouldn't it? Isn't the point of all this to get in touch with the people who are holding him so you can explain about the money?"

"I guess," she said.

A well-dressed couple walked past us and up the short sidewalk to the next building. Before entering, they paused and looked us up and down, probably wondering if we were solicitors. I reached across Charity and pushed the button labeled "Apartment 3." A woman's voice, faint and tinny, came from an intercom above the doorbells. "Who is it?"

Charity gasped and just stood there staring at the grid, so I took charge. "We're looking for Paul Redmun," I said.

"Who?"

"Paul Redmun. Is he there?"

The answer sounded like, "We're no dear bat cave."

"What did you say?"

"There's nobody here by that name," she yelled.

"This is apartment 3, isn't it?"

"What?"

I put my mouth right up to the intercom. "Are you in apartment 3?"

"Just a minute, I'll come down."

Charity was pale and shaky. I wanted to put my arm around her, but I settled for patting her shoulder.

Through the glass panel, we watched a woman descend the stairs. She was on the high side of middle age, covered neck to ankle in peach polyester. She had one of those Taco Bell dogs in her arms. They both looked us over before she cracked the door, holding onto it with her free hand.

"That damn loudspeaker isn't worth beans," she said through the crack. "Don't try to get in. Lobo bites."

The dog's eyes glittered like varnished black beads. I peered into them through the glass, looking for killer instinct. I didn't see it, but I've been wrong before and I have the scars to prove it.

I put my mouth close to the crack. "Ma'am, we're looking for Paul Redmun. The address we have is Five Wainscot Street, apartment 3."

"That's my address, but I don't know anybody by that name. He doesn't live in this building. You must have the wrong address."

"No. This is his address," Charity said. "I sent him a Christmas gift here, and I know he got it."

Maybe it was the mention of Christmas, but the woman eased up and gave us a whole foot to talk through. As soon as there wasn't any glass between us, the dog's ears flattened and he growled, showing rat-size teeth. "Easy, Lobo," she said.

"How long have you lived here?" I asked.

"Just since February. I never met the people who had the apartment before me—it was empty when I looked at it. It could have been your Paul whoever-you-said, I suppose."

"Have any of the other tenants lived here longer than that?" I asked her.

"Yes, but they're all at work. I can give you the phone number of the complex manager, if you want. I'll have to go back upstairs to get it."

"Yes, please," Charity said.

The woman pulled the door until the lock clicked, then she climbed the steps. Lobo watched us over her shoulder until they rounded the corner at the top.

In a few moments the intercom crackled. Loudly and slowly, the woman recited a phone number followed by, "Did you get that?"

"Yes. Thank you," Charity said, writing the number on a little pad from her purse.

"What?"

"Thank you!" I hollered into the intercom.

As we walked to the Ranger, I turned and looked back at what I figured must be apartment 3's window, just in case the woman had been one of the bad guys and a trussed and gagged Paul was banging his head against it to get our attention. The only thing I spotted, however, was Lobo—he was standing on the windowsill with his front paws against the glass, barking up a storm.

When we were back in the air-conditioned truck, Charity took out her cell phone and punched in the number from her pad. As she talked, she got more and more agitated. By the time she was done, the handle of her purse was twisted into a French knot.

She looked at me through narrowed eyes.

"What?" I said.

"The manager said Paul moved out of the apartment right after the new year. He didn't give them notice, and he didn't leave a forwarding address."

"Did he take his furniture?"

"He took everything including the lightbulbs from the fixtures and a few other things they considered theirs. Why didn't he let me know he'd moved? The jerk!"

I was astounded. This was the first time I'd seen her show anything but patient affection for Paul. I figured it was a good time to ask something I'd been wondering about.

"Charity, how could Paul get in debt for four million dollars? Does he gamble? Use drugs?" I tried to think of other things I didn't do because I was too cheap.

"He does have a history of drug use. He's been clean for months, though. At least he told me he was."

"So other than that, he's a stand-up guy? He's never stolen anything worse than lightbulbs?"

"We all have our faults, Jo. So do you want to know what I found out from the manager?"

"Sure," I said, wondering what Paul's faults might be, and if they might include extortion. Things sure weren't adding up in his favor.

"She gave me a good lead. She said she thought Paul had been friendly with the woman who lives in apartment 1."

"Biggers," I said.

"Yes. Gina Biggers. How'd you know?"

"It was right above her doorbell. Didn't you see it?"

"If I did, I don't remember. Anyway, she gave me Gina's work number."

"Great," I said.

Charity dialed and asked for Gina Biggers. After a minute or so she said, "Gina, this is Charity Redmun. I believe you know my brother, Paul. Could I talk with you? ...No, I don't have that much time. ...Yes, that would be fine." She wrote something on her pad and said, "We'll be there shortly."

"You're in luck, Jo," she told me after she hung up. "Gina Biggers works at a steakhouse."

Following Charity's directions, I drove about 20 blocks south to a restaurant called the Spittin' Grill. The street was so narrow and the parking lot so small, it was a lucky thing we weren't driving the ByVista.

We entered a small lobby decorated with cartoon cowgirls, and Charity asked the hostess for Gina Biggers. Soon a pretty brunette wearing denim overalls and not much else came out to and introduced herself. When Charity told her we'd have something to eat while we were here, she found us a table in her section, handed us menus, and in true waitress fashion said she'd be right back.

It was one of those trendy places where you can't hear normal conversation for all the noise bouncing off the walls. I wasn't up on my bands, but what was playing at way too many decibels might have been something by Nine Inch Nails.

"I think I'll have the prime rib special," I yelled to Charity.

"It's your birthday," she said. "Have the whole cow."

"Funny," I told her. "What are you going to eat?"

"A baked potato and a salad."

Gina came back and took our orders. After delivering our order to the kitchen, she sat down and said she had a couple of minutes to talk. We leaned forward and huddled our heads together in order to hear. "You're Paul's sister?" she said. "I can see the resemblance."

"Gina, do you know where my brother is?" Charity asked.

"Not really. I saw him a couple of weeks ago. He stopped in here for a bite. He told me he'd moved in with this guy he was running around with."

"What guy?"

"His name's Buck—I don't know his last name. I don't like him."

"Why?"

"He's always playing, you know, tough guy. He wears a pistol and talks against the government all the time. It makes my skin crawl."

"Does Paul carry a gun too?" Charity asked.

"Sometimes. He and Buck joined a group where everybody carries guns."

"My God," said Charity. "He never told me anything about that."

"This group he joined, do you know the name?" I asked.

"Yeah, if I can remember. They wear these caps with skulls that say, let me think…some kind of dog."

"Firedog Militia?" I said.

"Yes. How do you know?"

"Jo, how *do* you know?" Charity asked.

"The guys I told you about in the creepy gas station this morning were wearing hats like that."

"It's a good-size organization. You see those caps all over," Gina said.

"What kind of an organization is it?" I asked

"Paul told me they were raising money to train patriots, whatever that means. He asked me if I wanted to contribute, and I told him I didn't have any cash to spare."

Charity's eyes were big. "I can't believe Paul would get involved with a militia."

I, however, could believe it. The more I was learning about Paul, the less I wanted to find him. But for Charity's sake I asked Gina, "Do you know how we can find out where Paul and this Buck live?"

"All I know is he said it was somewhere down by Bisbee," Gina said. "And the rent was cheap. He was pretty broke."

"Doesn't he work?" I asked.

"Now and then. He never seems to keep a job for long. He was counting on a big inheritance, but he said his sister got it all. That must be you, huh?" She looked at Charity.

Charity nodded. "I was planning on setting up a trust for him after the estate was settled."

"Did you tell him that?" Gina said.

"Not yet."

"Well, maybe you should. He's plenty mad about the whole thing. Don't tell him I said this," she said, "but he told me he was going to get his, whatever it took. I'd watch my ass, if I were you."

One of the other waitresses came by and told Gina she had plates waiting in the kitchen. As soon as she was gone I said to Charity, "You got the whole inheritance?"

"I'm afraid so," she said, as if that were a bad thing. "Paul was estranged from my parents because of his drug use. Mom told me he kept hitting her up for money and even stole stuff out of the house to sell. Finally they cut off his allowance and asked him to leave. After that he pretty much dropped out of their lives. I didn't think they'd write him out of the will, though."

"They didn't even leave him a dollar?" I asked. "My grandparents left my father a dollar."

"Not even a dollar."

"But you kept in close touch with Paul?"

"Not exactly what you'd call close. Every so often he'd call asking for a loan and I'd mail him a check. That's how I knew he'd moved to Tucson and what his address was."

"Why'd he move here?"

"He joined a religious group back east. It sounded like a cult, the way he described it. The good thing was they got him to give up drugs. They sent him here to do missionary work of some kind, but he quit them a short time later. That was about nine months ago. I tried to call him every couple of weeks, but either he wouldn't answer or he was too busy to talk and said he'd call back, but he never did. Then in March he phoned and said it was too expensive for him to call me in Paris. He asked for $10,000 to buy a computer so he could e-mail me. I told him that was too much, and if he wanted a computer I'd order one for him and have it delivered. He told me to forget it, and that's the last I heard from him until he called about the ransom."

"Nice guy," I said under my breath.

"What?"

I was saved from having to think of something noncynical that rhymed with "nice guy" by Gina delivering our meals. The prime rib was good, if a little skimpy. Charity picked at her food, then said she had to go to the ladies' room. While she was gone, Gina and two other waitresses brought me a slice of chocolate cake and sang "Happy Birthday to You" at the top of their lungs in order to be heard over the loud music. I was terribly embarrassed. When Charity got back I read her the riot act and was rewarded with a smile. It was the first one I'd seen on her for a long time...and I know it sounds corny, but it made my heart skip a beat.

As we were driving back to where we'd left the ByVista, I asked Charity if she knew how to get to the intersection in the desert where she'd been told to leave the motor home. She said yes; the directions were in her purse.

"Why don't we drive over there, see if it tells us anything?" I asked her.

"You're not too tired?"

"I can sleep on the plane tomorrow."

"Sure, then," she said. "Why not?"

Following the instructions she'd been given, we struck out southwest into the desert, looking for the intersection of Nettle and Farley Roads. The problem was, there was no such intersection. We took Nettle Road from one end to the other, but it wasn't crossed by Farley Road or anything that sounded like Farley Road.

"I don't understand," Charity said. "Why would I be told to bring the money to a nonexistent intersection?"

I pulled to the side of the road and stopped. We got out the map, and sure enough, the intersection was nowhere to be found. We were surrounded by desert that was bare except for an occasional spiny plant. The sun was low, and the shadows were longer than the plants were tall. The road rolled out in front of us until it was lost in infinity.

"You know, Charity," I said, "a few years ago, my cousin Kimmy broke up with her husband, Mike. Not long after that I spotted him at a restaurant in Amherst, hitting on a sweet young thing. When I got home I called Kimmy and told her what I'd seen, and we had a good old time trashing him. The thing is, before long she and Mike got together again, and now neither one of them speaks to me."

After a moment, Charity said, "That's too bad, Jo. Why are you telling me this?"

"Because I don't want you to get mad at me. I don't want you to think I'm trashing your brother ."

"But...?" she said.

"Well, for instance, it worried me when Gina told us Paul said he was going to 'get his, whatever it took.' What do you think he meant by that?"

"It could mean he's going to start pressuring me to give him half the inheritance."

"You're going to give him some of it anyway, aren't you?"

"Sure, but he doesn't know that. And anyway, it'll be in the form of a trust that will pay him an allowance every month. That's a lot different than giving it to him in a lump sum. I know Paul—he'd blow it all and come back for more."

"So if he needed four million dollars and asked you for it, you wouldn't give it to him?"

"Of course not."

"To part with that much money you'd have to think he was in danger of being killed, right?"

"Jo, I *love* my brother. I've just lost my parents—he's the only family I have left. I'd do anything to keep him from being killed."

"Are you getting mad?" I asked.

"No, I'm not. So what are you saying? That Paul deceived me? He faked the whole thing to get the money?"

I shrugged. "You know him better than I do."

She watched her hands clasping and unclasping. "Well, just so you don't think I'm a complete idiot, I have to confess I've kind of been coming to the same conclusion. I fought it for a long time, telling myself he wouldn't do that to me. How could he? I was the one who stood by him after our parents wrote him off. I bankrolled him. I supported him. I love him."

"I know."

She raised her head and looked me straight in the eye. "What do *you* think Paul meant when he said he was going to get his?"

How could I say it? After a minute of mental phrasing and rephrasing, I said, "Charity, is Paul your heir?"

"Of course. Are you suggesting Paul would hurt me? Kill me for the money?"

"Like I said, you know him better than I do."

"Yes, I do…and I'll have to admit, Jo, I'm terrified." She covered her face with her hands and started sobbing.

I felt sorry for her, having to be terrified of someone she loved so much. To empathize, I pictured my mother as a crazed ax murderer. Would I still love her? Sure, but I wouldn't let her anywhere near me with an ax.

I turned the Ranger in the direction of Tucson and busied myself with driving. Ten miles later Charity was still crying. I couldn't stand it. I pulled to the side of the road, turned off the engine, and pulled her against me. While she drenched my shoulder, I stroked her hair. Her soft hair. I'd never felt hair that soft. I buried my face in her golden curls. They tickled my nose, caressed my cheeks. I closed my eyes and inhaled deeply, holding her scent in my lungs until it had time to enter my bloodstream.

I pretended we were lovers. *There, there, darling, dry those tears. We'll go on home now and crawl in our own little bed, and I'll give you something to smile about.*

Of course, the part about *me* loving *her* wasn't pretending. I knew that now. I also knew she was arrow-straight.

Back when I was training to be a nursing assistant, I struck up a friendship of sorts with a fellow lesbian who was in several of my classes. She told me she was madly in love with a woman who was married and uninterested in a relationship.

"Sounds pretty hopeless," I told her.

"Not at all," she said. "I'll just hang around and take what she can give, and someday she'll see the light."

"Yeah, right," I said, and wrote her off as a total fruitcake.

What scared me now as I sat with Charity folded in my arms was that the fruitcake's philosophy was starting to make sense.

"Stupid, stupid, stupid," I told myself. I must have said it out loud because Charity pulled away and said, "What did you say? I'm stupid?"

"Not you," I told her. "It's me. *I'm* stupid."

"Oh," she said. "Do you by any chance have a tissue?"

I found one in my pocket and handed it to her. Then I started the engine and pulled back on the road. The highest tips of the mountains around Tucson glowed bright orange in the last dregs of the sunset.

"Pretty, huh?" I said.

"What?"

"The mountains."

She gave herself a little shake. "Why, yes, they are. You know, Jo, I was thinking about what you said after the money disappeared, how it was odd there weren't any signs of a search."

"I know! It doesn't make any sense. Deputy Conway kept us in that room at the substation for no more than 15 minutes. Whoever took the money knew you had it, and they knew where to look. Did Paul know about that space under the bed?"

"Of course. He's the one who told me to put it there. He said it was the safest place in the motor home." She laughed bitterly.

"They were in it together, weren't they, Paul and those guys? I was never meant to get to Tucson with that cash."

"Looks like that to me. They probably had it all worked out to stop you on some pretense and take the money."

"A pretense like a 'lost' license plate. But how would they know I'd be on Interstate 10, and at what time?"

"What other route could you take from Charleston to Tucson and get there by Friday? You said yourself you'd never make it in time by taking back roads."

"That's true."

"As far as knowing *when* you'd be there, maybe they've been watching us. Maybe that couple in the Wellaway are connected to all this."

"The Wellaway?" she said. "Oh, sure, that makes sense. And here I'd thought..." She stopped.

"What?"

"It doesn't matter anymore." She actually looked relieved.

I considered pressuring her to tell me about it, but I decided not to. Maybe tomorrow.

As I pulled into the gas station and aligned the Ranger behind the ByVista, Charity looked at me. "But Jo, why couldn't Paul wait for the money until I got to Tucson?"

"Because he had no way of being sure you hadn't told someone."

"Like the police?" she said.

"Of course. You could have had a whole battalion of cops with you, for all he knew. And in my opinion, you should have."

"I know your opinion," she said.

The motor home's interior was hot as a blast furnace. Charity said we'd better start looking for a campsite with hookups, but first she wanted to stop in the mini mart to thank them for letting us leave it there.

"Good news," she said when she returned carrying a six-pack of Diet Coke and a newspaper. "The manager says we can stay here for the night, and we can even plug into an electrical outlet on the side of the building."

"That's real nice of him," I said.

"It's not without strings," she told me. "He wants me to go out for a drink with him when he gets off at 9."

"You're not going, are you?"

"I am. I need to pick his brain."

My stomach soured. It was one thing to accept that she liked men but another to send her off on a date with one. I ran out to plug in the ByVista. It took me a while because the motor home had a 505-amp system and the outlet was only 15. Poking around in a storage bin, I found several different-size adapters and cords. As I piggybacked from 50 amps to 30 to 15, I remembered reading in one of the manuals that you should never do this kind of thing because you could blow your whole electrical system. Charity's dad must have done it, though, or he wouldn't have had the adapters.

Charity was wearing a red sundress when I got back. She was a knockout. I wondered why she was still single. "Charity, do you have a boyfriend back in Paris?" I asked.

"I'm happier by myself. Anyway, I was married once. It was short and not too sweet."

"You were married? What was his name?" I was learning a lot today. Too much.

"Brad. And no, Jo, I don't want to talk about it." She picked up the business section of the newspaper and gave it her undivided attention. I grabbed the comics and did the same.

At 9 sharp, there was a rap on the door. Before opening it, Charity said, "You want to come with us, Jo? I'm sure he wouldn't mind."

I wasn't as sure as she was. "No, thanks. I'd like to meet him, though."

His name was Pete, and he seemed like a nice-enough guy, although I'd have liked him better if he'd had at least one hair out of place. To his credit, he invited me to come along, but he looked relieved when I said no. I watched as they got in his white Camaro. Then I went inside and wrote his description and license plate number on a piece of paper.

My body was dog-tired, but my brain was buzzing. Charity had been married! *Brad and Charity. Charity and Brad. Was he handsome? Rich? Did he cheat on her? No, that's silly—who would cheat on a woman like Charity? Maybe she cheated on him! Whatever it was, the ending was bitter enough that she took back her own last name—if she ever gave it away in the first place.* Curiosity nipped at my heels like Great-aunt Concetta's shih-tzu.

I checked my laundry that was still in the clothes dryer and was relieved to find it hadn't mildewed. Blessing Pete for letting us plug in, I started it tumbling and went to see what was on TV. When I turned the set on, however, everything went dark. Oh, my God, I blew the system!

I grabbed the flashlight and flipped to the troubleshooting section in the manual. It told me to check the fuses in the box under the refrigerator. I did and found that a major one had blown. I replaced it from a container of fuses that was stuck in the corner of the box, and everything came back on. I switched off all but the dryer, hoping my clothes would dry before it tripped again. The alternative was hanging them out the windows of the ByVista, and I was sure Neat Pete wouldn't appreciate that.

Without air-conditioning, the place was getting hot fast, so I opened every window and vent I could find. Sweating profusely, I sat in the dark until the dryer buzzed.

It was another hour and a half before the Camaro pulled up. By then I had dared turn on the TV again and was watching Conan O'Brien. Pete kept Charity talking in the driveway 15 minutes more. She finally came in and flopped in a chair. "I am so tired," she said.

"Did you have a good time? What did you have to drink?"

She gave me an irritated look. "Diet Coke, and I didn't go to have a good time. The guy's a self-centered boor. I was able to find out a few things about the Firedog Militia, though. The woman who was tending bar knew a lot about them—she's from down by the border and used to date one of their members. She said the militia started out as a group of ranchers protecting their property from illegal migrants crossing over from Mexico. But now there's a new bunch of guys taking over the group. They're the kind you don't want to mess with. They're more into stockpiling arms and training quasi-soldiers than helping the ranchers. And guess what, Jo, the leader of the militants is a man called Buck French, and he's mean as hell. She said he even served time, but she didn't know for what."

"Buck French? Is that the same Buck your brother moved in with?"

"It could be," she said. "So how was your evening?"

"Boring. Uneventful. Nothing happened at all." I turned off the TV and started unfolding my bed, although I was so tired I probably could have slept standing up.

Charity started for the bedroom. "Good night, then."

"Wait," I said. "What are you going to do tomorrow?"

"Since the money's gone and we've figured out Paul's game, I might as well go back to Charleston."

"Good idea."

"Unfortunately, it's not that simple. I thought I'd be leaving the ByVista in the desert and would never see it again. After making sure Paul had been released, I was planning to drive back in the Ranger. But now we're going to have to get the motor home back east."

"Who's we?" I said.

"We. You and me.

"Oh, no. I can't."

"I'll pay you another thousand."

"I can't do it, Charity. I'm supposed to be in Florida this weekend to pack up Mrs. Phipps."

"Who?" she asked.

"Why don't you save your money?" I said. "Find an RV dealer in Tucson and sell the motor home. What the heck, sell the Ranger too and get yourself a flight all the way to Paris."

"I'd love to do all that, Jo, but I can't, not until the estate is settled."

"Wait a minute," I said. "You sold four million dollars worth of art, but you can't sell a motor home?"

"Not legally."

"Oh," I said. "Is that why you keep saying you can't go to the police? You sold that art before the estate was settled?"

"That's it. You figured it out," she said in a tone that told me I hadn't.

Damn. I wasn't going to be on that plane tomorrow. I was way too nosy and way too crazy about her to abandon her now. I was in this to the bitter end.

10

In the morning we walked to a family-style restaurant down the block for breakfast. The waitress said, "If you want water, you're going to have to ask for it. We've got a real shortage."

I told her a cup of coffee would be fine, and I felt guilty even ordering that. Charity asked for orange juice and the yellow pages. I watched over the top of my menu as she opened the book near the front and traced down a column with her finger. Then she took out her cell phone and punched in a number. I heard her tell someone she had an emergency, could she come in right away? They must have told her no, because she tried another number and repeated it. On the third try she wrote something on her little pad, chug-a-lugged the juice, and said, "Have a nice breakfast, Jo. I have to run an errand. I'll be back as soon as I can."

"You're not going to eat?"

"Get me a bagel. I'll have it later." She didn't close the phone book, so after she left I turned it around. From the page headings, I deduced she'd gone to consult either an astrologer or an attorney.

As I finished my stack of pancakes, I looked at my watch. It was 9:10. At this very moment, a plane was taking off from the

Tucson airport bound for Atlanta, Georgia, and there was an empty seat in first class with my name on it.

On the other hand, maybe it was like in those movies *Sliding Doors* and *Run, Lola, Run*—every time there's a fork in your road, you split in two, and each of you heads in a different direction. If so, there was another Jo Jacuzzo out there and she was on that plane right now, shaking out her cloth napkin. I got a serious case of goose bumps.

I paid and walked back to the ByVista. As expected, the Ranger was gone. I hoped Charity would be back before too long or she might have to go out with Pete again tonight. After an hour and a half or so, she finally drove in and pulled up behind the motor home. She stuck her head through the open window and called, "Hitch it up, Jo, we're moving out."

When it was hitched, she went in the mini mart to say good-bye to Pete and came out with directions written on the back of a pink flyer. "Pete told me about a great place we can spend the night," she said. "He even called and made a reservation for us in his name. He said he was sorry he couldn't take off work and meet us there."

I'll bet he was. "Meet us where?'" I asked.

"It's in New Mexico. We're going to take the back roads this time, through the desert and into the mountains. We don't want to run into Deputy Conway again."

We both shuddered.

"Did your errand go well?" I asked.

"Oh, yes. It was just a bit of business with an attorney."

So it had been an attorney. Not that I'd seriously thought Charity would go to an astrologer, but you never know about people. I took care of a woman once who wouldn't even make a dental appointment without calling her astrologer. To her credit, she was 92 and still had her original teeth.

I wondered what "bit of business" Charity had done. Maybe she'd set someone on the trail of her missing brother and her missing money, both of which would no doubt be found in the same place.

Using Pete's directions, Charity directed me through the busy Friday traffic to the north edge of the city, where Oracle Road (no lie) took us out of town, across streets with names like Orange and Tangerine. I waited for Grapefruit, but it never came. Many of the parking lots we passed were decorated with puddles of smooth river rocks. With the water shortage, it may have been the closest they could come to real puddles.

After a zillion stoplights, things finally got less congested. The long mountains that flanked the road looked like great lizards basking in the sun, and the houses that clung to their foothills belonged to the kind of people who could afford ByVistas. I spotted a sign that told how to get to Biosphere II.

"Is that *the* Biosphere? I asked Charity.

"It must be."

"Wow. That would be something to see."

She checked the hand-drawn map. "Pete doesn't have us going that way. Anyway, we don't have time to stop. I want to get to Silver City in time to do some soaking. It's going to be slow going on these back roads."

"Silver City, New Mexico? Where the big copper mine is?"

"I guess you know more about it than I do."

"Do you think we could have a look at the mine? I've got a flyer in my backpack that tells how to find it. I picked it up when we were in Deming."

"Maybe tomorrow, if it's not too far out of our way," she said.

"Great... Wait a minute—did you say you're going to do some soaking? Soaking in what?"

"A hot mineral pool," she said. "Have you ever been in one?"

"No."

"You're going to love it."

We went for miles through a mountain-rimmed desert. The highway was such a straight shot, I had to use the cruise control to keep from speeding. I slowed down every once in a while and looked back to see if the Wellaway might be following. It wasn't.

We saw a sign for a memorial in honor of Tom Mix. I told Charity he was an old movie cowboy, and she gave me permission to pull off the road for a quick look. It was a statue of a sad horse with a marker saying Tom Mix had died on that spot, but it didn't tell what he'd died from.

After a while I had to slow down for a town called Florence where there was a huge prison complex. The chain-link fence around it was topped with vicious razor wire. A sign cautioned us not to pick up hitchhikers. I wondered if Tom Mix might have been killed by a hitchhiker.

We crossed the Gila River, which didn't have a drop of water in it, and soon turned east on another highway that climbed and wound through a rugged mountain pass where great golden boulders lined the road, glowing in the sunlight. On nearby peaks, groups of wind-carved stone figures stood tall, watching us go by.

We changed highways again in a city called Globe. It was a good-size place and, because it had lots of stoplights, a real slow-down. We fueled up and stopped for a bite to eat, then struck out into bona fide sky-high mountains with switchback curves and sheer drop-offs that had me driving in the middle of the road and praying.

Somewhere in the middle of all this we crossed the line into New Mexico and caught still another highway that would take us to Silver City. We didn't go all the way there, though. Charity checked her directions again and after a few miles told me to turn off on a private road with a sign that said BIG BEAR BUTTE SPA.

After paying at the office, we drove down a lane to the campground. There were 20 or so sites, almost all with tents or RVs in them, plus a bank of charming log cabins over to the side. We were high enough that there was real grass and big trees with deep green leaves. It was like coming home.

As we pulled into our site I looked around but didn't see any bodies of water. "Where's the hot mineral pool?" I asked.

Charity looked at the little map she got at check-in and pointed to our right. "There's a path to it over there. Pete told me the water is very hot and very therapeutic. I can't wait—I haven't had a good soak since last summer in Switzerland. You will go in, won't you, Jo?"

"I'll give it a try," I said.

I went out and took care of the hookups, after which I changed into a tank and cutoffs. Then I grabbed a towel and set off with Charity to find the pool. It wasn't far. A sign on the outside of the enclosure said SUITS OPTIONAL. I figured that was good news because what I was wearing wasn't exactly a suit.

As soon as we passed through the gate, Charity dropped the big towel she'd wrapped around herself and slid her bare body into the pool. My eyes bugged—I had no idea she didn't have a suit on under there. I snapped my head away, but not before noting that the curls in her sweet triangle were as golden as those on her head and looked to be just as soft. I stumbled to a nearby bench and sat, looking everywhere but where I really wanted to. I heard her introduce herself to the people who were already soaking, and they chatted away like they all had clothes on. Among other topics, they compared the mineral content of the water of spas they'd visited in other states and countries.

Gradually my thoughts quieted to a dull roar, and I noticed I was in an extraordinarily beautiful place. The walls around the pool were constructed of natural rock in a soft green hue tinged with turquoise. It was the color of the ocean on the one sunny day of my vacation last summer at the Jersey shore. Succulents had been planted in the cracks between the rocks. The word *grotto* came to mind, but I'm not sure why, since I'd never seen one.

"Jo!"

I looked before I remembered not to.

"Come on in," Charity said. "It feels great." The others, who I knew from the introductions to be Bill, Jeff, and Melissa, turned their heads and smiled.

It was either get in or leave, and I didn't want to leave. I walked around to a corner of the steaming pool that was as far from the crowd as I could get, and tried a toe. It was hot but not scalding, so I climbed in. The water came up to my neck. Immediately the aches and stiffness of the road faded away. It was all I could do to keep from groaning in ecstasy.

I sat on an underwater ledge, closed my eyes, and pretended I was Eve in the Garden of Eden. Or Adam, I didn't care. I knew there was a poison apple out there. One bite and I'd be back to stolen securities and scheming brothers and the Phippses, but that was tomorrow. Tonight was sublime comfort and innocent bliss.

After everyone had left but the two of us, Charity floated over and sat next to me, her bare thigh touching mine. "Just look at the stars," she said. "I don't know when I've ever seen so many."

"My, yes, look at them," I said, staring at her round breasts. They were actually floating. What if the nearest nipple floated over and touched my arm? I might have a hands-free orgasm. I forced my eyes upward. She was right—there wasn't an inch of sky that wasn't filled with pinpoints of light. "There's the

Big Dipper." I pointed to it. Charity snugged into me, so when my arm came down, it had nowhere to go but around her. And then she kissed me. It wasn't a "thanks, Jo, for all the laughs" sort of kiss. It was the lip-grinding, skin-pressing, I-want-you-baby sort. I had to grab on to rocks with both hands to keep from going under. Then she whispered in my ear something that sounded like "I love you so much." *What?! Did I hear her right?*

When she drew back, I reached for her, my body crying *More! More!* But she was climbing out of the pool.

"Let's have champagne," she said. "I've got a bottle I was going to share with Paul after he was released. We may as well drink it."

"We don't need champagne," I said.

She wrapped her body with a towel. "I do, Jo. Believe me, I do. I'll ice it up a bit and be back before you know it. Do you have the keys?"

I fished the ByVista key ring out of my shorts pocket and held them out of her reach. "Let me come with you."

"Don't be silly. Enjoy the water, and I'll be back before you know it. Come on, Jo, give me the keys."

She was sounding exasperated, so I handed them to her. For one blissful nanosecond her fingers touched mine. "Can I bring you anything?" she asked.

"Just your sweet self," I said.

And she was gone.

I felt lighter than air. It was a wonder I wasn't skimming the surface of the water like a soap bubble. *What a kiss!*

I'd been too startled to respond, but I'd be ready for the next one. In fact, I intended to initiate the next one. My lesbian classmate had been right! If you hang around and take what they can give, eventually they'll see the light.

Deliriously happy, I lay my head back and watched the stars crawl across the sky. Moonlit clouds begged to be dissolved, but

I'd sworn off cloud-dissolving for life. It was getting quite cool. Foggy wisps curled from the water into the air.

When I got bored of the stars, I tried doing laps. But the pool was so small, I was across in two strokes. The water was too hot for exercising anyway, so I splayed my arms and floated like a water bug.

After a while I started wondering why Charity hadn't returned. Had she changed her mind about coming back? Maybe she was waiting for me to come there.

I toweled off and climbed the path to the campground. When I was about a hundred yards from the ByVista, I stopped short. A few sites away, a forked branch caught in a TV antenna was silhouetted against the low moon. It was the Wellaway. There were no lights on, no shadows on the curtains tonight. Roy and Lois must have trundled off to their separate beds.

I ran to the ByVista. The lights were on, and the door wasn't locked. "Charity!" I called as I entered. "It's the Wellaway, the one that's been following us. It's here at the campground!" I tripped over something just inside the door. It was Charity's towel.

"Charity?" I ran to the bedroom. The clothes she'd worn that day were scattered across the bed. I knocked on the bathroom door, then opened it and poked my head in. Empty. I ran out and all the way back to the pool, startling a soaking couple in the middle of something really intimate. "Sorry," I muttered.

I was shaking in my wet clothes. I went back to the ByVista and checked the bedroom again. This time I saw her. She was lying on the floor on the other side of the bed, wedged between it and the long drawer under the closet. She was nude except for her belt, the narrow black one she'd been wearing earlierer. But it wasn't at her waist now—it was wound tightly around her neck. With some difficulty, I pried it loose and put my thumb on her pulse point. There was no pulse. I half-carried, half-dragged her to the living room, where there was enough room to perform CPR. I knew it well. I also knew when it was no use. Charity was dead. She'd been dead for a while. I sat back on my heels. *What now?*

Nothing, Jo. Nothing now. Nothing at all.

I lifted her hands and buried my face in them. They cooled my burning cheeks. *Oh, God! Charity!*

After a while reality hit me: I had to get out of there. What if I was next? I closed her eyes and fetched her towel, tucking it closely around her. I couldn't bring myself to cover her face, her beautiful face. I leaned down and kissed her lightly on her lips. How different a kiss from the one I'd intended to give!

I told myself I had to notify someone. But first I had to get my things together. It seemed extremely important to get my things together. I went to my cupboard, quickly changed into dry clothes, and packed my backpack. I found some plastic grocery bags under the sink. In one I sealed the wet clothes I'd just taken off and stuck them in a side zipper pocket. In another I put the jar of peanut butter and the rest of the loaf of bread. I'd finished off the small glass of jelly yesterday.

Slinging the backpack over my shoulder, I opened the microwave. The purse was still there. I guess Charity was right, it was a safe place to keep it. I poked around in it, looking for her cell phone, but it was gone. I looked in the charger, but it wasn't there either. It wasn't on the dash or next to the TV where she'd left it before. Finally I saw it. It was on the bedroom floor near where she had been lying. She must have been trying to call for help when… *Don't think about when!*

As I bent to pick it up, I looked out the window and saw the Wellaway. Only now the lights were on, and a shadow danced on the curtain. One of the Parkers was getting a midnight snack. Or maybe it was Jo's turn to die.

I didn't want to die. I was only 27. No wait, yesterday had been my birthday. I was 28 now. Somehow that seemed to make a difference—who knew at what age the odds turned? Self-preservation seized me. I picked up the phone and ran to the cockpit, jumping over Charity's body.

I threw the phone in the purse where I could find it later and pawed through it for the ByVista's keys. Not there. I got the flashlight and darted the beam in dark corners until the keys glinted at me from under the table.

Snatching the curtain from the windshield, I jumped in the driver's seat, fired up the engine, and put it in gear. There were a series of tugs as the hitch tightened and the hookups let go. By the dim light of the lanterns at the side of the dirt lane, I made my way to the highway. I switched on the headlights and turned toward Silver City, going as fast as I dared. In the outside mirrors I saw the electric cord and torn hoses streaming out behind me, illuminated by the lights of passing vehicles.

As soon as I got to town, I turned down a side street and drove two-thirds of the way around a block, where I parked, got out, and walked back to the highway. Hiding in the shadows of a tall bush, I forced myself to be still and watch. It wasn't easy—I was so tense, I was jerky.

In less than five minutes the Wellaway shot past like a cannonball. As soon as it was out of sight, I ran to the ByVista. After disconnecting the torn hoses and stowing the electric cord, I drove north out of town, back the way I'd come. All I had in mind was to get as far from Roy and Lois Parker as I could, as fast as possible.

When I passed the Big Bear Butte Spa campground, all was dark and quiet. You wouldn't have known someone had just been murdered there. The campers were deep in their pool-induced slumbers. I wondered if they slept naked too.

I drove for hours, uphill and down, rarely seeing another vehicle, the whole time trying to keep my mind off the fact that Charity was dead in the back of the ByVista. Instead I focused on reconstructing what might have happened. I pictured Charity walking up the path to the campground, not noticing the Wellaway. Roy and Lois were probably hiding behind the ByVista, waiting. As soon as she unlocked the door, they jumped out. Roy dragged her into the motor home and strangled her while Lois kept watch in case I came back. And where was I? Gaily frolicking in the hot tub. *What an irresponsible dummy!*

What I couldn't figure out was how they'd found us. Had they followed us from Tucson after all?

When I reached the road we had taken over those mountains, I didn't turn onto it. The last thing I wanted to do was to go back to Arizona. My intention was to continue north until I got to some state I hadn't been in yet. I pictured the U.S. map on my high school social studies classroom wall. What state was above New Mexico? Colorado? Utah?

"Oh, shit," I said out loud when several miles later my headlights illuminated a sign that said WELCOME TO ARIZONA.

There was no going back, so I kept going. The fuel gauge approached zero and beyond, and finally the ByVista started losing power. I pulled as far off the road as I could.

The plan that was hatching in my muddled brain was to walk away from the ByVista before calling the cops. After giving them time to fetch the motor home, I'd return to the highway and hitchhike back to civilization. I didn't normally approve of hitch-hiking, but I doubted if I'd see a taxi.

By the time they caught up with me, and they would (my fingerprints were all over the ByVista) I intended to have packed Mrs. Phipps, retrieved the Toyota, and be back home in Buffalo where I wouldn't have to face the situation all alone. That reminded me, I'd forgotten to call Mom. Oh, well, like Scarlet O'Hara, I'd worry about that tomorrow.

In darkness I went to where Charity lay. "I've got to leave now," I told her. "I'm borrowing your phone so I can call someone to come for you. I'm really sorry for what happened." I knelt and ran my hand across her cheek. "I love you too," I whispered.

Tears swelled behind my eyes, but I forced them back. This wasn't the time.

I started to take the phone from the purse. Then I threw it back in and took the whole purse. It wasn't safe here. What if I had driven back into Cochise County and Deputy Conway was the one who answered the police call? The purse would go the way of the four million, directly into Paul Redmun's pocket. Let him wait until the estate settled.

I stuffed the purse into my backpack and grabbed the flashlight and my bag of food. Realizing I might need something to drink, I went back and looked in the refrigerator for water. There was none—we'd forgotten to buy it. I dropped a couple of Charity's Diet Cokes in my plastic bag and went out. After locking the door, I hid the keys under a rock alongside the road. Then I crossed the road and walked away.

Mountain ridges zig-zagged along the horizon, pitch-black against the dark blue sky. I decided to head directly toward the highest peak, so that later I could walk directly away from it and arrive back at the road. It sounded like it would work, anyway.

I figured from the chill in the air that the elevation was still high, but not nearly as high as we'd been at Big Bear Butte Spa. There were fewer trees here, and they were shorter—the tallest was about the size of the well-trimmed apple tree in our backyard. There were several kinds of cactus and scrawny bushes with spines. Every few steps I stopped to wave the flashlight so I wouldn't run into them or trip over the sharp-edged rocks that lay everywhere. The brush became thicker, so thick I couldn't see the mountain range I was supposed to be using as a guide. If only I had a pocket compass! I made a mental note never to leave home without one again.

The flashlight beam picked up dark holes in the dirt. I wondered what creatures might be lurking in them. Scorpions? Our neighbors had brought one back from their trip to Mexico, frozen in a paperweight. Its long tail was arced above its body poised to sting, which made sense, considering it was about to be engulfed in liquid plastic.

I was shivering from the cold. I wished I'd brought my parka, but who'd have thought you'd need a parka on a trip to Florida? I stopped and put on an extra T-shirt and my Bills sweatshirt.

I walked for hours with a looped tape playing in my mind: *Why did I agree to drive Charity back to Charleston? But since I did, why did I go down to the mineral pool? But since I did, why did I let her go back to the ByVista alone? Run, Lola, Run.*

The flashlight was failing. It went dim, brightened when I shook it, and gradually went dim again.

The rocks I'd been walking around suddenly got bigger. Way bigger. Instead of walking around rocks, I was walking between them. As I emerged from between two particularly massive ones, my left hand brushed a cactus and came away with spines in it. The sharp pain brought tears to my eyes. I put everything I was carrying on the ground and pulled out the spines more by touch than by the faint beam of the flashlight.

After checking the ground for hazards, I sat down and drank a Diet Coke. When I went to get up again, I couldn't. I was tired. Not just regular tired—I was drive-all-day, steep-like-a-teabag, run-like-a-dog tired. It was time to make that phone call.

I took Charity's phone out of her purse and flipped it open. The screen was dark—no time, date, or cheerful "Charity Redmun." There was no dial tone either. I pushed all the buttons, including 911 several times, but nothing happened. My first thought was, *Why didn't I bring the charger?* My second thought was, *Duh.* My third thought was, *Do you see any cell towers around here, Jo?*

I returned the phone and purse to my backpack and ran through my options. It didn't take long. There was only one: stay here. Meanwhile, I was starving. I pulled out two slices of bread from the plastic bag, spread peanut butter on them with my finger, and washed it all down with the last Diet Coke.

I leaned against a boulder for a while, then decided that as difficult as it might be, I should try to get some sleep. I took out a rolled T-shirt to use as a pillow and curled my body around my backpack, pulling as much of my body into the sweatshirt as possible. Contrary to expectations, I drifted off right away.

When I woke, it was getting light, and I had the impression that what woke me was the sound of footsteps. I stood up and looked around. I was totally surrounded by boulders and cliffs. This was the West of woolly Westerns. *Watch out, Tex. Something's stirring in yonder gorge.*

A powerful thirst hit me. I'd never been so thirsty. I would have even drunk another Diet Coke, but there weren't any left. Just in case, I looked in the food bag, but there were just the two empties.

You woke to the sound of footsteps, Jo?

Oh, right.

I stood stock-still and listened. I tried to think—what animal would be large enough to make footsteps heavy enough to wake me up? I ran through a roster of large animals associated with the American West: buffalo, wild horse, big-horned sheep, wolf, mountain lion… Then I realized I was freaking myself out, so I started picking up my things. If there was a large animal around here, the best thing I could do would be to take myself someplace else.

As I hoisted the pack to my shoulder, I thought of two more large animals who might be in Arizona: Roy and Lois Parker. If they had found Charity and me at Big Bear Butte Spa, they could find us anywhere.

I picked up the food bag and ran. It wasn't easy. There were sharp rocks and lethal plants everywhere. As I rounded a boulder, I got a glimpse of a figure coming around the other side. It was a man, Roy maybe—I didn't hang around to make sure. I could hear him behind me, getting closer and closer. I dropped the things I was carrying and was able to pick up a little speed. I'd almost convinced myself the footsteps were fading when I tripped on a rock and went down on my knees. As I pushed back up, a blow behind my ear took me out.

11

I was euphoric. Charity, the ByVista, Arizona—they had all been part of a complicated nightmare, quite real at the time but now fading. In a minute I would get up and they'd be gone, nothing left of them but a lingering sense of sadness. *I had the weirdest dream,* I'd tell Mom.

Then I fully woke up, and it all came rushing back. I remembered everything, right up to the blow on my head. The mass of sadness that was Charity's death resettled in my chest.

I told myself to open my eyes, but the thought nauseated me. Curiosity won, though, and I eased them open. I was lying on a bed of some sort in a room of some sort. I moved my head, and the room did a couple of twirls before settling down to a slow rocking. I waited until it stabilized. Then, shifting nothing but my pupils, I looked around. The ceiling and walls were of particle board, and the one window I could see had translucent plastic stretched across it. I seemed to be in a rustic cabin. On second thought, it looked more like a shed.

I smelled the strong odor of peanut butter. Now, I love peanut butter, but this didn't smell good at all. In fact, it was making me sick to my stomach. Or was it the pain in my head that was making me sick to my stomach, and the peanut butter was guilty by association? That would be better, because I tended to have more peanut butter than pain in my life. So far.

I wondered if I could sit up. I gave it a half-hearted try and moaned as I sank back in a blur of vertigo.

"Better lay still." It was a man's voice.

"Roy?" I said. *Doesn't matter. If he kills me, he kills me.*

"The name's L.J. Who's Roy?"

I slowly turned my head. A person I didn't know sat on a stool at a chrome-legged table eating a sandwich and drinking an Old Milwaukee. He had a snarled red beard, and his clothes looked like they'd never met a Maytag. "Is that my peanut butter?" I asked.

"Yeah, but I like creamy better. Who's Roy? Your boyfriend?"

"Hardly," I said. My mouth was so dry, I had to peel my tongue off the roof as I talked. "Look, I'm really thirsty. Can I have some water?"

"Sure." He poured from a gallon jug into a mug and brought it over. "Drink it slow."

"Why?"

"I don't know. That's what they say in the movies."

Good, the man's civilized.

He helped me sit up. My head pulsed with pain, but I didn't care. I grabbed the mug and downed its contents in one gulp. "More," I said. He filled the mug again. This time I drank it more slowly, taking time between sips to notice that the mug had a bright yellow smiley face above the words "Love 'n' Succor Mortuary, Loma Nueva." When every drop was gone, I handed it back and touched the side of my head. An area by my right ear felt spongy, like one of Rose's gel-filled insoles.

"Somebody hit me on the head with something. I think it was Roy," I said. "Did you see him?"

"No-o-o." He sounded like he had more to say but thought better of it. He returned to his sandwich, and I closed my eyes again because the act of seeing made my head hurt.

I tried to puzzle things out, like why hadn't Roy finished me off? But it took too much energy, so I went back to sleep. When I woke, the light had changed. Sunshine was now streaming from the other side of the room.

L.J. was nowhere in sight, at least not in my limited sight from my flat position. The water jug was on the table, tantalizingly close, and the smiling cup sat next to it.

"L.J.?" I called. "Hello?"

I sat up and threw my legs over the side of the cot-like bed. The pain was still there, but it wasn't as bad. Holding on to the edge of the mattress, I swung my rear up so I was sort of standing. If I'd stayed in that position, I might have been fine, but I had dreams of walking. I pushed my upper body off the bed. As soon as my head got higher than my shoulders, my vision faded and I hit the floor.

When I came to, I was back on the bed and L.J. was standing over me. "You know, Charity," he said, "maybe I'd better get you to a doctor. You might have a concussion."

Charity? Charity's here? Maybe I was wrong, she didn't die. Or maybe I died. Ignoring the pain, I sat up and looked around the room. "Where is she?"

"Who?"

"Charity."

"I thought *you* were Charity. Why do you have Charity's purse if you're not Charity?"

"You looked in her purse? Did you take anything?" The nerve of him! Seemed I wasn't doing a better job of protecting Charity's purse than I'd done of protecting her.

"I didn't take anything," he said. "I'm not that kind of guy."

I backed off a bit. I knew what it was like to be unjustly accused. "Well, you did take my peanut butter," I told him.

"I'll buy you a new jar, for Chrissake. So what is your name?" He poured a cup of water and brought it to me.

"Jo." I took the cup and drank. "Thanks for taking care of me, L.J. I really appreciate it. I could have died out there."

"Yep." He crossed to a rusty utility cart in the corner, popped a beer from a six-pack, opened it, and took a long pull.

"When you rescued me, did you by any chance notice a motor home anywhere around with the name Wellaway on it?" I asked.

He dropped on the stool and burped. "You were in the middle of the high desert. How would a motor home get there? Anyway, what were you doing without any water? Committing suicide?"

"I had some Diet Cokes."

"Yeah. I buried the cans with my garbage, that all right with you?"

"Couldn't you redeem them or put them out for the recycle?"

"What's a recycle?"

"A truck that comes around for your cans and bottles, stuff like that."

"When does it do that?"

"Every week in Buffalo. But the soda cans, you can take back to the supermarket and they give you a nickel."

"That's nice of them."

"Not really, you paid it when you bought the soda."

"Buffalo sounds like a complicated place. So who's this Roy guy, and why would he be hitting you on the head?"

"I'm not sure. He and Lois have been following us. Of course, it could have been Paul."

"Hoo, boy, old Roy has his hands full, doesn't he! You and

Charity, and now Lois. I don't know about this Paul, though, unless Roy swings both ways." He giggled.

"Roy and Lois are married, at least they say they are. Where are we, anyway?" I asked him.

"See, that's the thing, Jo," L.J. said. "I can't tell you."

"You can't tell me? Why?"

"I got my reasons."

I was feeling dizzy again, so I lay back down and closed my eyes. I don't know if I lost consciousness or not. If so, it couldn't have been for long, because when I opened them again L.J. was sitting in the exact position he had been before.

"Welcome back," he said. "Look, Jo, I been thinking. I don't want you blaming Roy. I'd feel crappy if you and him broke up because of what I did. Of course, if he really is married to Lois, that might not be a bad thing. Anyway, I want you to know it was me that bopped you. I didn't know you were a girl."

"It was you? You hit me?"

"I'd never hit a girl. You should wear a dress or something, let your hair grow."

"You thought I was a guy, so you hit me? Why?" I wished I'd felt well enough to display proper indignation.

"I thought you might be with the Feds."

"Feds?"

"This is government land, see. I'm not supposed to be living here."

"You thought I'd come to kick you off the land?"

"Sure. Or you could have been looking for gold."

"You have gold?"

"No," he said quickly.

"Can you at least tell me what day this is?"

"Saturday. I think." He checked a calendar on the wall. "Yeah, Saturday."

"April twentieth?"

"Yeah."

It seemed an eternity since I'd abandoned the ByVista, but it had only been a matter of hours. I desperately needed to make that call to the police. "Do you have a phone?" I asked L.J.

"No. But you do. I mean, Charity does."

"It doesn't work. Is there a pay phone somewhere?"

"Pima Center. That's where the doctor is too. Why don't I take you there, have your head looked at?"

"I'd appreciate that. But first could I use your bathroom?"

"I don't exactly have one. I do my business in the desert. Let's see, how can I say this?...Will there be anything to bury?"

"No."

"Then, since you're under the weather, I'll let you water my garden." He helped me up and outside, to the far side of a shoulder-high tarp-covered pile. I didn't see any garden.

"You going to be okay?" he asked.

"I think so." After he went back around the pile and turned his back, I lowered my Levi's and squatted.

"Watch for rattlers," he called. "I saw one in that vicinity the other day."

Yeah, that helped me relax. That and the fact that a four-legged animal, possibly a mule, was watching me with great interest. I repositioned and looked across the dirt of the desert. That's all the desert seemed to be: dirt, dirt, and more dirt. Where had I got the idea that it was all sandy?

When I finished, I found I was able to get back around the pile on my own. I took my time and did a little of what Deputy Conway would call "wavering," but I got there. "Who's your friend?" I asked L.J.

"That's Marguerite. You should thank her. She carried you here."

"After you bopped me."

"Like I said…"

"Never mind." My head was pounding again. "Maybe you should be getting me to that doctor." I went back in the shed and drank more water. I wanted to lie down in the worst way.

My backpack was leaning against a table leg. I sat on the floor and unzipped it. I thought I'd better look through Charity's purse to make sure nothing was missing, although I didn't know how I'd know if anything was, or what I could do about it.

The phone was right on top. I tried it again just in case, but it was definitely dead.

Her billfold was there, with a 50, two 20s, and a couple of ones in it. Her pen and little pad were there. A couple of phone numbers and directions to the Spittin' Grill were written on it in neat script. Was it just yesterday we were sitting in the Ranger outside the apartment complex and Charity was on the phone, writing down those directions? I blinked back tears and turned the page. The name "Edwina Meek" was written there, along with a Tucson address. That must have been the attorney Charity had done her "bit of business" with.

I dug deeper and found a red leather checkbook with graduated pouches holding credit cards and a bunch of business cards, some in foreign languages. There was a small matching address book too. I flipped through it. Other than her parents and Paul on the "R" page, there wasn't a name in it I recognized.

In a transparent zipper bag were several makeup and grooming items, including a hairbrush with golden strands wound in the bristles. *If only cloning was a done deal!*

Way down in the purse's depths were the keys to the Ranger. I kicked myself for not leaving them under the rock with the ByVista's key ring.

As I put everything back in, I wondered how L.J. was planning to transport me to Pima Center. Marguerite was the only mode of conveyance I'd seen. I hoped Pima Center wasn't very far.

I was drinking a final cup of water when I heard an engine start. I grabbed my backpack and went outside. L.J. had taken the tarps off, and the shoulder-high pile turned out to be a beat-up Jeep with a roll bar.

Before letting me get in, he went in the house and brought out a dingy dishtowel. "You need to wear this." He tied it around my eyes. "Can't have you bringing the Feds out," he said.

"I wouldn't do that! Honest!"

"If you're so honest, why do you have Charity's purse?" He tightened the knot and tucked the edge of the towel around the bridge of my nose.

"Yuck, it smells."

"It's just for a while. Don't you peek, now—I'll be watching. The ride's going to be a little bumpy. I'm taking a roundabout route."

He guided me into the passenger seat. I heard a slamming of doors, a gunning of engine, and we were off. I wanted to argue some more about the dishtowel, but I was too busy holding on. L.J.'s roundabout route must have been across a lava bed. Just for meanness, I tried to keep track of the turns, but all we did was turn. I think we even made a few circles. Every time we hit a bump, my head felt like it had been struck by lightning. I tried to keep myself from bouncing around by bracing myself between the door and the dash. It didn't work.

"Where's my seat belt?" I asked.

"Good question," he said

After a while the bumping eased off, and L.J. told me I could remove the blindfold, which wasn't as easy as it sounded, he'd knotted it so tight. When I finally got it off, I saw we were on a paved road. I wondered if it was the same one I had been on last night. If so, it was possible we might come across the ByVista. That was such an awful thought, I was tempted to put the blindfold back on.

We traversed miles of winding, hilly roads and passed through breathtakingly colorful canyons. L.J. entertained me by identifying the layers in the sliced rocks at the side of the roadway and naming the lichens and minerals that gave the mountains their hues. He seemed to know a lot about it.

A roadside sign told us we were leaving the national forest, and I wondered at what point I had entered it. Houses dotted the landscape, many with two or three horses watching from behind fences. Suddenly we were in a town. A sign said WELCOME TO PIMA CENTER, HOME OF THE DESERT ROSES.

"What are desert roses?" I asked L.J.

"They're mineral crystals shaped like flowers, or it's their high school soccer team, or it's some enterprising ladies in a house on the south side of town—take your pick."

After driving past churches, bars, storefronts, and gas stations, L.J. turned up a side street and stopped at a house with a metal shingle hanging from the porch roof. It said ALBERT COELHO, M.D.

"This guy's good," L.J. told me. "He patched me up last year after I fell down a shaf…after I had a fall. Come on, I'll help you up the steps."

When we got to the door, there was a handwritten note taped to the inside of its little window: "Dr. Coelho is away on vacation until April 29. In case of emergency, he suggests you go to Loma Nueva Hospital."

L.J. stomped his scuffed brown boot on the wooden porch. "Loma Nueva, that's another 50 miles. A person could die."

"Look, I'm not going to die. Truth is, I'm feeling a little better now. What I need you to do is take me to the police station. Do you know where it is?" I figured I may as well show up in person and get it over with. It was no fun being a fugitive without Charity.

L.J. grabbed me by the shoulders. "Look, Jo, there's no reason to go to the police. It was an accident, like I told you. I'm really sorry. How can I make it up to you?"

"Don't worry, L.J., it's not…" *Hold on! Why shouldn't he make it up to me?* In 10 minutes we were sitting in the Downtown Diner, and I was ordering from the "Breakfast Anytime" menu. It wasn't until he'd paid for my cheese omelet with toast, hash browns, and coffee that I explained that my reasons for seeing the police had nothing to do with him.

He dropped me off in front of a flat stucco building. The sign over the glass door read: PIMA CENTER MUNICIPAL POLICE. L.J. asked me not to go in until he was completely gone because he and they had some unfinished business. Now I understood why he was so upset when he thought I was going to turn him in for "bopping" me. I should have made him take me somewhere classier than the Downtown Diner.

12

When L.J. had sped out of sight, I pulled at the door, but it was locked. I found a doorbell on the side and rang it. A woman in a police uniform peered out and unlatched the door.

"I need help," I told her.

"Let's see what we can do." She ushered me to a chair by a desk. I sat, placing my backpack on my lap. She took the chair behind the desk and hit some keys on a computer keyboard. "I'm Officer Lydia Ortiz," she said. "May I have your name, please?"

"JoDell Jacuzzo," I told her. "I'm from Buffalo, New York. I'm here about a friend of mine." That was bad phrasing—it made me remember the time Charity told me she liked it when I called her my friend. Tears stung my eyes. "Her name's Charity. She was murdered last night in New Mexico. I don't have any proof, but I think the murderers may be a man and woman who are traveling in a motor home called a Wellaway. They say their names are Roy and Lois Parker and they look like regular folks, but they followed us all the way here from Parsee, Georgia." I started shaking.

"Wait a minute. I need to call someone." Officer Ortiz picked up the phone.

I couldn't stop. It was like the words were under pressure in my head and I had to say them or explode. "The last time I saw the Wellaway was last night in Silver City," I said. "It followed me out of the spa and went south toward Deming. I think the Parkers may be in league with Charity's brother, Paul, who wants her money so bad he pretended to be kidnapped." My voice was rising in pitch. "You see, the reason we went to this campground in the first place was because we thought we'd be safe there, but I knew she might be in danger and I let her go back to the ByVista alone anyway, and now my Charity is *dead*!"

She put down the phone and looked at me. "Are you all right, dear?"

Her tone was too kind. I totally lost it, exploding into great wrenching sobs. I sobbed about everything that had gone wrong in the last several weeks: the Goddard affair, my lost career, the shattered piston, my aching head, and Charity, dear, dear Charity. Why hadn't I been nicer about the birthday cake?

I slumped over the backpack and wailed.

At some point a wad of tissues was shoved in my hand, but I was too distracted to remember what they were for. They remained crushed in my fist, while my nose dripped freely.

When I finally looked up, I was being stared at by Officer Ortiz and two men, one uniformed, one not. The not-uniformed man took advantage of the lull in my waterworks to say something that sounded vaguely familiar. He said it again, and I realized it was my last name. He said it once more: "Ms. Jacuzzo?" He saw he had my attention, so he told me his name and the other guy's, but I didn't catch them. Then he said, "You told Officer Ortiz someone had been killed? Someone named Charity?"

I took a deep breath and said, "Yes, Charity."

"Last name?"

"I don't remember. Red something. Redlund?" Geez, I knew it as well as my own. "Wait, I've got her purse in my backpack." I quickly added, "I didn't steal it. She was already..." My damn eyes started filling again.

Officer Ortiz stooped and put her arm around me. "May we see the purse, Ms. Jacuzzo?"

"Please call me Jo."

"The purse, Jo?"

I used the tissues I found in my hand to wipe my eyes and nose, and I stuffed them in my Levi's pocket. Then I unzipped the backpack and took out Charity's purse.

Before taking it, Officer Ortiz donned a pair of plastic gloves from her top drawer. Then she opened the purse and took out Charity's billfold. Finding a driver's license, she showed it around. The men nodded.

Not-Uniformed said, "We'll need you to give us a preliminary statement, Jo, and we'll be recording it. Is that all right with you?"

Preliminary? Preliminary to what? I told them it was all right.

They took me to a small room,where I sat at a table across from Not-Uniformed. Uniformed stood against the wall. Officer Ortiz had stayed back at her desk, itemizing stuff from Charity's purse at her computer.

Silently begging Charity's forgiveness for betraying her trust, I answered all their questions. I told them how I was sure Paul had hired the Parkers to do her in. I included a description of Roy and Lois and the Wellaway, and as many of the numbers on their New York license plate as I could remember.

I told them about the stolen four million and the Ranger's missing plate. Reciting the rhymes to myself, I gave them directions from the Interstate 10 exit to Deputy Conway's "substation." I shared my suspicions that Conway was in cahoots with Paul Redmun.

Finally, I told them about leaving Charity's dead body in the ByVista, and under which rock they could find the motor home's keys.

They asked permission to see the contents of my backpack. I watched as my things were laid out on the table, thankful I wasn't carrying any sex toys. I didn't tell them the flashlight was Charity's. I intended to treasure it, care for it, treat it to a set of new batteries.

They asked me how I got to Pima Center, and I told them I'd hitchhiked. Then my synapses started firing like crazy. What if they gave me a lie detector test and found out there were things I didn't tell them, like my omission of L.J.'s role in my flight and how Charity had let on she was in some kind of trouble with the police? What if they cross-checked with Buffalo and learned about my problem with the Goddards? What if they figured out the flashlight was Charity's and came to the conclusion I stole her purse too?

"Miss Jacuzzo," Non-Uniformed said sternly.

I jerked to attention. "What?"

"You realize, don't you, that you should have reported Miss Redmun's death immediately?"

"I know that now. I'm sorry. I wasn't thinking straight. I was only concerned with saving my own skin." He didn't say anything, just looked at me accusingly for a while. "I'm *sorry*," I said again.

Uniformed removed the tape from the recorder, telling me he was taking it to be typed up so I could sign it. While he was gone, the other guy asked me more questions disguised in a chatty manner. "Is this your first time in Arizona, Jo?"

"Yes, if you don't count leaving it for a few hours and coming back," I said.

"Do you know anybody in the area?"

"No."

"Do you know where you're going to stay while we conduct our investigation?"

"No." I was relieved to hear it wasn't going to be in a cell.

"In that case, we'll arrange a motel room for you. Don't leave town until we say you can, all right?"

"All right." I didn't want to know, but I had to ask, "Am I a suspect?"

"At this point, everybody's a suspect," he said.

"I didn't do it," I told him.

He didn't show any sign of having heard me.

When the statement was ready, I signed it and asked if they had a pay phone. I desperately needed to call Mom. It was Saturday; she would be home.

The men returned me to Officer Ortiz, who offered to let me use her phone. She even dialed for me, for which I was grateful. I was still shaking. I looked for Charity's purse, but it wasn't in sight.

Rose answered. "Jo, is that you? We've been so worried. Wait, I'll get your mother. She's upstairs." I heard her holler, "Delia? Quick, pick up the phone. It's Jo." She came back. "Happy Birthday, Jo, a day late."

"Thanks, Rose."

Mom picked up. "Jo, are you all right? Where are you?"

"I'm fine, Mom. I'm in Arizona."

"What are you doing in Arizona?" It was Rose. She hadn't hung up.

ME: "It's a long story that I can't tell you right now because I'm borrowing somebody's phone. The thing is, I can't leave Arizona yet, so I'm going to be late getting to Mrs. Phipps.'"

MOM: "How late?"

ME: "I'm not sure. A couple of days, maybe more. Will you let Gerald know?"

MOM: "Of course. But how are you getting there? Is your truck fixed?"

ROSE: "Even if it is, it takes more than a couple days to drive from Arizona to Florida."

MOM: "Not the way Jo drives."

ROSE: "You've got a point."

MOM: "Are you still staying with your new friend? What's her name again?"

ME: "Charity. ...No." A hiccupy sob plowed through my defenses.

MOM: "Jo, are you crying?"

ROSE: "You're right, Delia, she sounds like she's crying. Are you, Jo?"

ME: "It's nothing. I'm fine. Please don't worry."

MOM: "Don't worry about what? Jo, I need you to tell me what's going on, right now!" It was her Secretary-to-the-Principal voice.

ME: "I have to go, Mom. I'll call you tomorrow. I'm fine, really."

MOM: "Are you in some kind of trouble?"

ROSE: "Do you need money?"

ME: "I really have to go. I love you both. A lot."

I hung up. I offered to pay Officer Ortiz for the call but she said no, it was on the county.

She told me she'd made arrangements for me to stay at a motel at the edge of town. She sent me over in a squad car, a later model than the one I'd ridden in back in Buffalo. But the seats were more stained; I didn't want to know with what.

But neither this vehicle nor the one in Buffalo could hold a candle to Deputy Conway's classy black Buick. *Good grief, Jo, you've become a connoisseur of police cars!*

The driver stopped in front of a rundown motel and opened the back door for me. He had to—there were no handles inside. I climbed out, relieved there was nobody around to see. When I got to the desk, the clerk looked me up and down. "Bad day, huh?' she said.

"Pretty much," I said, handing her my credit card.

She shook her head. "The county's paying. They must want you to stay in town real bad."

"What county is this?"

"Mariposa."

"Are we close to Cochise County?"

"Not very."

"That's good," I said. She gave me a key and a motel diagram with my room circled.

First thing I did was take a long, hot shower. Before leaving the bathroom, I got my wet tank and cutoffs out of the backpack's pocket and hung them over the rod to dry. That got me thinking about Charity again, and fresh tears gathered. I'd known her only four days, but it had been an intense four days. I missed her like crazy.

Then I remembered she had never paid me. I was counting on that money. How was I going to pay for the Toyota's new — well, good-as-new—engine? Now I really felt like crying.

I took the traveler's checks from my backpack and counted them. Because Charity had paid for almost all our expenses, I had a couple hundred dollars' worth left. Of course, if I didn't get to Tampa pretty soon Gerald Phipps would want his front money back, and he'd pay my thousand to somebody else, somebody who'd actually show up. I was sinking into the red real fast.

My head started to pound. I shoved the pillows from the bed and lay flat on the cardboardy mattress, gazing at the streaked beige ceiling. I'd never felt so alone.

At some point I fell asleep and had a nightmare. I was lying on an operating table hooked up to a strange machine, and there were aliens standing around, talking about all the things they were planning to do to me. One of them smacked me on my cheeks and said, "Jo?" *How do they know my name?* Another lifted my right eyelid and shined a laser in. It sliced through my eye and deep into my brain, laying it wide open. I screamed and struck out. The alien let go of my lid.

"Good, she's awake," another voice said. "Jo? Can you hear me, Jo?"

Both voices were female. *They're out there, Fox and Dana, and they're women!*

I cracked an eye and looked around. "Where am I?"

"You're in Loma Nueva Hospital." The speaker was wearing a doctor's coat. "Can you follow this?" she asked, drawing an arc of light over my head.

I scrunched my eyes against it. "No."

In spite of the pain, I was feeling lightheaded and childish. *What kind of medication had they given me?* I tried to sit up.

"Careful of your IV!" said the woman on my other side.

"Try to lie still," the doctor said. "You may have a concussion."

"That's what L.J. thought," I said, cracking my eyes. The light was gone, so I opened them all the way.

"Can you tell me how your head was injured? I have to include it in my report." She took a tiny tape recorder from her coat pocket.

"It was L.J. He didn't mean to do it, though, and he bought me an omelet to make it up... Oops, I wasn't supposed to tell anyone. Oh, well, you'll never find him. I was wearing a blindfold." Now I knew what they'd given me—truth serum.

"Jo," said the doctor, "are you telling us you were a victim of domestic violence?"

"Of course not. I just met him."

"Who?"

I fought against the serum. "Look, here's what happened. I was in the desert, and I fell and hit my head on a rock."

"What about the man you said you just met? What did you call him? L.J?"

"He found me and took me to Pima Center. He may have saved my life."

"And the blindfold?"

"It was my idea. The light was hurting my eyes. Like now."

The doctor switched the recorder on and spoke into it. "The patient reports that she fell in the desert and hit her head on a rock. A man she just met provided a blindfold at her request and took her to Pima Center." She didn't believe a word of it.

I looked down and was surprised to find I was wearing one of those backless things hospitals call gowns. "How did I get here?" I asked.

"A policeman brought you. He found you passed out in a motel. Do you remember anything about that?"

"No," I said. I closed my eyes. "Excuse me, I have to sleep now."

Only they wouldn't let me sleep. Before leaving the room, the doctor told the woman who'd been holding my left hand since I threatened the safety of the IV, "Make sure she stays awake. I'll go order the tests."

The woman nodded solemnly. "If she closes her eyes I'll pinch her."

"What tests?" I asked.

"Nothing exotic," the doctor said, and left.

The woman really meant it about pinching me, but she did it in a manner that would never get her convicted. Each time I started to drift off she took my blood pressure, squeezing the black ball with a vengeance. My eyes not only opened, they bulged.

After a while a policeman came in carrying my backpack.

"Uniformed!" I said.

"What?" he said.

"Sorry, I didn't catch your name last week."

"It's Officer Olmstead, and it was yesterday. How are you feeling?"

"Tired and achy. They won't let me sleep. Are you the one who brought me here?"

"That was me. When you didn't answer the phone this morning, they sent me over to check on you. The maid let me in your room, and we found you unconscious. I hope you don't mind, but I let the people here make a copy of your insurance card."

"I don't mind." My insurance had been through the Can-Care Agency, and I doubted if it was still valid. At any moment the billing department might show up to throw me out on the street.

"They tell me you may have a concussion. How did that happen?" he asked.

"When I was in the high desert, I fell and hit my head on a rock."

He gave me an incredulous look. "You hit it on a rock?"

"What? It never happens?" I said.

Officer Olmstead put my backpack next to me on the gurney. "I've got to get back to Pima Center," he said. "The doctor says unless your tests show something she doesn't expect, they'll discharge you tomorrow. Call us when they do, and we'll come pick you up. We want to clear up a few things."

"What things?"

"I'm not sure. We've been in communication with the New Mexico authorities. They may have some questions."

Geez, now I was in trouble with the authorities of still another state. "Okay," I told him. I wondered if they'd found Charity, but I didn't want to trigger any more questioning right now. I wasn't up to it.

He gave me a card with a phone number and left. Pretty soon a guy in scrubs came to fetch me, and I spent a couple of hours in a sub-basement shivering while I waited for X-rays and blood tests. After that, I was taken to a room, transferred to a bed, and told I could sleep. But I wasn't sleepy anymore. I pushed myself up and looked around the room. The other bed was crisply made, ready for another maimed body.

I heard the clanking of trays far down the hall and smelled hot food. I was reallly hungry. To make the wait more bearable, I switched on the TV mounted high on the wall across from the foot of my bed. The only working channel was giving a tour of the hospital, narrated by a Martin Landau clone. For all I know it could have been Martin Landau. California was right next to Arizona. He could easily have popped over for the taping.

Martin had finished up Musculoskeletal and was in the middle of Neonatal when a nurse brought me two pain pills. They must have knocked me out, because I never made it to Pediatrics. I didn't get my dinner either.

When I woke up, my mouth tasted like I'd been sleeping for days. I lay with my eyes closed, wondering which I wanted more, food or a shower. Then it occurred to me that I wasn't going to get either if I didn't let somebody know I was awake. I groped around for the buzzer that had been clipped to my sheet. When I didn't find it, I opened my eyes. It was being held out of reach by a man standing next to my bed.

"Jo Jacuzzo," he said.

It wasn't a question, so I didn't say, "Yes." Actually, all I could do was stare at his hat, a black baseball cap with a smoke-belching skull embroidered on it.

He saw the direction of my gaze and smiled. It was a cold version of Charity's smile. "You're familiar with the militia?" he asked.

"Not really. You must be Paul Redmun," I said, looking him over. His curly blond hair was Charity's, but his eyes weren't. Charity's eyes had been wide and soft; Paul's were narrow and flinty. He was thinner than her, and not as classy a dresser—

Charity would never have let her underwear stick out over the top of her khakis or worn a cigarette behind her ear.

"You're not going to get away with it, you know," he said.

"Get away with what?"

"My sister was a gullible fool, but I'm not."

"Wait a minute—you don't think I killed her?"

"You know what I think."

"I'd never hurt Charity," I said. "I was her friend."

"Oh, is that what you call it?"

"What do you want from me?"

"Nothing for now, but I'll be back." He threw the buzzer at me and left.

Grabbing the bedrails, I pulled myself to a sitting position and inched down to the end of the bed. The familiar wooziness struck, but it soon passed, so I hung my legs over and slowly stood up. So far so good. Dragging the IV stand, I took a couple of steps and a couple more, and then I almost fell over in shock. There was a body in the next bed.

I moved closer. It was a very old woman. Her deeply lined face was white as the pillowcase that framed it. I took her pulse. It wasn't much as pulses go, but she was alive. A sign was tacked to her headboard: DO NOT RESUSCITATE.

I continued to the window and peered out, hoping to catch Paul walking to the parking lot. I thought it would be a good idea to find out what kind of car he drove. The only thing I could see, though, was an adjacent hospital wing. The vertical blinds in its windows were the same morning-urine-yellow as mine.

I knew I had to get away from here before he came back, but was I strong enough? The IV stand and I paced the room. I felt my strength return with each step. *How could Paul think I killed Charity?* I wondered. *Wasn't he in league with the Parkers?*

A food cart rumbled loudly to my door. The aide who carried

my tray was thrilled to see me looking so well and said I could sit in the chair to eat if I liked. She pulled the bed-table over to it. I could hardly wait for her to take the cover off the plate. The last time I'd eaten had been at the Downtown Diner in Pima Center with L.J. How long ago was that?

The meal of pasty oatmeal, lukewarm scrambled eggs, white toast, and undercooked bacon was the most delicious I'd ever had. I could have put away two more just like it. After scraping the plate of every egg bit, I laced the cup of coffee with all the sugar packets on the tray and tossed it down.

The shower would have to wait. I removed the IV needle from my hand, took my backpack from the closet, and looked through it. Everything seemed to be there, including my wallet and traveler's checks. Officer Olmstead had even fetched my now-dry tank and cutoffs from the motel shower rod. The clothes I'd been wearing when I fell asleep were hung neatly on hangers, even the socks and Jockey-for-Hers. The outfit was anything but fresh, but so was I—I put it on.

Nobody seemed to notice me leave, least of all my roommate.

Holding the backpack low, I edged along the wall until I found a stairwell. Holding tightly to the handrail in case wooziness decided to strike, I descended two levels to a door stenciled with the words GROUND FLOOR: CAFETERIA.

Several tables in the cavernous room were occupied by what looked to be family groups. Uniformed hospital staff sat at others, chatting in hushed tones. A few had their noses buried in books. Easing around the perimeter, I passed through a doorway to an outside patio where there were more tables. From there, I crossed a grassy area to a street in back of the hospital. Shouldering my backpack, I walked for several residential blocks. The hot, dry air sucked moisture from my pores.

The homes I passed were squat frame structures sided with

stucco. Decorative wrought iron bars guarded doors and windows, making me wonder if this was a high crime area. I kept my pace up so I wouldn't look like a loiterer.

A few of the yards had patches of sickly grass growing in them. Others consisted simply of hard dirt or were carpeted in pastel gravel. The plants that poked through were olive-green and spiny like those in the desert. There was an exception, though: a flowering bush I'd also noticed in Tucson. It was growing everywhere, sporting huge red blooms of the kind Rose would call showy.

A sun-bonneted woman was pulling weeds out of her patch of gravel, so I stopped to ask what the red-flowered bush was. "Bougainvillea," she said. "It's awful. The petals fall off and lodge everywhere."

"It's pretty, though."

"Pretty," she said with no enthusiasm.

She seemed fairly friendly, so I asked, "Do you by any chance know where I could find an airport or a bus station?"

"Far as I know, we don't have an airport, just an airstrip where they give flying lessons, and they could get rid of that, as far as I'm concerned. Those little planes buzz around here like mosquitoes. It's that irritating."

"How about a bus station?"

"I wouldn't know. I never take buses. If you go three—no, four blocks that way," she pointed in the direction I'd been going, "you'll come to a gas station. They might know."

Since I still didn't have my full strength back, four blocks sounded like 400. I had to pee too. I considered asking the woman if I could use her bathroom, then decided against it. I didn't want her remembering me that well. So I took off, walking slowly and with my legs crossed, so to speak.

Approaching the gas station was like coming home. I hadn't

been to one for a whole couple of days. After using the facilities, I walked around, communing with the glass-front cooler, the drink machines, the rows and rows of colorful snacks. The clerk kept a careful eye on me, probably because of my backpack. I selected a bottle of root beer and a Snickers bar and held them in exaggerated plain sight as I took them to the register. While I was paying, I asked the clerk about the bus station. He said it was in a strip mall near downtown, about 10 blocks away. At my request, he called a taxi.

The taxi driver was the curious sort. In the guise of polite conversation, he asked where I'd come from, what I was doing in town, and where I was planning to take a bus to. He wasn't wearing the cap, but he still could have been militia, so I told him nothing. Anyway, my destination was unknown even to me.

At the bus station I asked the woman in the ticket booth what the nearest city was that had a good-size airport. "That'd be Phoenix," she said, looking as me like I'd just crawled out from under a cabbage.

Using a traveler's check, I bought a ticket and settled down on one of the battered benches for the two-hour wait. Soon, however, paranoia set in, and I went outside to see if anybody I recognized was around, like Paul Redmun, for instance. Or Officer Olmstead—the hospital staff would surely call to tell him I was gone. Or Deputy Conway and/or the Hats. Or my favorite fun couple, the Parkers.

Across from the bus station was an Odd Lots store. I crossed the parking lot and went in. With the change from my bus ticket I bought a pink knit blouse with white daisies stamped around the hem, a black denim mini-skirt, black pantyhose, a pair of black sandals with wedge heels, and the biggest sunglasses they had. To set the outfit off, I got some Pinkly Pearl lipstick, Blacker than Blue eye shadow, a bag of five plastic razors, and a knit straw cap to pull down around my face. When I came out of the bus station bathroom half an hour later, my own mother wouldn't have recognized me. She really wouldn't.

I boarded the bus, looking for a seat companion who wouldn't be likely to ask me a lot of personal questions. First I considered a boy who looked to be about eight but decided it would be too high a price to pay. I settled on a 50-ish woman who was busy reading a book. She looked up and smiled when I sat down. I smiled back. By the time we got to Phoenix, she'd told me all about the book's characters, described the plot and all the sub-plots, given a play-by-play account of each scene, and shared the way she figured it was going to end. She was wrong—I'd seen the movie.

13

The Phoenix bus station was big and modern. It was also very near the airport, which was cleverly named Sky Harbor. I asked a clerk where the American Airlines ticket counter might be. "Terminal three," she said in a robot voice. "Shuttle now leaving."

As I exited the shuttle, my left wedge heel landed sideways, dropping me heavily on the side of my foot. I felt around, but nothing seemed to be broken. It was awfully painful, though. I decided as soon as I got off the plane at Tampa, the wedgies and the rest of this stifling getup would be history.

I hobbled inside and got in line at the ticket counter. While I waited, I looked through my backpack to make sure there was nothing that could be construed as a weapon. I also made sure my driver's license and credit card were handy. I panicked when I realized I looked nothing like the picture on my license. Then I remembered I never looked much like it anyway.

When I had moved up to fourth in line I heard noisy confusion in the area behind me. I turned and peered over the heads of my neighbor rubberneckers. Wedgies were good for something, anyway.

What I saw was appalling. A man was dragging a woman by her

neck to the outside door, and she was screaming bloody murder.

"Shut up, cunt!" he hollered. "You're not going anywhere." She screamed again, and he socked her in the face. "You're fucking dead!" he said.

Two security guards jumped him. There was a scuffle, and he was handcuffed and taken away. Holding her hand over a bloody nose, the woman was led off in the opposite direction by one of the ticket clerks. All the people around me started talking to one another. There's no ice-breaker like a little violence.

I was totally shaken. It was one thing to see this kind of thing on TV and another to see it in person. The man's rage had filled the room. I could still feel it.

Would he kill her in the end? Was she, as he'd put it, *fucking dead*? From what I'd read, when a man threatens a woman's life, he often carries through. Or tries to, anyway.

The airport carpet faded, and I saw Charity's nude body on the floor in front of me, felt the panic as I tried to loosen the belt that was cutting into the supple softness of her neck. Who had put it there? Who had wanted Charity *fucking dead*? And why? I'd told the police it was Paul and/or the Parkers. But that was just guessing, wasn't it? Like the officer had said, at this point everybody was a suspect.

Back when Charity asked me to drive her back to Charleston, I'd decided I was in it to the bitter end. *This is bitter,* I thought. *But it's not the end.*

I pushed along the rope, passing the people ahead of me. They attacked me with venomous eyes until they saw I wasn't cutting in—I was leaving. Following signs to the rental car area, I went from counter to counter until I found a Ford Contour that was available and relatively inexpensive. I had no idea how long I'd need it, so I used my credit card to pay for a week. The clerk gave me a map, highlighting the route to Interstate 10 south. After driving around the huge airport twice because I was always in the wrong lane to exit, I found my way to the interstate. I was on the road again, and my headache was back in full force.

A couple of hours later I passed through Tucson and stopped for the night at a motel on the south side. I found a phone book in a drawer and leafed through it, searching for a suitable alias. I figured I had to be careful—I didn't want to add identity theft to my list of punishable offenses. I ended up naming myself for two streets back home. Using the pen and stationery I found in the desk, I practiced writing "Sheridan Belmont" over and over.

My headache was better in the morning, so I went to the mall. First I found a beauty salon and became a kinky redhead. It was awful—I knew those hair chemicals smelled, but I'd never been smack in the middle of them before.

Since the stylist was having a light day, she took some time to show me how to apply eye makeup. She said the way I was doing it, I looked like a two-dollar whore. I told her I was one and proud of it.

Then I visited a bunch of shops and came up with some fun outfits, including a pair of ankle-high patent leather boots with no heel to speak of. As I signed the final credit slip, it occurred to me to wonder what the limit on my card might be.

To test my new look, I drove to the gas station where Charity and I had stayed overnight. As I was gassing up the Contour, Charity's date Neat Pete came out. "Hey there," he said. "Where've you been all my life?"

"Don't you remember? We met last week," I said.

"No way. I'd remember *you*."

"I was staying here in a big motor home with my friend, Charity."

"Oh, yeah, Charity." He almost drooled. "Is she around?"

" 'Fraid not," I said. "Well, I have to get going." I got in the car and started pulling the door closed.

"Did that woman find you?" he said.

I stopped in mid-pull. "What woman?"

"She came by in a motor home after you left, asking if I knew where you'd gone. She said you'd left your extension cord at a campground in Texas, and she wanted to return it to you. I figured you would want it back."

"So you told her we'd gone to Big Bear Butte Spa." I felt sick.

"Yeah, I hope it was okay. And I told her brother too."

"Whose brother?"

"Charity's. What's his name, Paul?"

"Paul was here too?" My stomach contracted. If he gave me any more good news, I'd have to use his bathroom.

"Yeah. He told me he heard she was looking for him. He even looked like Charity but, you know, not so pretty."

I peered at the surrounding buildings. There were windows, lots of windows, too many windows. They could have been watching us all the time we were here.

I pulled at the door again, but he caught it. "Are you busy tonight?" he asked.

"Extremely," I said.

It was a long time before the nausea went away.

My next stop was another station, the Pinto Gas and Repair. I wanted to get the phone number from the Firedog Militia poster.

It took a good part of the afternoon to get there. The barren landscape I passed through triggered a wave of longing for the deep-green lushness of western New York and cool moist air that didn't leave your eyes dry and your skin feeling like a shriveled apple peel.

The Pinto station looked even more deserted than it had the first time. The motorcycles weren't there. I hoped that meant the snickering guys weren't there either. Even so, I had to steel myself to get out of the car and operate the pump. When I went in to pay, the lone person in the place was the teenybopper who had manned the register before. Today she had her hair in a ponytail, probably so it wouldn't hide any of her four-inch hoop earrings. She looked bored.

"Hello," I said, and waited to see if she'd recognize me.

"Hi, there," she said. "How're you doing? Just the gas?"

"Just the gas." The candy bars looked like they'd been there since the place opened. I glanced to my left to check if the militia poster was still there. It was.

"That'll be $12.53," she said, checking out my purple tank and neon-green ankle pants. Her faded denim was dreary by comparison. But what she lacked in hue, she made up in brevity. Her halter top was two muffin cups and a couple straps.

As she counted out my change, I tried to think of ways to—as Charity would have said—"pick her brain." I spied a box of matchbooks on the counter. "Do you have any matches?" I asked.

"Sure." She pointed at the box with a blood-red fingernail. "Take two. I know what it's like to run out."

"It's the pits."

"Yeah," she said. "I've lit butts off the stove. Once I caught my frickin' hair on fire." She almost fell off her stool laughing.

I laughed even harder. Then I pointed to the poster. "What's that?"

"You don't know about the militia? Where you been?"

"New Jersey."

"No kidding? What're you doing in Arizona?"

"Things got a little hot for me back east, you know what I mean?"

"Yeah, well, it's frickin' hot here too."

"Hey, touché," I said. The girl was a frickin' riot. "By the way, my name's Sheridan."

"Sheridan? That's cool. Mine's Denise. Are you staying around here, Sheridan?" Her tone implied I'd be crazy if I did.

"I don't know where I'm staying. I just got in."

"How come your car's got an Arizona plate?"

She wasn't as dumb as I thought. "It's a rental," I said. "I flew in. Sky Harbor."

"You were in Phoenix? Cool! Did you hit any bars?"

"Couldn't take the time. I'm going back to Phoenix in a few days. Want to come with me? You can show me the hot spots."

"I've never been there, actually, but I'd love to go. What are you doing in the meantime?"

"Business," I said with a wink.

"What are you doing tonight?" she asked. "Want to come to a party?"

"Where?"

"Somebody's house. I'd have to show you. Then you can come home with me for the night if you want to."

"Won't your folks mind?"

"It's just me and Daddy. He won't care. I have friends sleep over all the time."

"Well, then, sure."

"I get off at 10. Why don't you stay here and keep me company?"

"Can't. I got things to do."

"Pick me up, then."

"I'll be here." I sashayed out and took the interstate back to the last exit I'd passed. In a few miles, the road led to a town. First thing I did was go in a drugstore to buy a pack of cigarettes to go with my matches. Didn't want Denise calling my bluff.

There was a diner next door, so I ate some French fries and a salad in honor of Charity. It was only 7 when I finished, so I asked the waitress where I could kill a few hours. She said there was a revival out on Wiggins Road, and she thought they were having services every night. I told her thanks and followed her directions because I was curious to see what a revival looked like. It turned out to be a big white tent with cars parked around it. I rolled down the window but couldn't hear anything.

On the way I'd passed a Kmart, so I drove back to it. There were a zillion more cars in their lot than at the revival tent. I went in and wandered around tossing things in a shopping cart: I got fresh batteries for Charity's flashlight, a pocket compass, a nail clipper with a little file in it, and nail polish. I wanted pointy red fingernails like Denise's.

Thinking of Denise, I tossed a romance novel in the cart.

After paying, I moved the Contour under a floodlight and did my nails—it wasn't much different than sanding and painting models. Still, I had a bit of trouble applying the polish with my left hand and got it all over the cuticles. After they dried I went back in the Kmart and bought a bottle of polish remover to neaten them up. I still had some time, so I did my toes.

The Pinto Gas and Repair was cheerier at night than by day. The pump area was lit by halides, and a warm incandescent glow poured from the window and door. I parked in front, went in, and gave Denise the novel. She stuck it under the counter to read "when it wasn't busy." I figured that was almost always.

"Who owns this place?" I said.

"My daddy." She stuffed the bills from the till into a zippered bag.

"You work here every night all by yourself?"

"I take turns with my sister, so half the time I work days. But don't worry, Sheridan, she'll do double shifts when I go with you to Phoenix. She's got a family, and she likes to make an extra buck now and then." She turned off the lights and locked the door. "We'll need to stop at the night drop on the way," she said.

"Who usually picks you up?"

"Daddy or my boyfriend, Alvy, but we're on the outs at the moment. I called Daddy and told him I was catching a ride with a friend."

Déjà vu, friend Charity.

After ditching the bag of money at a tiny bank in a minuscule town south of the station, Denise guided me south on deserted roads. She took out a cigarette, but I told her I had signed an agreement with the rental car people not to smoke in the car.

"Why'd you do a thing like that?"

"Discount."

"Oh. Well, how would they know? We could open the windows."

"The agreement said they'd be testing it with smoke-sniffing dogs."

"You're kidding? Dogs?"

"Do you have a dog, Denise?" I'd run out of lies, so I thought I'd try distraction.

"We've had a bunch of dogs. When I was a kid, we had a really nice one. She was a collie mix. We named her Lassie."

I let her ramble on about Lassie and all the other dogs in her life, which led to all the cats in her life and an unfortunate gerbil who'd been eaten by one of the cats.

When we had gone 40 miles—I was keeping track—I asked her how much farther we had to go. "We're getting pretty close," she said.

It was still another 20. On thing I'd noticed is that people who live in the country don't seem to think anything of driving long distances. I had a cousin who lived 50 miles from Buffalo, and she'd drive into town for a cup of coffee, whereas I needed a three-day weekend before I'd go out to visit her.

We parked in a field of dry grass next to a sprawling ranch house with brick arches framing a wide veranda. Fifty or so cars and trucks were already there, and country music was blaring.

Denise jumped out, lit a cigarette, and sucked deeply. I lit one too, and took a few faux puffs as we walked to the house. Groups of people were gathered on and around the veranda, chatting. As we picked our way through, I could see I was in the right place to observe the militia. The white skulls on the men's caps glowed in the moonlight.

We entered a living room packed with people. A girl with corkscrew curls shrieked and ran over to hug Denise, who introduced her to me as Heather. Heather told us Denise's ex, Alvy, was in the kitchen getting drunk, so we might not want to go that way. We dutifully went back out and walked around to the backyard with Heather in tow.

The backyard was where the real party was. The music was blasting from two concert-class speakers mounted on a hay rack. Several dozen couples were dancing on the cement patio or sitting at picnic tables drinking beer from a column of kegs over at the side. Many of the guys sported skulls, and some were wearing guns.

Denise offered to get me a beer, but I told her I wanted to start off slow. "I hear you," she said and ran off to spy on Alvy. Heather showed me where to get a can of pop. There wasn't any root beer, so I took a 7-Up. She took one too, and we stood by the cooler, watching the merriment. Heather was even younger than Denise. She had chick-down on her face and arms. "You live around here?" I asked her.

"Over by Tombstone," she said. "Where you from again?"

"New Jersey."

"Is that near New York City?"

"Real close," I tell her.

"Do you ever go to Broadway? I'm dying to see *Cats,* but I don't know when I'll get there."

"I don't think it's on anymore."

"No way!"

I shrugged.

She gave me a look like it was my fault and walked away. Before long I saw her dancing with a young fellow. They were pretty good. He had her twirling all over the place.

I looked around for Denise but didn't see her. Since my reason for coming down here was to gather information, I thought I'd better start introducing myself to people. There was an empty six inches on the end of the bench of the nearest picnic table, enough for one bun, so I took it. The woman I snuggled up to moved over. She was older than me, in her 40s maybe, with lobe-length brown hair that had been set on juice-can-size rollers and held in that shape with industrial-strength hair spray. She was wearing black slacks and a green long-sleeve Western-style shirt with silky fringe attached here and there.

"Hi," I said. "Nice blouse."

"Why, thank you," she said.

"My name's Sheridan. I'm Denise's friend," I told her.

"I'm not sure I know Denise, but it's nice to meet you. I'm Aggie."

"Hello, Aggie. I just flew in from New Jersey."

"You sure are a long way from home." She turned to the others at the table. "This here is Sheridan from New Jersey." She introduced me to her husband, Steve, a skull-wearer, and told me the names of the rest of my tablemates. Each nodded politely or said "How do you do?" This done, they took up the conversation

I'd interrupted, which seemed to be speculation about whether a certain Sunday-school teacher was having an affair with a certain student. The loud music drowned out lot of the details, but from what I could hear the case was highly circumstantial. I didn't think it'd make it to the grand jury.

In a while, an invisible DJ put on a slow tune, and everybody at our table got up to dance except Aggie, Steve, and me. "Go ahead, dance," I told Aggie, thinking maybe they were staying at the table to avoid leaving me alone.

"Oh, that's okay," Aggie whispered. "Steve don't dance." As she was telling me this, Steve got up and crossed the patio. After a word with a woman wearing a low-cut tee and hip-hugging pants, he swept her close in his arms and swayed to the music. Aggie was technically right, he wasn't dancing. I was embarrassed for her and excused myself, saying I had to go to the little girl's room. On my way to the house I reflected that Jo would never say "little girl's room," but it had rolled right off Sheridan's tongue.

The kitchen was crowded and messy. Every surface was filled with half-empty plastic cups and open bags of snacks, their contents spilling into puddles of beer. I spotted Denise. She was being pressed against the refrigerator by a guy I assumed was Alvy, and he was kissing her in a manner that led me to believe they'd made up. When the kiss finally ended, she saw me.

"Oh, good," she said. "I want you to meet my boyfriend. Alvy, this is Sheridan."

Alvy squinted at me, and I recognized him from my first visit to the Pinto Gas and Repair. He was the guy who told me it wasn't him who had the problem. In my opinion he *was* the problem, especially tonight, with a gun on his hip and an alcohol-soaked brain. I took a step backward.

"Don't I know you?" he slurred.

Denise gave him a playful punch. "No, silly. Sheridan's from New Jersey."

"Oh," Alvy said. He rummaged through the paper cups on the counter until he found one that still had beer in it and drained it.

"Listen, Sheridan," Denise said. "Looks like I'm not going home tonight after all. Do you think you could find someplace else to stay?"

Damn. This kind of thing had happened to me all the time in high school. "Oh, sure," I said, as I had back then. "Don't worry about it."

"I'm frickin' sorry," she said.

"No problem." I turned and almost ran into Aggie, who must have been standing there a while. If she had just come in, her fringe would have been waving.

"Did you find the bathroom?" she asked.

"No."

"It's upstairs. Come on, I have to go too."

I followed her up a flight of steps. Three women and a guy were queued up in the hall. I was tempted to say I didn't have to go that bad, but it turned out I did.

Aggie and I leaned against the wall. "I didn't mean to eavesdrop, but did I hear you don't have a place to stay tonight?"

"It's turned out that way. Do you know where there's a motel?"

"No, we're way out. By the time you got to a motel, it'd be morning."

"Maybe I'll sleep in my car." I should have rented a Wellaway.

"You have a car?" she asked.

"It's pretty small."

"I'll make a deal with you…what was your name again?"

"Sheridan."

"I could use a ride home, Sheridan. If you give me one, you

can spend the night on our couch. It's sort of lumpy, but better than a car seat."

"What about your husband?"

"Steve won't be home tonight. He's gone a lot."

I'll bet. I wasn't sure I wanted to get in the middle of a domestic situation, but Steve had been wearing the skull—maybe I could learn a thing or two. I told her sure, I was ready to go any time she was. She said how about as soon as we peed?

Her home was at least 20 miles away, mostly on dirt roads. I was glad I wasn't driving my Toyota. I was also glad I'd peed. As we rattled along, I asked Aggie how she would have gotten home if I hadn't been around.

"Somebody would have taken me. If not, my daughter Tracy would have had to come got me."

"How old is she?"

"Fifteen."

"And she drives?"

"She's got her learner's."

This led to a discussion about our families. Aggie told me she was from Kentucky and still had two brothers there. She came to Arizona many years ago to visit a friend in Bisbee. The second night there, she'd met Steve during happy hour at the Copper Queen Hotel, and she never went back home.

Besides Tracy, she and Steve had a six-year-old, Patty.

I made up Sheridan's story as I told it. I was raised in Trenton, but now I lived in an apartment in Newark with my boyfriend, Vinnie, and I worked for an importer. I was in Arizona on business, looking for markets for my employer's wares. I'd met Denise a few days ago, and we hit it off, so Denise invited me to the party. *Good story, Jo. Thanks, Sheridan.*

We were on yet another deserted road. I hadn't seen any kind of building for a long time. Suddenly a yellow glow popped over the horizon. As we got closer, the glow defined itself into windows.

"Look at that!" Aggie said. "She's got every light in the house on."

"Who does?" I asked.

"Tracy. She's baby-sitting her sister. She gets scared when we're gone after dark. The aliens are around at night."

"Aliens?" I tried to think how far we were from Roswell.

"You know, the aliens. Illegals. From Mexico."

"Oh. Are we near the border?" I asked.

"It's a couple miles south."

"Wow, I'd like to see it." That would be something to write home about, if I'd been the writing type.

"There's no proper roads to it. You'd do best if you headed for one of the border towns."

"What's it made of, chain-link?" I wasn't sure why I thought that. I must have seen a picture of it once, back in school maybe.

"Well, it's different depending where you go. Some places it's chain-link, and others just barbed wire. The stuff they're putting in now is corrugated steel. If you really want to see it, go to Douglas."

"Is Douglas far?"

"Not too bad."

The house was an L-shaped one-story affair. Half the two-car carport was taken up by a Dodge Caravan. Aggie directed me to find a place to park on the dirt, which was easy since the whole yard was dirt.

As soon as I opened my door and put a foot out, a dog started barking furiously. It sounded like a big dog. I pulled my foot back in and slammed the door. "Don't worry, Sheridan," Aggie said. "He's chained up out back."

Chains break. I'd have preferred if she'd said he didn't bite. I eased the door open. When the barking didn't get any louder, I got out of the car. Aggie told me to be sure to lock the door.

She used two different keys on the locks in the windowless door that led into the house. When we were inside, she locked them again, turned a deadbolt, and fastened a safety chain. I felt the bite of conditioned air.

"Tracy, it's me," Aggie yelled. I followed her from a kitchen into a family room where a teenage girl was asleep under a brown afghan on a burgundy plaid sofa. "Go to bed, honey," Aggie said, shaking her.

Tracy sat up, blinked, and scowled. "I thought you'd be home an hour ago. I have to go to school tomorrow, you know."

"I know. Go on to bed."

"Where's Daddy?"

"He didn't come home yet."

"No shit! Anybody we know?"

Aggie glanced at me, and Tracy followed suit. "Who the hell are *you*?" Aggie said.

"This is Sheridan, honey," Aggie said. "She gave me a ride and she's going to spend the night."

"Great," she said in a tone that let me know it was anything but. She got up and stomped out.

"Don't pay any attention to her, Sheridan," Aggie said. "Tracy's got a bug up her ass because Steve said she couldn't have her boyfriend over."

"While you were gone?" I thought that was pretty smart of Steve.

"Anytime, actually. Let's see, now, what do you need to know? The bathroom's that way." She pointed in the direction Tracy had gone. "The toilet doesn't flush very well. Just hold the handle down till you're satisfied. Feel free to watch TV if you like, and help yourself to anything in the kitchen. I'm tired. I got to go to bed." She wished me a good night and went out, turning off the lights as she went.

I was tired too. I took off my shoes, turned off the TV, shook out the afghan, and lay down. Like Aggie'd said, the sofa was lumpy, but they were soft lumps, still warm from Tracy. I was asleep in no time.

14

When I woke, the windows were full of light, and manic music filled the air. A young girl was lying on the floor much too close to the television in my mother's opinion, watching a cartoon cat beat up a cartoon dog. She must have sensed me looking at her, because she turned her head. I closed my eyes, but it was too late.

"Mommy said if you woke up, I was supposed to ask if you want a cup of coffee," she said.

I reopened my eyes. "Patty, I presume?"

She giggled. "Yes."

"The coffee's in the kitchen, I presume?

More giggles. "Yes."

"Thank you. I can get it." After folding the afghan, I reached for my boots and started to put one on.

"Don't forget to shake it, she said.

"Why?"

"Scorpions." She didn't add "dumbhead," but it was implied.

"You have scorpions in your house?"

"Sure. They're everywhere. If you look at the light in the entryway, you can see one. But don't worry, he's dead."

"Maybe later," I said, and shook both boots like crazy before putting them on. Then I used the bathroom and shook the towel before drying my hands.

When I got to the kitchen Patty was already there, spooning instant Folgers into a cup. She was a slip of a girl with toasted-almond eyes and long brown braids. She filled the cup with water from the faucet, gave it a stir, and stuck it in the microwave. She'd obviously done it before. Then she turned to me. "Want some Cheerios, I presume?" It was accompanied by so many giggles, she could hardly get it out.

"No, thanks. Just coffee. Is your mother around?"

"She went to the store. She'll be right back."

"There's a store around here?" I hadn't seen a store on the road I'd been on last night.

"A little one. Do you want milk and sugar, I presume?"

"Just sugar. How about your father? Is he around?"

"I don't know where he is." She took the sugar bowl from the counter and set it smack in the middle of the table where a dummy like me could find it.

"How about Tracy?" I asked

"School."

Good. "Do you go to school?"

"The bus comes in 10 minutes, but it's always late," she said, and went back to her cartoons.

I read refrigerator notes until the microwave dinged. You can learn a lot about people from their refrigerator doors—I'd found that out from working in patients' homes.

This refrigerator door told me Aggie was going to host her church group next week and was planning to serve egg salad sandwiches and orange sherbet punch; Tracy was going to have a summer job interview on May fourth and a tooth cleaning in July; and Patty got good grades, according to her last report card, and she wasn't a bad little artist. I wondered if Steve even lived here.

I heard a car door slam, and after doing the key routine, Aggie came in carrying a plastic bag. "Good morning, Sheridan," she said. "Did you have enough milk? I bought more."

"I don't use it."

She looked at my black brew and wrinkled her nose. "I got to have at least half milk for my ulcers. I bought eggs too. Want me to fry some up?"

"No, thanks. Not now."

"Let me know." She put the groceries away, made herself a cup of very white coffee, and sat across from me.

I hadn't seen her in the daylight before. Her skin was sallow and puffy. Fluid-filled bags hung from her eyes.

"How'd you sleep?" I asked.

"Not too good. How about you?"

"Like a rock. Thanks for letting me stay. I don't know what I would have done otherwise."

"Glad to help," Aggie said. "Thanks for the ride."

"I met Patty. She's real cute."

"Smart too." She glanced at a wall clock. "Lord, look at the time. Patty!" she yelled. "Are you ready for school?

Patty ran in. "Yes, Mommy, but I need lunch money." As she spoke there was a rumble and the window was filled with the golden glow of sun on the school bus.

Aggie grabbed her purse and dug for change. "Damn," she said, "I'm a quarter short."

I took a quarter from my pocket and handed it to Patty.

"Thank you, I pre-soooome," she said and, after waiting for her mother to unfasten the chain and turn the deadbolt, ran out. I wondered what these people would do in case of fire.

"What was that she said to you?" Aggie said, returning to the table.

"Nothing," I said. "Did Steve come home?"

"No. He probably went right to work from…his friend's house. He'll be in for supper."

"What does he do?"

"He works the ranch."

"What kind of ranch?"

"Cattle."

"Where is it?"

"You're in the middle of it," Aggie said. "It runs from the last cattle guard we crossed last night all the way to the border."

"What's a cattle guard?"

"It's a bunch of horizontal bars in the road. The cows won't go across them. They're afraid of getting their legs stuck between."

"Is that what those were?"

"What did you think they were?"

"I don't know. Storm drains, maybe?" I crossed to the window. All I could see was flatland dotted with dull green plants, and a long mountain range in the distance. "Where are the cows?"

"They're pretty scattered. There's not a lot for them to eat," she said. "They'd starve if they had only Bernie's land to graze. He leases lots of government land for them."

"Bernie?"

"Bernie Hollings, Steve's boss. Their house is four miles farther down the road. He and Barb would have been at the party last night, but one of their kids has strep throat."

"Speaking of last night," I said, "I noticed Steve was wearing a Firedog Militia cap. Is he a member?" I sat down again, glad for an opening to start my snooping.

"Oh, sure, all the men around here belong."

"What is it, a fraternal group like the Moose?"

"Sort of. But a lot of women belong too. I do."

"And you have meetings?" I asked.

"Sure. And parties, like last night."

"One thing I noticed at the party, so many of the men were carrying guns. Why would they need them?"

"Everybody in Arizona carries guns," Aggie said. "You don't need a permit unless it's a handgun, and not even then if you keep it in plain sight."

"No kidding? But why do they *need* them?"

"Well, if everybody has a gun, you wouldn't want to be the only person without one, would you?"

I thought there was something wrong with that logic, but I couldn't put my finger on it. "Do you carry a gun?"

"I don't need one. They wouldn't shoot a woman."

Suddenly I was happy to be Sheridan. No one would mistake *her* for a guy.

So far, Aggie hadn't said anything that would make the militia any worse than the Masons, so I tried another tack. "Back in Tucson," I said, "I heard that the militia was formed to help the border patrol keep people from coming across from Mexico."

"Well, you can't keep them from coming over. The fence is broken in so many places, they just walk in. What we do is watch for them and then call the U.S. Patrol to come get them."

"So you're not mad at the government?"

"Well, I don't know why anybody wouldn't be mad at the government. Aren't you happy with them?" She looked at me like I was a little off.

"Not really," I said. It was the first bit of truth I'd told for a while. "But that person in Tucson also told me militia members are stockpiling arms."

Aggie narrowed her eyes. "You're not a government agent, are you, Sheridan?"

"Of course not!" I laughed a little for effect.

"Steve says they've been down here nosing around."

"I'm not, honest. Mind if I have more coffee?"

"Help yourself." She shoved the jar over.

While the microwave hummed, I decided it might be a good idea to drop the grilling for a while and revert to Dumb Easterner. "Truth is, Aggie, I'm totally fascinated with this whole militia thing. We don't have one back home, at least I don't think we do. If we did, I'd join."

"Why? You got an alien problem back there?"

"Well, sure," I said, sitting down across from her. "What about those terrorists?"

She leaned forward. "They're a big worry here too."

"They are?"

"Well, they could be. Most of the aliens are guys looking for work. But if they can get through, what's to keep the terrorists from doing it?"

"I never thought about that."

"But even if they're not terrorists, the aliens cause a lot of damage here," Aggie said. "They cut our fences and kill our dogs. They steal our water. They break our security lights. And they leave trash all over the place." Her lips were stiff and her eyes were wide, and she pounded her fist on the table with every point she made. I wondered if this was why she had ulcers.

"Excuse me, do you mind if I take a shower?" I asked.

I went out to the car to get a change of clothes. Sheridan's finery was in the backseat in a paper shopping bag. Why hadn't I bought her a cute little suitcase at Kmart? I chose a navy blue and white checked tank and a pair of white bell-bottoms. There was only one more outfit left in the bag. If I was Sheridan past tomorrow, I'd have to do some laundry.

Aggie was waiting at the door when I went back in. "I'm sorry for getting so upset," she said.

"That's okay," I told her. "If I had all those things happen to me, I'd be upset too."

"Well, they haven't actually happened to me personally, except for our dog seems to bark a lot. And once Steve took me down to their gathering place, and there was a lot of trash around. The rest of that stuff I heard about at militia meetings."

"Have the…have they ever hurt anyone?" I was having a hard time saying "aliens."

"Not that I've heard, just dogs, and a cow once. The aliens are the ones that get hurt and even killed. Their rides don't come and they run out of water, or they die of the heat."

"That's awful," I said.

"Sheridan, remember back there when you said you'd heard the militia was stockpiling arms?"

"That was just through the grapevine."

"Well, the truth is," she said, "I don't know what's really going on here. Lots of things have changed lately, and I don't care for most of them. For instance, we didn't used to be the Firedog Militia. We were called the Ranch Security Patrol, and the only ones who belonged were the ranchers and people who lived around here."

"When did it change?"

"When the new guys took over."

"What new guys?"

Aggie was quiet for a minute. Then she said, "You know what? There's a militia meeting tonight. Want to hang around and come?"

"They'd let me?"

"There's new people coming all the time now. It used to be just us, but like I said, everything's changing. You can sleep on the sofa afterward, if you like. It wasn't too bad, was it?"

"It was very comfortable. Thanks, Aggie, that would be great."

As I undressed for my shower, I wondered why I wasn't feeling ecstatic. It looked like I was going to be getting what I wanted, a peek at the Militia in action. But all I felt was stressed and jittery. Was this how real spies felt? Of course, it could have been the caffeine—I couldn't remember the last time I'd drunk two cups of coffee in a row.

When I emerged from the bathroom, Aggie was waiting. "Since you're staying over, would you like to go see the border today? I've got errands to run in Douglas, and you're welcome to come along. We can get some lunch."

"I'd love to," I told her.

"The part of the border fence near the crossing is real pretty. They put in a new one a few years ago and painted it gold."

"Can I go across the border?"

"To Agua Prieta? You don't want to do that. It's a big city with lots of vagrants hanging around. Steve won't let me go over unless he's along," she said. "There's no reason to anyway, unless you have some prescriptions you want filled."

Unfortunately or fortunately, I didn't.

The city of Douglas was a busy place. Most of the people on the streets looked Hispanic, and a lot of the signs on the businesses were in Spanish. Aggie parked near the Gadsden Hotel and led me into the lobby, telling me, "You got to see the marble staircase in here. They say Pancho Villa rode his horse up it."

The staircase was huge—I could see how a horse could climb it, although I wouldn't want to be on his back when he tried to come down the slippery steps. Like a tour guide, Aggie pointed out the massive marble columns and the stained-glass domes in the ceiling, "People say they've seen ghosts in here too," she said, "but I wouldn't take that as gospel."

I spotted some telephone booths off to the side, and I asked Aggie if she knew what time it was. My sports watch was in the backpack with Jo's clothes.

She pointed to a big clock above the check-in desk that said 11:43. I calculated the time change and decided Mom would still be at work. That wasn't a problem, however. The school would accept the charges because Mom was the one who answered the phone.

"Oh, Jo," Mom said in her *Why did I ever want to be a mother?* voice. "I thought you were dead."

"It's only been four days since I called."

"Where are you?"

"I'm still in Arizona."

"You are? What are you doing there? Do you have any idea how many phone calls you've had?"

"Calls? From who?"

"A policewoman phoned from a town called something Center—I wrote it down, but it's at home. She said you fled the hospital. Why were you in a hospital, and why would they care if you fled?"

"I fell and got a concussion, but I'm okay now. The police wanted to ask me some questions about it. So how are you, Mom?"

"Awful. Some insurance company called too, about an accident you had with a dump truck. Was that what made you fall and get a concussion?

"No, it was just a fender-bender. I'll take care of it when I get home. Who else called?"

"I don't know. Rose took the messages. There were a few more."

I lowered my voice. "Was one of the callers named Paul?"

"Paul? I don't know. Who's Paul?"

"Just this guy. So he didn't call?"

"I don't think so. It's all written on the tablet by the phone. Call us at home tonight."

"I can't. I have to go to a meeting."

"A meeting? Wait a minute," she said, and I heard a man's voice in the background. "Jo, Gerald Phipps wants to know if you're ever going to get to his mother's.'"

"Yes. Yes, I am. Just a couple more days."

"Is your truck fixed? Where are you staying? Do you have a phone number?"

"No. Listen, Mom, if anybody else calls, tell them you haven't heard from me and have no idea where I am, understand?"

"Why?"

"Just do it, and tell Rose to do it too. Now, I've got to go. I'll call you in a couple of days."

"I thought you said you'd be at Elinor Phipps's house in a couple of days."

"That too. And I'll explain everything."

"That'll be the day."

"I love you, give my love to Rose."

"Jo, wait—"

I hung up, wondering what Mom did in a past life to deserve me.

Aggie and I wandered in a couple of shops near the hotel. I bought three little animals carved out of onyx for Mom and Rose, a bird of some sort, a turtle, and a howling wolf. I planned to tell them they were souvenirs from "almost Mexico."

The menu at the restaurant where we went to eat had two sections, one for Mexican food and one for American food. For the first time in my life I wondered why people living in the United States were called "Americans." People who lived in Mexico and Canada were also Americans, weren't they? And how about all those people in South America and Central America? They were Americans too. So wouldn't their food be American too?

Aggie saw me looking at that side of the menu. "Don't you like Mexican food, Sheridan?" she asked.

"I had enchiladas once. They were okay."

"They have wonderful enchiladas here," she said.

When my enchiladas came, I found out they weren't even

related to the ones I'd had in Buffalo. My eyes watered and my nose ran, and I needed four glasses of water to get them down. Aggie laughed herself silly.

Then, as promised, she took me to the border crossing. It was a complex of buildings in that southwest color I can only describe as "light rust." Cars crawled between them, bumper-to-bumper in both directions. The fence that abutted the gate, separating the U.S. from Mexico, was about 10 feet tall, constructed of vertical metal bars about four inches apart and angled inward at the top. Aggie had said it was gold, but it didn't look gold to me. It was more of a peachy beige.

"You should see it at night when it's lit up," she told me, pointing to a series of evenly spaced floodlights on portable generators. They were aimed at the fence and the homes on the other side. I pitied anyone in Agua Prieta who had a north-facing bedroom window.

I stared at the fence, wondering what would happen if it were to be torn down like the Berlin Wall. Would there be chaos? Would it be the end of the United States and Mexico as we know them?

Aggie interrupted my thoughts to say we'd better be heading for the Safeway so she could be home when Patty got there. She couldn't depend on Tracy, she said.

The Safeway was pretty much the same as Top's Market in Buffalo, except for the produce department, where there were two great mountains, one of pink pinto beans, the other of snow-white rice. There were also fruits and vegetables I didn't recognize and a great variety of peppers, fresh and dried. I wondered which ones had made my enchiladas dang near inedible.

Tracy was in the kitchen talking on the phone when we got back.

"Don't make any plans for tonight," Aggie told her. "It's meeting night. I need you to baby-sit."

Tracy handed the receiver to her mother. "I'll pick it up in the bedroom." She ran out. Aggie listened for a short time then hung up.

"Tracy's a pretty girl," I said as we put the groceries away.

"Yeah, but she's a handful. She has this boyfriend Steve absolutely hates. We fight with her about it all the time."

"So you don't like him either?"

"Not really, but I figure why make a big thing of it? They'll be breaking up soon. Kids do."

The school bus pulled up and dropped Patty at the end of the driveway. She gave her mother a kiss and another work of art for the refrigerator door, which made it necessary to remove an old one.

"You're really good," I told her. "Wish I could draw like that." I was serious.

"You want this one?" She handed me the displaced artwork, a brick-chimneyed house with flowers around it and a rainbow arching over it.

"I sure would. Is this a picture of your house?"

"It's my someday house. I'm going to have a cat. See him?"

I looked more closely. Peering out from a blue-curtained window was something with yellow stripes that could have been a car. "Is he a tiger?" I asked.

"No, he's a cat. I'm going to call him Oodles."

"Great name. Are you sure you want me to have this?"

"Sure. I can draw another one."

"Thanks. I'll hang it over my fireplace."

"No, you won't," she said. She turned to her mother. "Can I go watch TV?"

While I peeled potatoes, Aggie fried up a package of chicken parts and made biscuits. When dinner was almost ready, a big Ram pickup rolled into the driveway. "It's Steve," Aggie said.

I wondered if he'd remember me. He didn't. He stopped inside the doorway and looked at me with the same distaste that Tracy had last night. "Who's this?" he asked Aggie.

"It's Sheridan. We met her at the party, remember? She's a friend of…" She looked at me for help.

"Denise," I said.

Ignoring me, he said, "What's she doing here?"

"I needed a ride home last night," Aggie said, a hint of accusation in her voice, "so I invited her to stay. She's coming to the meeting with us tonight."

He glared at me. "You been before?"

"No, I don't live around here. I wish I did."

He was going to say more, but Aggie told him, "Dinner's on, honey. Go wash up. Tell the girls too."

He grunted and left the kitchen.

During the meal, Aggie entertained the rest of the family with tales of our day in Douglas, including the one in which my nose ran. Patty laughed along with her mother, but Tracy gave me a look that said I was a pathetic fool.

Steve acted like he hadn't heard—he gave his plate his full attention, refueling from the serving dishes whenever it got low. He was a large man, particularly thick around the middle. He was muscular too. The fabric of his short-sleeve shirt, the same one he'd had on last night, strained around his upper arms. His jowly face was deeply suntanned, and his buzz cut had recently been buzzed.

When Aggie ran out of things to say about our outing, she asked her daughters what they'd done in school. Tracy shook her head and went on eating. She was a chip off the old block. Patty picked up the conversation and ran with it through dessert.

When nothing was left of the Safeway cake except the cardboard circle, Tracy stood and told her parents, "I've got plans for tonight, so I called Michelle. She's going to sit for you. You'll need to go pick her up."

Steve rose so fast his chair fell over backward. "I don't think so," he said. "You go call her back."

"I won't," Tracy said. "It's not fair. I have a life too."

I looked at Aggie. Her face was white. "Steve," she said. "It's okay. I'll pick up Michelle."

"It's *not* okay!" Steve yelled. He glanced at me and lowered his voice. "Tracy, go in the living room. We need to talk." He put his hand on her shoulder. She shook it off and trounced into the family room. He followed, pulling the door closed behind him.

Aggie righted Steve's chair. "We'd best be getting these dishes done," she said, her voice trembling.

"I'll be glad to do them," I told her.

"Thank you, Sheridan. You wash and Patty can wipe, and I'll put away the leftovers."

Patty obediently took a dishtowel from a rack and stood near the sink. She kept turning her eyes toward the family room door. Now and then we heard a raised voice. Sometimes it was Tracy's but more often Steve's.

I'd finished the glasses and the silverware and was starting in on the plates when there was the sound of a door slamming in a far part of the house and Steve came back in the kitchen. "You can forget about picking up Michelle. Tracy's staying home," he told Aggie.

"What time are we leaving?" she asked.

"You girls can get yourselves there. You seem to have plenty of cars." He went out, and soon his truck backed out of the driveway, throwing gravel as it turned onto the road.

Aggie and Patty took deep breaths in unison. I wondered what hadn't happened.

15

Aggie told me militia meetings were held in a church basement in a town about 15 miles northeast. It wasn't *her* church, she said in a tone that let me know her church was better.

When we pulled in the lot was nearly full of vehicles, mostly pickups decorated with American flags and rifle racks. Steve's Ram was there, parked near the church door. With flag decals on its side windows and a rifle in its rack, it fit right in.

We entered the church and descended to a big hall. The walls were stained an uneven light brown, and the carpet had seen too many potlucks. Folding chairs were arranged in 10 or 12 rows, facing a podium flanked by two flags. One was a U.S. flag and the other was black with a smoking skull on it.

Fifty or so men and about half as many women were chatting in groups or standing in line to get coffee from a giant electric urn. Many of them were smoking, which probably explained the stained walls.

I recognized a few people from last night's party, including the woman Steve hadn't been dancing with. He detached himself from a group and approached her, slipping his arm around her waist as they spoke. Aggie saw it too and quickly looked away.

My attention was caught by a man in the group Steve had abandoned. He was obviously the top banana in the bunch—all eyes were on him, and his jaw was going a-mile-a-minute. He was wearing a big cowboy hat and a badge. It was Deputy Conway.

I turned my back to him and spied a LADIES sign on the other side of the hall. I tapped Aggie's arm. "Do you mind if we sit over by the bathroom? I don't feel too well."

"It's the enchiladas," she said with a chuckle.

As soon as the big hand on the laughing-Jesus wall clock went straight up, a man in an aqua shirt stepped to the podium and welcomed everyone. He must have had emphysema or something, because he had to pause every couple words and take a deep in-breath. He said his name was Warren Baker and he was the militia's president. He asked all the new people to stand up and say their names and where they were from. I was surprised how many were from other states. Several said they were boon-docking on so-and-so's ranch and were here to help. My ears perked at the word "boondocking."

I wasn't planning to announce myself, but Aggie prodded me until I stood and thrust my tiny breasts out as far as they'd go, hoping they'd divert Deputy Conway's attention from my face. "Hi, I'm Sheridan," I said in a tone half an octave higher than usual. "I'm Aggie's friend, and I'm here to help."

"Where you from [*breath*], Sheridan?" Warren asked.

"Newark," I said, and sat down. I sneaked a glance at Deputy Conway. He was leaning over to whisper in the ear of a shorter guy who had his back to me. I watched for a sign he might be talking about me, but I didn't see any.

I'd been the last of the newcomers, so Warren introduced the first speaker of the evening, Mayor Roger Keeney, who was the only man in the room wearing a business suit. A few people clapped.

Mayor Keeney started out by saying he knew the kinds of problems the ranchers were having he grazed a few hundred head himself. "But," he added, "we really need to be leaving the roundup of illegals to the border patrol. If you see anything suspicious, you can call the authorities and it will be investigated."

There was an explosion of laughter.

"I know, I know, they're seriously understaffed," he said, "but the government is trying to do something about that—they've more than doubled the number of border patrol officers recently. So we've just got to have patience. We can't be going ahead and forming posses like we've been doing. It doesn't look good for the area. I've got articles from all over the country." He held up a handful of clippings. "It's all over the World Wide Web too. They're calling us vigilantes and racists. They even say we're hunting people for sport. Who's going to come visit or live here after they read that?"

A man in the third row stood up. "Our kind of people, that's who," he said. He got a big round of applause.

The mayor looked right at him. "You may think that, but it's not true. All kinds of property is up for sale, and nobody's buying, not even 'your kind of people.' The tourists are going to stop coming too, and that's a major concern for many of our friends and neighbors."

"Not my problem," the man said, and sat down.

Aggie touched my arm, and I leaned my ear over. "Nobody likes the mayor. He's been helping the aliens," she said.

"How?"

"He drops off bottles of water at places in the desert where they gather. And he takes them blankets on cold nights."

"What a lowlife!" I whispered. "I'll bet he even gives them the Heimlich maneuver when they're choking!"

"What?" she said.

"Nothing." I returned my attention to the proceedings. A man in a camouflage T-shirt and a Marine haircut stood up and said, "What we're doing here is defending the borders of our country. The people of this nation should be thanking us."

"That's not the way it's being seen," the mayor told him. "Come over to my office tomorrow. I'll make you copies of these clippings. I'll show you the Web pages."

"And I'll show you where you can stick your Web pages," the man said, bringing the house down.

The mayor waited until things got quiet. Then he said, "Well, think about it, that's all I'm asking. Thank you." He stepped down and took a seat.

Warren came back to the podium long enough to say, "Okay, now it's time for Paul's report [*breath*] on our great training program [*breath*] and the progress on our boot camp."

Paul Redmun approached the mike, and I realized he was the man with his back to me Deputy Conway had been talking to. I slid down in my chair so fast I almost landed on the floor. Aggie whispered, "You know Paul Redmun?"

"No," I whispered back.

"He's one of those guys I told you about, who's trying to make us into something we're not. I don't like him."

I made a face that was supposed to tell her *I hear you* and *shhh* at the same time. The last thing I wanted to do was draw Paul's attention to our corner of the room. Aggie must have got the message, because she turned her eyes up front again.

"It's good to see so many new people tonight," Paul said. "As President Baker mentioned, we offer newcomers an excellent training program, and we urge all of you to take part. Let me tell you about some of our courses." He consulted a piece of paper in his hand. "You'll learn how to handle firearms in a correct and safe manner, and how to qualify for your concealed-carry permit. There's also a course in the use of tools that will facilitate your task—night-vision goggles and infrared motion sensors, for instance. You'll learn about the militia's mission and our growing network of communications. And that's just a few of them. Be sure to come to an introductory session tomorrow night right in this hall, same time as tonight. May I have a show of hands of those who plan to attend?"

Half a dozen hands shot up.

"Great." He folded the paper and put it in his back pocket. "And now, ladies and gentlemen, are you ready for some wonderful news? Due to a recent generous donation, we've been able to buy that piece of land we've been telling you about, and the building of the barracks will begin in the next few weeks. Also, we've ordered weapons for training purposes, and by November we're going to have an up-and-running boot camp."

Despite the stuffiness of the hall, I got a chill. Could the "recent generous donation" be Charity's four million? She must be spinning in her...wherever she was.

"My good friends John Conway and Buck French here are going to be in charge of the camp," Paul went on, "and they have some great plans, like an indoor *air-conditioned* firing range." There was much whistling and applause. Deputy Conway waved and the guy in the camo shirt stood up and took a mock-serious bow.

So that's Buck French. Cute.

When the applause finally died, Paul said, "If any of you would like to be involved in the planning and building of the camp, be sure to see me after the meeting tonight, because I'm going to be out of town for the next few days. And thanks for your support." He gave a parting wave and sat back down next to Deputy Conway.

Warren came to the podium again and introduced Bernie Hollings. "That's Steve's boss I was telling you about," Aggie whispered.

Bernie set in to organizing the "militia watch" for the week. Hands bobbed up and down as people volunteered for sectors and shifts. "Don't forget, you're going to need your lights, binoculars, cell phones, and radios. Also take your video cameras, if you have them. And be sure to remember your dogs and firearms—it's no picnic in the park out there. Now what did I forget?"

Several voices said, "Water."

"Oh, yeah, take lots of water." He looked at Warren. "Okay if I introduce Rick?" Warren nodded. "Okay, then. Rick's going to lead a business meeting, and I don't want anybody leaving until it's over."

There was a smattering of laughter as 50 percent of the audience got up and left or started milling around the room. Several went over to talk with Paul. A skinny fellow holding a couple of spiral notebooks approached the mike and started droning about an upcoming election and how they needed more volunteers for the nominating committee.

Aggie poked me, "Sheridan, do you see Steve?"

I rubbernecked in the direction of his favorite squeeze. She was there, but Steve wasn't. "Maybe he left," I told her.

"That's what I'm afraid of. Come on, let's go. I don't want him and Tracy getting into it when I'm not home." She took off in the direction of the stairs.

I followed, happy to be leaving the place. I jumped in the Caravan and Aggie backed it out, tires skidding. "Did you see?" she said. "Steve's truck is gone. I'll bet he's already home." We headed down the road at an unsafe speed.

"Why are you worried? Would he hurt Tracy?" I asked.

"He never has yet."

"But you think he might?"

"I don't know. Her mouth is getting smarter every day, and she won't mind us at all anymore. Steve's capable of hurting people, that's for sure." Steering with her right hand, she used her left to unbutton her cuff and push her sleeve way up. "Look at this."

"It's too dark," I said.

"Go ahead, touch it."

I ran my hand over her arm. From her elbow to her shoulder, it felt way too smooth and slightly pebbly. I'd had a schoolmate who'd been in a fiery crash when she was eight, and her skin felt like this.

"Is it a burn?" I asked.

"Sure is. He threw me in the fireplace. He's kicked me a bunch of times too, even broke my pelvis once."

"Aggie," I said, "that's awful. Why are you still with him?"

"Who else'd have me?"

"Have you? Nobody has to *have* you. You can get a job, support yourself."

"Steve says I'm a half-wit and could never get a job."

"He's wrong. You're a wonderful person, and plenty smart too."

"Well, thanks, Sheridan." She sounded doubtful.

"I mean it. You don't have to keep taking it from him. If you're scared to fight back, you need to leave."

"The thing is, I'm no angel, either. I got plenty of faults."

"Like what?"

"I'm pretty lazy. I'd rather watch TV than vacuum, for instance."

"Who wouldn't?" I said. "What else?"

"Well, this is a little personal, but Steve doesn't turn me on like he used to, if you know what I mean."

"Okay. But did you ever kick him or burn him?"

"Of course not."

"Then it's not the same."

"It doesn't make any difference," Aggie said. "I couldn't leave without the girls."

"Take them with you."

"Steve'll never let them go. He's said as much."

"That's not for him to decide. Anyway, they'd be better off without him, believe me. Every time he beats you, they get hurt too."

"I know it's a bad situation. But look at it this way, Sheridan, Steve provides for us really well. We got a house and two cars. We got food and nice clothes."

I pushed her sleeve down and buttoned her cuff. "And that's worth getting beat up for?"

"I can take it. But if he hurts a strand of hair on the head of my girls, I'll take them and leave, and that's a promise."

"I wouldn't wait for that to happen, Aggie."

"Let's not talk about it anymore, okay?"

"Okay."

We traveled in silence for a while, and then I said, "What can you tell me about that guy Paul Redmun? Do you know who he got that big donation from?"

"I don't know much about him," Aggie said. "Deputy Conway brought him and Buck French to a meeting about six months ago, and they just took over. All of a sudden our name was the Firedog Militia and everybody started wearing those stupid hats with the skulls on them. Then they put up recruiting posters,and even ran advertisements in magazines, telling people they could come here and stay on the land for free if they volunteer to patrol the border or donate toward the boot camp. But tonight was the first I'd heard about a big donation. You could ask Steve."

No, thanks. "By any chance have you heard Paul mention the name Charity?" *Charity!* I hadn't said it out loud for a long time. It tasted sweet on my tongue so I said it again under my breath, "Charity."

"Charity's a name?" Aggie said.

"Sure."

"I guess people name their kids Faith and Hope, so why not? Sonny and Cher even named their daughter Chastity. How'd you like to go though life with a name like that? What guy would want to have sex with a girl called *Chastity*?"

"I'm guessing that doesn't bother her too much," I said. "I'm wondering about that boot camp. Do you think Paul and Buck might have something in their minds besides border-patrolling?"

"Like what?"

"I'm not sure. Why would they need a boot camp and arms and so many recruits if the purpose is just to round up the illegals and wait for the border patrol?"

"You're right, Sheridan. It's getting completely out of hand."

"What do the other ranchers think about it?"

"I can't speak for all of them," she said, "but Steve and Bernie are having a real good time. They took the whole course of training sessions, and now they go out in the desert practicing their shooting day and night."

"What do they shoot?"

"Birds and snakes, things like that."

"Scorpions?"

"You'd have to be a real good shot to hit a scorpion. They're little."

"Patty tells me they're all over your house."

"That little rascal. They're not *all* over. It's a good idea to shake out your shoes, though."

My skin was crawling. I considered taking my boots off and shaking them again, just in case. Then I'd like to shake out all my clothes, and after that shake out Aggie and the vehicle we were in.

The pavement gave way to rutty gravel, and Aggie had to give all her attention to driving, which gave me time to sort things out. Seeing Paul and Deputy Conway together was significant, although it didn't prove anything. Their boot-camp windfall didn't prove anything either. It could be Charity's money, or it could be from somewhere else—I had no way of knowing. For now these were simply facts to file away. Maybe someday I'd be able to fit it all together and have something substantial to go to the police with.

Meanwhile, I'd better be careful. Two of my archenemies were in the area—no, three—I'd just added Steve. It was almost disappointing that I hadn't seen the Wellaway.

The undercurrent of violence at the meeting had really upset me. I understood that the ranchers were having problems because of the illegal border-crossers, but your average citizen didn't need to be running around out there with a gun. Anything could happen. And the boot camp and the other stuff Paul talked about sounded like bad news for everybody concerned. I was glad I was leaving the area tomorrow. I was tempted to take off tonight.

"Oh, my God," Aggie said as we approached the house. Steve's truck was in the driveway, and another vehicle, an old Honda Civic, was parked in front of the house. "Whose car?" I asked.

"Carlos Morino's," she said, skidding past the truck and into the carport. The door to the house stood open.

"Who's Carlos Morino?"

"Tracy's boyfriend."

As we ran through the kitchen, we heard Tracy yell, "Daddy, don't!" We made it to the family room in time to see Steve punch a half-nude teenage boy in the back with the butt of a rifle, knocking him to his hands and knees.

"I'll fucking teach you to screw my daughter, you Mexican bastard!"

The boy grabbed a pair of pants from the floor and scrambled to his feet. He ran past Aggie and me, digging a set of keys from a pocket as he went. In a few seconds we heard the squeal of tires.

Steve glared at Tracy, who was sitting on the sofa holding the afghan across her front. "You little bitch!" he said. "I'm going to fucking kill him!." He backhanded her across the face and started for the door. Tracy dropped the afghan and leaped onto her father's back. She clawed at his face and clamped her teeth into his arm. He reached around and picked her off, hurling her to the floor. Blood ran from her mouth.

Steve touched his arm, and his hand came away bright red. "Fucking bitch!" He drew his foot back to kick her.

"No!" Aggie hollered, throwing herself over Tracy and taking the brunt of the blow.

"That's it, Aggie. You're fucking dead!" Steve pulled his foot back for another kick.

Up to this point I'd been paralyzed. I was the little girl hiding under the covers in another room, waiting for the awful noises to stop. It was the words "You're fucking dead!" that mobilized me. It's what the guy in the airport had said as he beat up on "his" woman. It may have been what Charity's killer said before he choked the breath out of her. It's what my father would have said to my mother before beating her senseless, except he was such an upstanding guy, he didn't cuss.

All my life I'd been doing the same thing I'd scolded Aggie for. I'd been taking it and taking it and taking it.

As the foot started its forward swing, I ran behind Steve, reached around, and poked my thumbs in his eyes. He gave a howl, dropped the gun, and covered his face with both hands. I swung in front of him, picked up the rifle, and drove the butt deep in his stomach. He bent over and howled again.

I took a few steps backward and pointed the barrel at him. I'd never held a gun before. The carved arc in the smooth wooden stock fit right on my shoulder. I aimed for his eyes so he could see right into it, if he could still see. "Get your dumb ass out of here, Steve!" I hollered, as loud and as mean as I could. "I'm giving you till three. One."

He took his hands from his face and looked at me through bloodshot eyes. He reached down for his rifle and then realized I had it.

"Hey, give me that," he said.

"Gladly," I said, adjusting the barrel so I was aiming at his heart. "Two."

He folded his arms on his chest. "Look, I don't know where you come from, but you sure don't know how to hold a shotgun. If it went off, you could do some real damage to me and my house and my family. So I'm just going to leave for a while, because I have some business to take care of. And when I get back you'd better be gone, or you're dead meat."

So it was a shotgun, not a rifle. Live and learn.

He limped out, and I heard his truck roar and pull onto the road. None of us moved until the sound faded in the distance, then Aggie climbed up from the floor, using one of the end tables for support.

"Okay. That's it, kids. We're out of here," she said. "Sheridan, will you go fetch Patty and get her dressed? Her room's the first door to your right. I'll get Tracy cleaned up." Holding her kicked side with one hand, she used the other to lead her daughter toward the bathroom, looking back once to say, "Thanks, Sheridan."

I carefully set the shotgun on one of the tables. It felt like I'd removed a mantle of power, and I suddenly understood why people like guns.

16

There was no answer when I knocked on Patty's door, so I opened it and looked in. Patty wasn't in bed. I finally found her in her closet sitting on a pile of clothes, holding her pillow around her ears.

"Come on," I said. "We're going on a little trip. What do you want to wear?"

"What did you say?" she said, loosening one side of the pillow.

"We're going on a little trip with your mommy and Tracy. You need to get dressed."

"What about Daddy?"

"He's not going."

"Okay," she said, and stood up. I had a déjà vu of the glorious moment I found out my own dad was out of the picture. "It's not your fault, you know," I told her.

She nodded, but I could tell she wasn't convinced. Together we picked out a blue gingham pedal-pusher set, white socks and sneakers, and a yellow jacket. I told her it was a smashing outfit. We took turns in the bathroom and went to the den, where Tracy was lying on the sofa, dressed in jeans and a long-sleeve Henley. Her cheek was red and swelling.

"Where's your mom?" I asked. She pointed her thumb toward the kitchen.

Aggie was making bologna sandwiches. The door to the outside was standing open. "Are you all right?" I asked her.

"Yeah. I may have a bruised rib or two, but nothing feels broke."

"We ought to get going," I told her.

"I'm ready," she said. "Patty, will you bag these, please?" The phone rang. Tracy ran into the room, but Aggie got it first. "Hello?... Oh, Mrs. Morino." She looked at me and winced. "Did Carlos get home all right?... No?... Why, sure you can." She handed the receiver to Tracy.

"Yes?" Tracy said into it. "Say that again?... Okay, I've got it. Thanks." In one motion she hung up, grabbed a set of keys from a hook by the door, and ran out. By the time the three of us got outside, the Caravan was out of the driveway and accelerating up the road.

"Damn," Aggie said. "Now I've got to go get her. Will you take me?"

"Where?'

"To the Morinos', I suppose. Mrs. Morino said Carlos didn't come home yet. Tracy probably went there to wait for him."

"What if she won't come with you?"

"She's got to. In any case, I need to get my car." Just then we heard three faint pops that sounded like they came from somewhere in back of the house. The chained dog started barking furiously.

"What was that, Mommy?" Patty said.

Aggie shook her head. "Shhh." She went outside, crossed to the edge of the carport, and looked south. Patty and I followed, holding hands.

I peered into the darkness but couldn't see anything. All at once, a moving light appeared, and between barks I heard the faint hum of a motor that grew louder by the moment. The light soon resolved itself into two sets of headlights. They were coming in our direction.

We ran back in the house, turned off the light, and watched at the window. In a few seconds, two pickups, one white and one black, drove out of the desert a short distance from the house. When they reached the road, they turned right and soon disappeared over the rise.

"Do you know who that was?" I asked Aggie.

"The white Ford is Bernie's. I don't know who the other one belongs to, but I sure know who was driving it."

"It was Daddy," Patty said.

"Dang, child, you inherited my good eyes. Now will you go get your pillow, please, and your blanket?" When Patty left the room, Aggie told me, "We have to go back there and take a look."

"Back where?" I asked.

"In the desert. Somebody got shot, and maybe he's still alive."

"Do you think it's Carlos?"

"That's who got his life threatened, isn't it? I don't suppose that car of yours has four-wheel drive?"

"No."

"Well, the road isn't good, but it isn't all that bad either. The worst part will be getting through the two washes."

"What are washes?"

"You know, dry streambeds. They're all rocky on the bottom. But we'll probably make it."

"Probably? Aggie, it's a rental car. I'm afraid if I wreck it, they'll make me buy it." The other thing I was afraid of was finding Carlos's body with bloody holes in it. Sheridan might faint.

"Okay, then, I'll walk," she said. "You stay here with Patty." She opened the door and stepped out.

"All right, all right, we'll take the car," I told her. *Anything to get out of this god-awful house.* I went to the family room and picked up the shotgun. I didn't want it, but I didn't want Steve to have it either.

Aggie settled Patty in the backseat after I removed Sheridan's bag of clothes.

I put it and the shotgun in the trunk. While I was in there, I got out Charity's flashlight and the new batteries. Aggie was already at the wheel, so I got in the passenger seat and handed her the keys. She told Patty to lie down and keep her head below the window. When she started the engine, I leaned over to check the gas level. It was half full.

Aggie pulled across the dirt and onto a rough lane heading south into the desert. It got a lot rougher as we went. I tore the fresh batteries from their package and inserted them in the flashlight, then had a hard time getting it back together because of all the lurching. As I struggled with it, Aggie told me we were heading toward a feeding spot for the cattle. "It's a major lay-up."

"A what?"

"They call it a lay-up. It's where the aliens gather to wait for rides."

"Rides from who?"

"I don't know. I've never seen them."

"They must go right by your house if they take this road." Calling it a road was generous of me.

"They don't take this one. They try to stay away from people's houses. There's a whole network of roads in here. This one gets you to the main road fastest, though. It's the one you'd use if you just shot somebody."

Patty stuck her head between our seat backs. "Who shot somebody?"

"I said *if*. Now get your head down."

"How far is it to this place?" I asked.

"About a mile. From the direction of the shots and the time between when we heard the sound and when we saw the trucks coming toward us, I figure that's where they were."

"Don't ever let anybody ever tell you you're not smart," I told her.

"I'm smart too," Patty said.

"Yes, you are," Aggie and I said in unison.

When we came to the first dry wash, Aggie slowed way down and maneuvered slowly over the craggy rocks. She had to back up once, but other than that we had no trouble.

She drove on for a while longer, then stopped the car. "I need you to get out, Sheridan."

"Why? What's wrong?"

"Nothing's wrong. This wash is deeper than the other one—we have to lighten the car, get the floor as high as we can. Is there anything heavy in the trunk?"

"Just the spare tire, and it's probably one of those little fakes," I said as I climbed out.

"Watch for critters," she said.

"Scorpions?"

"Scorpions won't kill you, Sheridan. Rattlesnakes will."

Thanks. I feel a lot better.

I closed the door after me, turned on the flashlight, and swept the beam around.

Aggie gave the Contour some gas and started across the dry streambed. From the underside of it came the sound of metal scraping on rock. I hoped the rental people wouldn't put it on a hoist until it had been rented a few more times.

She took it an inch at a time, turning this way and that to avoid the largest rocks. She was almost home free when a rear tire slid off a slanted rock and the fender caught on the edge of it. Aggie tried spinning the wheels, then rocking forward and back. "Put it in forward," I told her through the open window. "I'll try lifting."

I went to the caught fender, planted my feet as square as I could, and pretended the Contour was Mr. Baumgartner, a 300-pound-plus fellow I'd had to maneuver in and out of bed every day for several months. Unfortunately it didn't work. The car was easier to get a grip on than Mr. Baumgartner, but it was quite a bit heavier.

Aggie got out and told Patty to get in the driver's seat. She had her press her foot firmly on the brake, and then she snapped it in gear. "Okay, now," she told her, "the pedal on the right is for gas, and the one you have your foot on is the brake. When I holler 'right pedal,' press your foot on the gas until I holler 'left pedal.' Then you push on the brake."

She came back to where I was standing. "This is not a good idea," I said.

"I'm out of good ideas, Sheridan. Get ready to lift."

We took hold of the fender. "Press the right pedal, Patty!" Aggie called. We heaved as Patty revved the engine, but the car didn't budge. "Okay, Patty, left pedal." The wheels stopped spinning. "Good girl," she said.

"And I thought Tracy was too young to drive," I said.

"You know what, Sheridan, we need ourselves a lever. Is there anything in this sorry excuse for a car we could use as a lever?"

Why hadn't I thought of that? I reached in the window and pulled the trunk release. I took out the jack handle and wedged the chiseled end under the fender as close as I could get to the part that was caught. The dumb Sheridan pants didn't have room for the flashlight in their tiny pockets, so I stuck it in my waistband. I put both hands on the other end of the handle. Aggie placed hers next to mine and yelled, "Right pedal!" Patty gunned the engine. We pushed down, putting our combined weight on the handle. The fender hopped off the rock, sending the jack handle flying. It missed my face by not more than an inch before clattering down between the rocks. The car took off across the desert like a startled rabbit.

"Left pedal, Patty! LEFT PEDAL!" Aggie screamed as we scrambled out of the wash and took out after it. Patty must have heard, because the car took a nosedive and skidded to a stop. Aggie ran to the door and reached in through the window. When it was safely in park, she pulled Patty from the car and held her close, and they both cried for a while. I teared up a bit myself.

Aggie asked, "Did you get hurt, Sheridan?"

"No," I said, "but I sure don't want to buy this car now. It doesn't even have a jack handle."

We soon arrived at the lay-up. "See all the trash the aliens have left?" Aggie said as she pulled to a stop.

I had to admit, there was a good bit of it. In the beam of the headlights, I could see water bottles everywhere. Blankets and articles of clothing were strewn on the dirt and tangled in bushes. Plastic grocery bags and pieces of paper flew around in the wind.

"Do you think anybody's here?" I asked.

"I don't know. We made enough noise back there to drive off a herd of elephants." She backed up and drove forward a couple of times, angling the headlights in different directions. "I don't see anybody," she said. She killed the engine and opened her door.

"Wait, Aggie," I whispered. "Over there. Something moved!"

"Where?"

I pointed to a dark shape about 50 yards from my side of the car.

"It's a cow, Sheridan."

"Can I see the cow, Mommy?" Patty asked. She was flat on the seat with her blanket bunched up, hugging it like a teddy bear. Driving must have been a frightening experience for her.

"You've seen cows, honey," Aggie said.

I directed the flashlight to the creature's nether regions and saw great udders. "How'd you know in the dark that it was a cow and not a bull, Aggie? Is that what cattle are? Girls?"

"Cattle are both boys and girls, although most of the boys aren't really boys anymore, if you know what I mean." She shifted her eyes to the back, telling me to drop the subject.

Patty stuck her head between the seats. "She means they've been castrated," she said.

Aggie turned. "Patty, will you lay down and be quiet?"

"When are we going home?"

"I'm not sure we're going home tonight, but we'll be going someplace in a little while. Are you tired?"

"Uh-huh."

"You go on and sleep then. I have to go check something. I'll be right back. Do you want to come, Sheridan?"

I didn't want to, but I did.

Aggie locked the doors, telling Patty not to unlock them for anybody. "And keep your head down!" she told her.

We walked between piles of debris, flashing the light back and forth on the ground. "Do you remember what he was wearing?" she asked.

"Carlos? A white T-shirt, I think," I said. "And his pants were light-colored too. Chinos, maybe?"

"I don't see anything like that around here."

"Me neither." What I was noticing, though, was that there were no mosquitoes. I hadn't seen a mosquito since we hit Arizona. On a warm night like this at home, I'd have been chewed to a pulp.

Aggie stopped and pointed. "What's that?"

I looked. Something on the ground was reflecting the dull light of the quarter moon. It looked wet. I went closer and shined the flashlight on it. The wetness was bright red. I knelt down and, being careful not to touch it, took a whiff. "It's blood, and it's real fresh," I said. I'd had experience with blood that wasn't.

"Is it people blood?"

"I don't know."

"Look over here," Aggie said. About 10 feet to her right were three plastic crates with gallon bottles in them. A fourth was on its side, the bottles spilled out. She lifted one. "They're full of water. Roger must have been here."

"Who's Roger?"

"Mayor Roger Keeney, who spoke at the meeting tonight. Remember, I told you he sometimes brought out water for the aliens?... Oh, Sheridan, I just had a horrible thought."

"What?"

"Maybe that's whose truck Steve was driving. Roger's got a black one like that. I remember wondering why somebody smart enough to be elected mayor would be so dumb as to buy a black truck. They just soak up the sun, you know."

"Maybe Roger was in the truck too. Did you see anybody besides Steve?" I asked.

"No. Not sitting up, anyway. Of course, if he was bleeding, he might have been laying down...or dead."

There was a noise over to our left. Without looking to see if it was the cow, an alien, or Roger's ghost, we turned and made a beeline back to the car. Aggie drove like she was one of the Unsers. The only time she slowed was to cross the killer wash, taking a different path than before. I heard a lot of serious scraping, but nothing got hung up. I looked back to see how Patty was faring. Incredibly, she was fast asleep.

Aggie drove out of the desert and pulled up in front of her house. "Why are we coming back here?" I asked.

"I have to get my purse and our sandwiches."

"Leave them, Aggie. Let's get going."

"It'll only take a minute. I know where Steve hid some cash. We're going to need it." She went in the house, taking my car keys with her. No way was anybody going to run off with her daughter.

My head whirled with images of what might have happened out there in the desert tonight. Steve and Bernie were out there with guns, maybe target-shooting. The mayor came along and started unloading cartons of water bottles. There was some kind of an accident, and the mayor got shot. Steve and Bernie lifted him into his truck. When we saw them, they were rushing him to a doctor. Sure, that's what happened.

In your dreams, Sheridan.

Headlights appeared over the road's rise. After looking back to make sure Patty was still sleeping, I scrunched down as far as I could. The approaching vehicle slowed down and pulled into the driveway. I peeked over the bottom of the window frame.

It was the Ram. Steve got out and ran in the house, leaving the driver's door wide open. I ducked back down, frantically wondering what I should do.

I could get the shotgun out of the trunk and go shoot him. If I did, I'd have to shoot to kill, and since I'd never shot a shotgun in my life the odds of killing him were slim. If I wounded him or missed completely, Aggie and I would be, in Steve's words, dead meat. Even if we got away, he'd be sure to chase us, and in a race between a Ram and Contour, hands down I'd bet on the Ram.

But wait, what if I were to disable his truck? I took the nail clippers from the glove compartment, where I'd stashed them after my nail job in the Kmart lot, and ran over to the pickup. Directing the beam of the flashlight under the dash, I found a bunch of brightly colored wires. Using the clippers, I cut through every one of them, and then, in case I'd only disabled his wind-shield wipers or turn signals, I pulled out every fuse in sight. I was looking around for something else to render inoperative when I heard Aggie yell, "I want you out of here!" I raised my head and saw Steve backing out the door and down the steps.

"Aggie," he said, "I'm warning you. You try and leave me and I'll hunt you down like a dog."

"You gonna kill me like you did Roger, and maybe Carlos?" Aggie started moving toward the car. I saw the glint of a pistol in her hand.

"That's none of your fucking business, Aggie. Now give me that thing." He lunged at the gun. There was a shot, and Steve went down on one knee. Aggie ran for the Contour, and I followed, shining the flashlight in Steve's surprised eyes as I passed.

Aggie jumped in the driver's seat, handed me the pistol, her purse, and the bag of sandwiches, and started up the motor. As we took off, I saw Steve push himself up and start hopping around the truck.

"I thought you didn't have a gun," I told Aggie.

"It's not registered. Don't tell anybody."

"You said you didn't need a gun."

"Guess I was wrong," she said. "Did you do something to the Ram?"

"Yeah, something," I said.

The Morino house was on a dirt road a few miles off the road we'd taken to Douglas. No lights were on. Four dogs the size of Cujo met us at the end of the driveway and ran around the car as we pulled in, barking and growling like crazy. Several vehicles were parked near the house, none of which was Aggie's Caravan.

Aggie honked, and we waited silently. In a couple of minutes, an immense angel came out of the dark house and floated across the porch. When she got closer, I saw that it was a woman in a plus-size terrycloth bathrobe. Her black hair was held back by a wide white headband. There was a flashlight in her hand and a shotgun under her arm.

"*Silencio!*" she hollered at the dogs, and immediately they quieted. I would have too—this was clearly an alpha female.

As she approached the Contour, she turned on the flashlight, shining it on Aggie's face and then mine. Aggie rolled down the window a couple of inches. "Is Tracy here?" she asked.

The woman shined her light on the sleeping Patty before answering in a heavy accent, "No. She did not come here."

"Do you know where she is?"

"She went to Mexico to be with Carlos."

"Mexico? Why?"

"It's safer for them there," said Mrs. Morino.

"So they're both all right?"

"Yes."

"Please tell me where she is," Aggie said. "I've got to go get her."

"Your husband is a brutal man," she said. "He will kill them."

"He won't know anything about it. I've left him. Please tell me where she is."

The woman stared at her for a while. Then she said, "Did Tracy tell you she's going to have a baby?"

"That's not true!" Aggie said.

"Believe what you like. You can pick up your car in Douglas, near the crossing." Mrs. Morino returned to the house, taking the dogs with her.

"Aggie," I said as she headed back to the main road, "do you think Mrs. Marino is right? Could Tracy be pregnant?"

"Of course not. She'd tell me. I'm her mother."

"If she told you, what would you do?"

She looked back to make sure Patty was still sleeping, then said, "I'd take her somewhere for an abortion. My God, if Steve ever found out…" She was quiet for a few minutes. Then she said, "Do you suppose Tracy wants Carlos's baby?"

Duh. "That might be the case," I said. "How would you feel about that? Would you be able to accept it?"

"I guess I'd have to, wouldn't I? But Steve never would. I don't know what he'd do to her."

"Then maybe Tracy's better off where she is, for now."

Aggie looked at me. "What am I going to do?"

"Why don't you start by reporting Steve to the police?"

"That's not going to do any good. He's in real thick with them."

"He is?"

"Sure. He's an honorary deputy. A lot of the militia members are. That's what worries me. Deputy Conway has access to the police computer. They can track me down anywhere I go."

Dang! I'd been wondering how Paul Redmun knew I was at Loma Nueva Hospital. All it took, probably, was for his buddy Conway to check the computer and make a call to Officer Olmstead in Pima Center. I was as vulnerable as Aggie was.

"I've got an idea," I said. "What do you think about seeing a lawyer? I know of one in Tucson, a woman. A friend of mine went to see her, and she liked her fine. She might be able to find Tracy for you."

"You think so?"

"It's worth a try. And we can tell her about the blood in the desert, and how we think Steve was driving Roger Keeney's truck, and she could tell the Tucson police."

"Do you think they'd lock Steve up? I don't want him locked up."

I gave her an incredulous look. "Why not?"

"Well, he is my husband."

"Aggie, are you thinking of going back to Steve?"

She thought for a while, then said, "No. I can't. I have to protect my children."

"So do you or don't you want to talk to the lawyer?"

"I do."

"Fine. We can drive to Tucson tonight and go see her in the morning."

"What about my car?" she asked.

"Leave it in Douglas. From what you tell me, it sounds like it might be easy for Steve to trace it."

"All right," she said, and fell into a brooding silence for the rest of the trip.

17

It was almost 3 A.M. when we checked into a motel in Tucson. I wrote "Mary Smith" and a fake license plate number on the room registration, and Aggie paid in cash. Aggie and Patty went off to the room while I took the Contour down the street and parked it behind of an all-night restaurant.

As I walked back to the motel with a bag containing Sheridan's last clean outfit, I found myself darting from shadow to shadow, wondering how I had come to lead a life of false names and hidden motives. I felt a royal headache coming on.

When I got to the door of our room, I gave the three quick raps that Aggie and I had agreed on. She let me in and crawled back in bed with the sleeping Patty. One of those infomercials was on TV. Models who looked no older than 19 were selling wrinkle cream. Or maybe they were 60 and the cream really worked.

Aggie was asleep when I came out of the bathroom. She'd put a sandwich on my pillow, but my head was pounding too hard to eat. I turned off the TV and got in the other bed, but I didn't sleep for hours.

In the morning I put on the outfit I'd brought: a coral sleeveless shirt and matching knee pants. Aggie told me she'd spit nickels to be able to wear something like that.

Using the motel's yellow pages, I found the address for Charity's attorney, Edwina Meek. I remembered the name from seeing it in her purse back at L.J.'s. I decided to forget about calling ahead—it was better to just show up. If she didn't have time for us, maybe she could send us to someone who did.

After making sure the Contour hadn't been towed away from the all-night restaurant, we went in and ate breakfast as a thank-you. I asked the waitress if she happened to know where the Murray Building was and, as luck would have it, she did—her husband's Uncle Walter had an office there. He was a bail bondsman. I asked her for his last name—the life I'd been leading, who knew?

The Murray Building was constructed of brick and obviously built before the Arizona Congress or whoever decided all buildings should be one-story. Edwina Meek's office was on the third floor. The receiving room was small, with green tile on the floor and white walls. There wasn't room for all the plants and trees sitting around, and but they were there anyway. Three of the eight orange plastic chairs that lined the walls were unusable due to overhanging branches.

There was a desk in the corner full of flowering plants—the computer, phone, and mugful of pens looked like interlopers. The desk chair was empty. I was wondering what to do when a woman wearing a red-flowered pantsuit bustled in from the hall. She was holding a capped cup of Starbucks and a little white paper bag. She smiled at Patty and said to Aggie and me, "Excuse me, are you sure you're in the right place?"

"Are you Edwina Meek?" I asked.

"No," she said. "By the way, it's Edwina, rhymes with Tina," she said, and brushed past us to the desk. "Do you have an appointment?"

"No, sorry," I said. "But we need to see her. It's sort of an emergency. She saw a friend of mine on a moment's notice last week, so we thought we'd give it a try."

"I'm sorry, but Ms. Meek's not in today. What's your friend's name?"

"Charity Redmun."

For the first time, she looked at me like I might be somebody. "And what's *your* name?" she asked.

"Jo Jacuzzo," I said. Aggie looked at me funny, so I leaned over and whispered, "It's an alias."

"Good thinking," she whispered.

"Oh, Ms. Jacuzzo, you must have finally got our messages," the woman said.

"What messages?" I said.

"Give me a minute." She picked up the phone and punched. Soon she said, "It's me. There's a woman here says she's Miss Redmun's friend, Jo Jacuzzo... Yes... Just a minute." She looked at me. "Can you come back at 1 P.M.?"

I looked at Aggie. She nodded. "Sure," I told the woman. She relayed that to the mouthpiece. When she hung up I asked her, "What kind of messages were they?"

"I'll have to let Ms. Meek discuss that with you."

We asked her what we could do in Tucson with a kid for four hours, and she suggested the Desert Museum and gave us directions. Before we left, she opened the bag and gave Patty half an oversize blueberry muffin. Patty said thank you and wolfed it down, which I thought was amazing considering she'd just polished off a big plateful of French toast.

"So how long you been using that alias?" Aggie asked me as we drove across a mountain to the Desert Museum. The road we were on was so winding and steep it made me hope we hadn't scraped anything off the brakes in the killer wash.

"I've used it a long time. An alias is a handy thing to have."

"I suppose so. Should I use an alias?"

"That's up to you. What name would you use?"

"I've always liked Caroline. Maybe I'll be Caroline Jeckle. Jeckle's my maiden name."

"Good choice," I said.

It was a hot day and the museum was mostly outside, but there was shade available, and I learned a lot. I got a chance to see some of the animals I'd been worried about running into in the desert, plus a few others I hadn't even known I was supposed to worry about—a real ugly wild-pig kind of animal called a javelina, for instance.

They had desert plants there too, including a zillion kinds of cacti. I found out the spiny thing that speared me in the high desert might have been a jumping cholla—a good name for an attack plant if I ever heard one.

There was also a tunnel affair Patty went through at least 10 times. Befitting my adult status, I stopped at seven.

We didn't want to leave so soon, especially considering what it had cost to get in, but we had no choice. When we got back to the lawyer's office, Flower Lady was gone and another woman was leaning over her desk looking at something. When she straightened up, I saw she was very tall. Everything about her was tall: her face, her neck, and especially her legs. The inseam of her gray slacks had to be 34 inches or even more.

"Hello, I'm Edwina Meek," she said, looking from one of us to the other.

"I'm Jo," I said. We shook hands. I gestured at Aggie. "And this is Caroline Jeckle. She's really the reason we're here." Aggie shook hands with her too.

"I'm Minnie Mouse," Patty said, holding out her hand. Aggie turned red, but the lawyer and I cracked up.

When we were settled in her inner office, which was pretty stark compared to the waiting room, I said, "Ms. Meek, Caroline here needs some advice."

"Please call me Edwina," she said and turned to Aggie. "How can I help you, Caroline?"

Aggie turned red again and 'fessed up to her real name. She'd have made a lousy criminal.

She told Edwina about leaving her husband, who regularly beat her, and how she was scared he might use his ties to Deputy Conway to find her. She described what we'd found in the desert the night before and shared her suspicions about what might have happened to Mayor Keeney.

"Let me take a minute to check on something," Edwina said. She asked Aggie for the mayor's full name and the town, then called information. His home number was unlisted, but she called the town hall and was told the mayor wasn't in and his duties had been taken over by the chairman of the town council.

"That's interesting," Edwina said as she hung up. "What else would you like to tell me?"

Aggie turned to me. "Sher…Jo, would you mind taking Patty to the waiting room for a while?"

I did mind, especially if she had something juicy to say about anybody in the militia, but I didn't have much choice. For the next hour, Patty and I sat in the plastic chairs and drew mustaches and worse on people in old issues of *Time* and *Family Circle*, using pens we borrowed from Flower Lady's desk.

At one point I asked Patty how she was feeling about leaving home and all.

Her mouth drooped and her chin puckered. "I just don't want Daddy hitting Mommy anymore. But I miss him, and I 'specially miss Tracy."

"I know you do." I gave her a hug and drew a big sunbonnet

on a high-mucky-muck politician. I got the laugh I'd hoped for.

When Aggie finally came out, she said, "We need to get Patty's stuff out of your car, Sheridan. Edwina's arranged for me and her to stay somewhere for a while. We're being picked up in a few minutes. Edwina's going to try and find out Tracy's whereabouts too, so I can let her know I still love her."

"That's great!" I said. When we got to the car and she was folding Patty's blanket, I said, "What about Steve's shotgun? It's still in the trunk."

"Oh, God. I forgot about that. Give it to Edwina. She wants to talk to you anyway. I already gave her my pistol." She balanced the blanket on the fender and threw her arms around me. "Thank you so much, Sheridan."

Patty hugged me too, which wasn't easy since she was holding the pillow. I got the shotgun out of the trunk, and we walked back to the Murray Building. Aggie'd been told to wait for their ride just inside the door. We said goodbye again at the bottom of the stairs, and I started climbing.

I went in the waiting room and knocked on Edwina's door. "It's me, Jo Jacuzzo," I hollered.

"Come in, Jo," she called.

"Okay, but first I want you to know that I'm carrying a shotgun. I don't want to scare you."

I heard the click of footsteps on tile, and she opened the door. "Thanks for warning me," she said. "Is it yours?"

"It belongs to Steve, Aggie's husband. I had to take it away from him because he was hurting people. I forgot I had it."

She looked around the room. "Why don't you prop it in that corner?"

As I carefully set it down, I said, "I don't know what you're going to do with it, but if the police check it for prints, you'll explain why mine are there, won't you?" I'd been leaving prints all over the state of Arizona. Maybe my next purchase should be a pair of gloves.

"I'll take care of it." She sat at her desk and motioned me to a chair.

"Another thing, I don't know what you want to see me about, but I need to know how much it's going to cost. I don't have a lot of money."

She laughed, which I thought was sort of rude. Then she said, "Don't worry about it, Jo. I won't charge anything you can't pay. By the way, do you know the police are looking for you?"

"Yes. I was supposed to go back to Pima Center for questioning, and I couldn't."

I was noticing Edwina's desk was taller than most desks, probably so she wouldn't bump her knees. It reminded me of the mahogany dining room table at Great-aunt Concetta's. The top of it hit me right in the nipples. It took a lot of upper-arm calisthenics to eat.

"Maybe I can help you with that problem," Edwina said. It took me a couple of seconds to realize she was talking about the police and not Great-aunt Concetta's table.

"You mean square it up with the police? That would be great," I said.

"Perhaps. The reason I wanted to talk with you, however, concerns Charity Redmun."

"You know that Charity's dead?"

"I do. She was brutally murdered, and I'm aware that you were the one who found her body."

"How'd you know? Was my name in the paper?"

"Hers was, but yours wasn't."

"Thank goodness." I sure didn't want Mom to hear about it that way. *Buffalo native JoDell Jacuzzo is implicated in the strangling death of a South Carolina heiress. "If it weren't for my mother, I wouldn't even be here," she tells Arizona police.*

"Jo," Edwina said, "when Miss Redmun came to see me last Friday morning, she said she had reason to be afraid of her brother Paul. However, she couldn't go to the police…"

I interrupted. "Why? Why couldn't she go to the police?"

"I'm afraid I can't tell you that right now. As soon as I can, I will. In any case, what she wanted me to do was draw up a new will that left nothing to Paul unless she got back safely to Paris. Did she tell you about that?"

"No."

"Well, we did draw up such a will. The problem was, it was important that we get a copy to Paul immediately so he would be deterred by it. Since Charity had no idea where he was, she asked me to hire a private investigator to locate him. Unfortunately, it was Saturday afternoon before the investigator was able to find Mr. Redmun and deliver the will, and, as you know, Charity was dead by then."

"So that's what he meant!"

"Who?"

"Paul came to see me in the Loma Nueva hospital last Monday morning. He told me I wasn't going to get away with it. I didn't know what he meant, but maybe he thought I persuaded his sister to change her will."

"I suppose he did, especially since you're the beneficiary."

"The what?" *Damn that L.J. That blow to the head messed up my hearing.*

"Charity named you sole beneficiary of the new will."

"That can't be right," I said.

"She left you the entire estate except for one dollar, which she insisted on leaving to her brother. I'm not sure why."

"I do," I said. "I told her it's what my grandparents did." *Thanks for the message, Charity…Oh, yeah, and thanks for the estate. Now, stop it, Jo. It's all a big mistake. But what if it isn't?*

Edwina rose, crossed to a window, and looked out. "So Paul threatened you? That worries me, Jo. He's a dangerous man."

"Is he the one who killed Charity?"

"The police think so," she said, "although I don't know what evidence they're basing that on. There's a warrant out for his arrest, but he's disappeared again."

"I saw him last night."

"Where?" She came back and sat down.

"At a meeting of the Firedog Militia. He was talking to Deputy Conway."

"Deputy Conway? Aggie told me about him. He and Paul Redmun are friends?"

"Partners in crime would be more like it. Didn't Charity tell you Deputy Conway pulled us over on the interstate and took the money she was bringing for Paul's ransom?"

"Paul's ransom?"

"She didn't mention that?"

"No. All she said was she wanted a new will, and she wanted Paul to receive a copy right away because she was afraid of him. She wouldn't say why." Edwina grabbed a yellow pad and a pen. "So tell me everything."

I did. When I finished, she said, "Look, Jo, I've been contacted a couple of times by a Sergeant Tomaso of the Tucson police. I'm sure he'd like to know about your seeing Paul last night. If I get him on the phone, will you talk with him?"

"I guess so."

When she had Sergeant Tomaso on the line, she told him, "This is Edwina Meek, the attorney who was working with Charity Redmun shortly before her murder. I have her friend Jo Jacuzzo here in my office, and you might like to speak with her. She's seen Paul Redmun recently down by the border." She handed me the phone.

Sergeant Tomaso introduced himself in a deep, friendly voice and asked exactly where I'd seen Paul, so I told him about going to the militia meeting and the location of the church where it had been held, adding that Paul said he was going to be out of town for a while. I also told him that Paul was good friends with Deputy Conway and therefore had access to any information that might be entered into the police computer. The sergeant said he'd take that into consideration. Then he asked if he could meet with me in person to clear up a few things. I put my hand over the receiver and relayed that to Edwina.

"I think it's a good idea," she said. "Why don't we ask if we can do it here at my office?"

"That would be okay," I said. Good. I'd been hoping to meet one more cop before leaving the state.

She motioned for the phone and said, "This is Ms. Meek again. Ms. Jacuzzo has agreed to meet with you tomorrow in my office." She looked at a book at her desk. "No, I've got to be in court in the morning. How about one?" She looked at me, and I nodded. "Fine, we'll see you then."

Before leaving, I asked Edwina what she knew about the situation down by the border. "Do you think the ranchers are wrong to want to protect their property?

"I don't think there's ever a good excuse for vigilantism, Jo."

"That's what I think too," I told her.

She pushed up her glasses, massaged her closed eyes, and said, "You see, the reason people are crossing over here to work is because there *is* work. There's work for them on farms, in construction, in factories. Some of our industries would fall apart if it weren't for low-cost laborers from across the border. So instead of spending all that money on rounding them up and sending them back, our government should be setting up work agreement programs with Mexico and having the employers provide buses and decent housing, not to mention a living wage."

"Would that solve the problem?" I asked.

"It would certainly alleviate it," Edwina said. "People are dying. They pay guides to bring them across, and often the guides abandon them in the desert without water. It can get way over a hundred degrees out there. And now because of the increase in border patrol officers and the militia squads, the guides are taking them further out into the wilderness, where they have even less chance of making it. Even little children are dying."

"Children?"

"Yes. Whole families come over, and sometimes they all die. I've heard some horror stories. Jo, when you were down there, did you get the feeling that members of the militia might actually be preying on and killing these people?"

"I don't know, but they're sure training their members to kill. With the boot camp and all, it sounds like they're preparing for war."

"Maybe they are. I've read that some people believe Mexico is planning to rekindle the Mexican-American War and try to get their land back."

"No kidding?" I said. "They believe that? That would explain a lot."

As I walked the two blocks to the Contour, I promised myself that if I really did end up inheriting the Redmun estate, I'd put some of it toward good causes like supporting a lobby for Edwina's work agreement idea.

I wasn't counting on the money, though. The whole thing could turn out to be a mistake, or somebody in Charity's family might contest it and win. I just hoped it wouldn't be Paul.

It was lonely in the motel without Aggie and Patty. Without someone to talk to, I found myself obsessing about Charity.

The kiss. The inheritance. Had she loved me after all? What if she had lived?

I looked around for the TV remote and found it firmly attached to the bed stand—they must have heard about me and the Goddard's safe. After scrolling through a couple dozen channels, I ended up watching one of those true forensic shows, where they convicted a guy because they looked in his car trunk and found a hair from the victim's mother's cat. How incredible is that?

I wondered what kind of tests the investigators might be running on the ByVista right now, and if they'd ever put it on TV. What if they showed Charity's dead body? I took an oath to stop watching true forensic shows.

I considered calling Mom but didn't. There was too much I couldn't tell her.

In the morning I took a shower and put on a burgundy T-shirt and a pair of Levi's from my backpack. They were horribly creased, but I didn't care. I felt like I was in my own skin again.

I left Sheridan's clothes in the motel room with a note that said if anybody could wear them, they should help themselves.

18

Flower Lady was in Edwina's waiting room when I got there the next morning. Today she was wearing pink on the bottom and candy-stripes on top. She pushed a button and told me to go right in.

Edwina was at her desk, and a man in a police uniform was sitting in one of the chairs in front of it with his back to me. Two other people were there too, sitting in orange plastic chairs they must have dragged in from the waiting room. They turned their heads when I walked in and smiled. It was Roy and Lois Parker of Wellaway fame.

"Come on in, Jo," Edwina said. "And close the door, please."

I didn't know whether I should come in and close the door or make a run for it. Then I realized that although I might be able to outrun the Parkers and the policeman, I'd never outrun Edwina, with those long legs of hers. I pushed the door shut and took the empty seat. I shifted my eyes to the corner of the room where I'd put the shotgun yesterday. It was gone.

Edwina smiled at me and said, "This is Sergeant Tomaso, and this is Esther Burgess and Robert Higley of the Cultural Property Program of the National Central Bureau. They work in conjunction with Interpol. Did I get that right?"

Lois/Esther and Roy/Robert nodded.

"Interpol?" I said. I knew I was in trouble with the Arizona, New Mexico, and New Jersey police, but who had I annoyed at the international level?

"They work in conjunction with Interpol," she repeated. "Sergeant Tomaso invited them to come today."

I pulled my gaze from the Parkers, or whoever they were, and gave Sergeant Tomaso a dirty look. He ignored it and started talking fast, like he had a lot to say.

First he told me they'd followed up my lead on Paul Redmun but hadn't found him yet. Then he said, "The reason I wanted to meet with you, Ms. Jacuzzo, is because I've been authorized to finish your debriefing concerning the Charity Redmun murder. But first, Ms. Burgess and Mr. Higley want a word with you. They're on a tight schedule." He waved the proceedings over to them.

Lois/Esther did all the talking. To my relief, she said nothing about my charade as actor Delia Frank the night I visited them in the Ariel's Pond campground. Maybe they hoped I wouldn't mention it either.

"Ms. Jacuzzo," she said, "may I ask if Ms. Redmun told you anything about some works of art she'd recently sold?"

"She told me she sold some, but that's all."

"Did she tell you they were stolen property?" she asked.

"She stole them?"

"She didn't personally steal them," Lois/Esther said, "but they were part of her father's collection of illegal paintings. By illegal, I mean that each of them had been, at one time or another, taken from a gallery or museum. We'd had our eye on him for a while. We were waiting for him to sell something, but he never did, and then, of course, he was murdered. We were preparing to approach Miss Redmun about returning the paintings to their rightful owners, but before we could she sold three of the paintings to one of our undercover agents."

"Did she know the art was stolen?"

"Of course she did. She was an expert in that kind of thing. However, she had never done anything unethical up to that time, and now Ms. Meek tells us she was under pressure to pay her brother's debt because she thought he would be killed if she didn't."

"That's true," I said. "Otherwise I'm sure she wouldn't have done it. She wasn't that kind of person."

"In any case, we were hoping she'd lead us to where the rest of it is hidden."

"Was that why you were following us?"

"That and the fact that she had four million dollars of our money, which Ms. Meek tells us was stolen from her motor home."

"Yes, it was, and now I think the Firedog Militia has it." I told them about Paul's "generous donation." "Can you get it back from them?" I asked.

"We're certainly going to try. Now, Ms. Jacuzzo, we understand you've inherited Ms. Redmun's estate."

"I guess so, but I'm sure some relative will contest it." I looked at Edwina.

"No, Jo," Edwina said. "I'm good at what I do. The will is incontestable. In any case, I've been in touch with Ms. Redmun's attorney in Charleston, South Carolina, and he tells me Paul Redmun is the only relative she had left. She was married once, but the marriage was legally dissolved." She smiled. "Like it or not, the estate is yours."

Lois/Esther said, "So that brings us to our business with you. We think the rest of the contraband art may be somewhere in the Redmun home in Charleston, perhaps in a hidden room. We need your permission to go in and look for it."

"Of course you can look for it. Take it. I don't want any stolen art."

That was all they needed. Roy/Robert whipped a prepared statement out of his briefcase and handed me a pen. I scanned it. It had my name in it in several places, and there was a big X by a line on the bottom of the page. I looked at Edwina.

"I've already examined at it, Jo. I recommend you sign," she said.

I signed, and Edwina and Sergeant Tomaso witnessed my signature. "How are you going to get in?" I asked. I didn't want them battering down "my" front door.

Edwina answered, "The attorney in Charleston has a key for them. He's going to send you a copy too, so you can check out the house at your leisure."

The Parkers/Interpol agents took off, and it was Sergeant Tomaso's turn. After turning on a tape recorder, he asked what seemed like a thousand questions, reeling them off from a stack of papers. A lot of them I had already answered in Pima Center, but I answered them again anyway. Maybe they wanted to see if I'd answer the same way.

As an added perk, I told him everything I'd learned from going to the militia meeting and from Aggie, although I didn't identify her. The Sergeant was especially interested in the proposed boot camp and the blood in the desert.

When he finally ran out of questions, I signed a statement that everything I'd said was, to my knowledge, true. He packed his stuff away in a black leather briefcase, telling me to keep Edwina informed of my whereabouts in case any more questions came up. Then he left.

I turned to Edwina. "So that's why Charity couldn't go to the police? Because the art she sold was stolen, and she was afraid she'd be put in jail?"

Edwina nodded. "It was a valid fear. I wish she would have

confided in me about it. But that's all water under the bridge now, isn't it? And you did the right thing, Jo, when you gave them permission to search the Redmun house—which is now your house, of course."

"I still can't believe it."

"It's true. I don't know how much you'll inherit, but it's in the tens of millions, plus the house and a lot of artwork…"

"Legal?" I asked.

"Perfectly legal. There are also several vehicles, including a motor home, although it's presently impounded."

"The ByVista? I don't want it." I'd never be able to go in it without seeing Charity's lifeless body. I thought I might like to get a motor home someday, but a smaller one. It was a great way to travel, once you figured everything out.

Edwina said, "The motor home and anything else you don't want can be sold. Now, I need to know what your plans are. We'll need to keep closely in touch for a while."

"I'll be going back to Buffalo, but first I have to go to Tampa and pack up Mrs. Phipps, although someone else may have done it by now. I guess what I really need to do is call home."

"Be my guest," she said, and pushed her phone over.

"Thanks. I'll call collect."

"Don't bother." She rose and crossed to the door to the waiting room. "Come out when you're done."

I picked up Edwina's phone and glanced at her calendar. Friday, April 26. I'd left home two weeks ago today. Remarkable. I noted the time, did an adjustment for the difference, and dialed Mom at home.

"Hello," she said.

"Hi, Mom! It's me," I said, and mentally ducked.

"Jo!" she said happily. "I'm so glad you called."

"Why?" I said warily.

"Your friend stopped by the house last night. He is *so* nice. Good-looking too."

"What friend?"

"You know. Last time I talked to you, you asked if he'd called."

"Mom, you don't mean Paul Redmun?"

"Of course I do. Why wouldn't I?"

"Where is he now?"

"I don't know, but I told him you'd be home in a few days. You will, won't you?"

"A few days? You told me I should go to Universal Studios."

"How could you spend more than a few days there? Rose and I only lasted three hours. So are you done with Mrs. Phipps?"

"No. I'm still in Arizona."

"Arizona? You haven't even gotten to Tampa yet?"

"I thought you'd be aware of that," I said. "Hasn't Mr. Phipps been in touch with his mother?"

"He's in Seattle, at a conference. He'll be back Monday. What am I going to tell him?"

"I'll tell him myself. I'm coming home." I hung up and went out to inform Edwina that I was leaving and why.

"Jo, be careful," she said. "I'll call Sergeant Tomaso and tell him Paul has been seen in Buffalo."

"Thanks," I said.

Flower Lady gave me directions to the Tucson Airport. When I got there, the car rental guy didn't like the idea of accepting a Contour that had been rented in Phoenix. However, when I told him I was going to drive it to Buffalo otherwise, he scowled and took it, charging me an extra fee even though I hadn't used up the full week I'd already paid for.

I got a seat on a red-eye after being patted down and having the contents of my backpack spread all over the counter. They kept the nail clippers, which irked me because they had senti-mental value as wire cutters.

As the plane descended to the Buffalo Airport at 3 A.M., the pilot announced that it was 30 degrees outside. As Charity had said in the Parsee Home-Cook Diner a thousand years ago, "Oh, brrr!" I dug out my sweatshirt, still stained with desert dirt.

I caught a taxi home and banged on the front door rather than using my key, figuring that would scare Mom and Rose only *half* to death. In a little while the living room curtains rustled, then the door flew open and Mom and Rose said in unison, "What did you do to your hair?"

I hugged them each for a long time, then sat them down at the kitchen table and gave them a much edited version of my recent adventures. I told them about the inheritance but didn't even hint at how much it might be. I ended with a dire warning to never let Paul Redmun in the house, and if he came to the door or phoned, to call the police immediately.

After that we were too keyed up to sleep, so we sat in the kitchen the rest of the night and they brought me up to date on everything that had happened at the high school while I was gone. The physics teacher announced her engagement to the art teacher, which was a surprise to nobody, and two sophomore girls got into a fight wherein one stabbed the other several times with a protractor. They both were suspended, but the stabbee would be coming back to school in a week while the stabber would probably finish high school somewhere else, which suited Mom and Rose just fine.

As soon as it got light, Rose sneaked out for doughnuts. When she got back, Mom stuck a candle in the middle of a chocolate frosted, and they sang "Happy Birthday" while I blew it out. Then they brought out my gifts, a new Bills sweatshirt from Mom ("How did you know?" I said) and a video game from Rose. I dug the carved onyx animals out of my backpack. Holding them out of sight under the table, I wrapped them in a napkin before presenting them. It was just like Christmas.

At 9 A.M., the phone rang. We turned our heads in unison and watched until the answering machine turned on. When a man's voice said he was a detective with the Buffalo police, I ran over and picked it up. He told me he'd been alerted by the Tucson authorities to keep a watch out for a Paul Redmun, who was wanted for questioning in three deaths.

"Three?" I yelped. "Charity Redmun and who else?"

"Let's see." I heard the click-click of a keyboard. "Says here it was more Redmuns, George and Martha of Charleston, South Carolina."

"I thought they caught the guy who did that."

"Let's see." More clicking. "Evidently the man in custody agreed to a plea bargain. He admitted to committing the murders of Mr. and Mrs. Redmun and implicated Paul Redmun as the person who hired him."

"No kidding!"

"In any case, Tucson told us Redmun has shown up at your house recently and might do so again, so we'll be stepping up our drive-bys. And if you see or hear anything, call me." He gave me his number and hung up.

I relayed what he had said to Mom and Rose and taped his number on the wall next to the phone.

"I can't believe it. That Paul was such a nice fellow," Rose said.

"Well, I don't know," Mom said. "He seemed a little shifty-eyed to me."

19

I took my backpack to my room and unpacked. Patty's drawing of her "someday" house was folded up in one of the pockets. I smoothed the wrinkles out as best I could and tacked it onto the wall over my bed. It wasn't exactly a fireplace, but it would do for now. I wondered if the Redmun house had a fireplace, then told myself to stop counting my chickens.

It took 15 minutes to look at the mail that had come while I was gone. I checked my e-mail and tried out my new video game, but I couldn't get into it. I spent the next hour walking around the house and peeking out the windows.

"Stop it, Jo," Mom said after my fifth circuit. "You're making me crazy."

"I'm making *me* crazy too. How about loaning me your car?"

"My car? Do you think you should be leaving?" she said. "What'll we do if *he* comes?"

"Same thing I'd do. Keep the door locked and go call the police. Anyway, if Paul comes at all, it won't be for a few days."

"Why do you think that?"

"Didn't you tell him I wasn't expected home for a few days? You said that on the phone."

"If you say so, honey. Where are you planning to take my car?"

"I thought I'd drive over to the Goddards, check out the place."

"Do you think that's wise? You wouldn't want to run into that daughter of theirs, what was her name?"

"Mom, in the last two weeks, I've met people that make Dora Farr look like Mother Teresa. I'll be back real soon."

"All right." She reluctantly handed me her car keys.

When I got to the Goddards' house, I drove past without stopping. Despite what I'd told Mom, I had no wish to run into Mrs. Farr. It puzzled me that there weren't any cars in the driveway. It was Saturday—Mrs. Farr should have been there. I wondered if the plan to take Mr. Goddard to the nursing home and Mrs. Goddard to the Farr condo had been carried out.

I parked in the next block and waited until the rain shrank to a misty drizzle. Then I walked back to the house and peered in a garage window. The Goddards' massive black Lincoln was still sitting there gathering dust—Mr. Goddard couldn't drive anymore, of course, and Mrs. Goddard had never learned. I tried to imagine what it would be like going through life without being able to drive, but I couldn't.

The front door to the house was shut tight, and the street-side shades were drawn. I looked around for a FOR SALE sign but didn't see one. I walked down the side of the house to the backyard and garden and saw that the door to the potting shed was open. I peered in at the very moment Mrs. Goddard came out. Both of us jumped.

"Oh, my goodness, Jo!" she said, her hand pressed to her chest. "I almost had a stroke." Then she realized what she'd said, and added, "Not like Ralph's, of course."

"How are you, Mrs. Goddard?"

"I'm just fine. How are you? I like your hair. Come in, you're getting wet." She backed into the shed and I went in. I was hit by the earthy smell of plants and loam.

"Are you home alone?" I asked.

"Yes," she said. "Dora took Ralph to the dentist."

"So there hasn't been an opening for him at Box Elder?"

"It looks like he won't be going there after all. I took your advice and called a lawyer. He's in the process of getting our power-of-attorney back."

"Congratulations, Mrs. Goddard. How's your daughter taking it?"

"Dora's not happy, but what can she do? As soon as I can, I'm planning to hire a second aide for a few hours in the evening so she won't have to be over here all the time. It'll still be cheaper than the nursing home. Maybe we'll have to go someday, but I'm going to put it off as long as I can."

"I'm so glad for you. So it looks like you'll be here to put in your garden this spring. What have you got started?" I surveyed the sprouted seeds and plants in pots of all sizes that covered the shelves and floor of the glassed-in half of the shed.

A plant in one of the pots on the floor looked familiar. I looked closer. "Is that the azalea I gave you? What happened to it?" Last time I'd seen it, it had been in its original green plastic pot on the kitchen windowsill, where it could get the morning sun. Now it sat in the middle of a gigantic redwood container, looking like a little kid in a big bathtub. Unfortunately, it was dying—the leaves were turning yellow, and several of them were lying under it on the dirt.

"I repotted it," she said. "It's not doing too well, is it?"

"No, it isn't. Wasn't that the redwood pot your ficus was in?" The ficus, or weeping fig tree, had been her pride and joy. It sat in the front entryway and was taller than the door itself.

"Yes, that's the pot," she said. "I never liked that old ficus. I threw it out."

"You threw it *out*?"

Mrs. Goddard placed her body between the azalea and me. "Why don't you come in the house, Jo? I'll make you a cup of nice hot tea."

"In a minute." I edged around her, knelt down, and surveyed the azalea. "Maybe it's not getting enough water," I said, sticking my finger in the potting soil. About an inch down, my hand hit something hard. I dug it out. It was a 1916-D Mercury dime.

I looked up at Mrs. Goddard. "Look what I found in the dirt," I said, handing her the coin.

"Really?" she said, staring at it as if she'd never seen it before. "My goodness, how'd that get in there?" She took it and dropped it in her jacket pocket.

I stuck my finger in the dirt again. This time I hit the corner of a plastic bag. I dug around it and pulled it out. It was a Ziplock, probably quart-size, filled with sparkly jewelry. "Look at this!" I said. "How do you suppose *this* got in there?"

Mrs. Goddard examined her shoes for a long time. Finally she said, "Okay, Jo, I was the one who robbed the safe."

"You robbed your own safe? Why?"

"I had to. Remember when we were talking that day, and I said that losing control over your money was like losing your life, or something like that?"

"I remember."

"Well, after I said that, things got even worse. You probably don't know, but Ralph and I were in the habit of keeping quite a bit of cash in the safe in case of emergency."

"I *do* know. I found out when the police were grilling me."

Her cheeks turned red. "Oh, Jo, I'm so sorry. It must have been awful for you. You don't know how many sleepless nights I've had over this. Did you get another job?"

"No."

"Oh, dear. Well, anyway, one day I caught Dora in the closet with the safe open, helping herself to some of our money. I confronted her, and she said she had the right to take whatever she wanted, since she had power-of-attorney. She said neither Ralph nor I was capable of handing our own affairs."

"That's not true," I said.

"I know! I was furious. One evening she left early because she and Jim had a social engagement. When Ralph was sound asleep, I opened the safe and took everything out of it. First I tried to bury it in the dirt under the ficus, but there wasn't enough room—there were too many roots. So I ended up bringing everything out here and pulling the ficus out of the pot. I put the bags of money and stuff in, added some dirt, and planted the azalea."

"How'd you get the ficus out of the house? That was a big tree."

"The pot has wheels. I just tilted it back and rolled it out. Getting it over the sill of the sliding-glass door was the hardest part. When I got it out here, I cut the ficus up with the pruning shears. What a mess I made!"

"Didn't the neighbors see you?"

"Oh, no, it was quite dark by then."

What a picture! I could just see this tiny woman steering this pot with the huge tree in it through the house, over the sill, and across the yard in the dead of night.

"So the coins and cash are in the pot, and the rest of the stuff from the safe too?

"It's all in there. I put it in bags to protect it from the damp. But I was still afraid to water the azalea too much, poor thing."

"Didn't Mrs. Farr notice the missing ficus?" She'd sure noticed everything *I* did.

"No. She comes and goes through the kitchen door. Anyway, she's never cared about plants or gardening or anything like that."

"And Mr. Goddard didn't miss his coin collection?"

"Luckily he hasn't asked to see it. If he had, I guess I would have run out here and dug it up. Actually, I thought about telling him what I'd done, but that might have made him an accessory. We could have both ended up in jail."

"The two of you could have shared my cell," I said.

"I would never have let them incarcerate you, Jo. If that had happened, I would have confessed. Nevertheless, I did get you in a lot of trouble, and I'm terribly sorry for it. I need to come clean to the police, for your sake and mine."

"That's a very good idea," I said.

"Do you think it will hurt my case for voiding the power-of-attorney? I'm sure Dora will say this proves beyond a doubt that I'm incapable of handling my own affairs."

"I suppose she might." The thought didn't please me at all. I wanted my name cleared, but I didn't want the process to help Dora Farr in any way, shape, or form. Talk about your mixed emotions. "Mrs. Goddard," I said, "how long does your lawyer think it will be before the power-of-attorney will be voided?"

"He didn't say. Not too long, I hope."

"Well, look," I said. "I have to go to Florida for a while, and maybe South Carolina, so I'm going to make you a deal. If I let it go for now, will you promise to go to the police the minute the order is voided?"

Mrs. Goddard looked tremendously relieved. "Oh, yes, I promise, Jo. In fact, I'll sit down this minute and write a confession, so you have something to show them in case I die. I'm no spring chicken."

"Aren't you afraid I'll take the confession directly to the police?"

"Why, no, Jo. I trust you."

Her saying that could have made it all worth it, but it didn't.

I pushed the plastic bag down in the dirt and smoothed it over, and we went inside the house. While I washed my hands at the kitchen sink, she put on water for tea. Then she sat at the table and wrote up a statement describing what she had done.

Later, as I was driving out of the subdivision, I passed Mrs. Farr's car going in the opposite direction. I had a big smile ready, but she didn't look my way.

Before going home, I stopped to have a burger at Marlo's Diner, where my buddy Weezie was manager. When she finished guffawing at my hair, she said, "Good gravy, Jo, what have you been up to?" We sat down in a booth and I told her, including a lot of the details I'd left out of Mom and Rose's version.

Weezie had to get up a few times to put out fires—figuratively speaking—but she hurried right back, saying, "And then what happened?"

Sunday was a hard day. Mom and Rose got more and more nervous by the hour. ...Okay, I did too. None of us had slept very well.

Rose baked a ham, but not much of it got eaten. By 3 in the afternoon, we decided we had to get out of the house. It was a chilly day with temperatures in the 40s, but at least it had stopped raining. We bundled up and went for a brisk walk in Delaware Park. By the time we got home I had settled down enough to microwave some popcorn and watch a couple of reruns of *Law & Order*. Usually these kinds of shows served to put my own troubles in perspective, but tonight I could identify.

20

I was up early Monday morning pacing the floor and planning what I was going to say to Mr. Phipps. I promised Mom I'd call him at 9 on the dot and explain why I was back in Buffalo and his mother was still in Florida. When I got him on the line, I apologized all over the place. Luckily he was fond of Mom and Rose, and agreed that concern for their safety was a good enough reason for my return to Buffalo.

"I'm still planning to go to Tampa," I told him. "Hopefully Paul Redmun will show his face in the next couple of days and they'll arrest him. As soon as that happens, I'll be on my way."

"Well, Jo," he said, "how about this—if you haven't left by next Saturday, I'll hop a plane and go to Tampa myself. And in that case, I'll want my $300 back that I fronted you for expenses."

"Deal," I told him, watching the thousand dollars sprout wings and fly into the ether. Maybe at some point I wouldn't need it, but I'd found in my limited experience that estates took a long time to close.

Mom had ridden to work with Rose, leaving her car so I could pick up Great-aunt Concetta at 1:30 and take her shopping for underwear. She'd been asking everybody in the family, and they'd all suddenly got very busy. A few left town.

Around noon, as I was getting out of the shower, the phone rang. Since we'd agreed not to pick up until we knew who was calling, I threw on my robe and ran downstairs to the answering machine. My wet foot slid on one of the polished wood steps, and I almost fell and broke my neck. I reached the kitchen just in time to hear Rose's voice tell the machine, "...so let me know if you hear from her."

I grabbed up the receiver. "Let you know if I hear from who?"

"Your mother."

"Isn't she at school?"

"We can't find her. Gerald said she stopped answering the phone half an hour ago. He thought she'd probably gone to the lady's room, but she's not there."

"Maybe she went out for lunch with somebody."

"Without telling me? She wouldn't do that."

"You're right," I said. "Do you think I should come help look for her? I could cancel Great-aunt Concetta," I said hopefully.

"No, we've got the kids mobilized. Just call if you hear."

"And call if *you* hear. You've got me worried."

I went back upstairs and got dressed. The phone rang just as I was bending over to tie my sneakers. I had a moment of indecision. Should I take my shoes off again and take the chance of my socks slipping on the steps, thereby breaking my neck? Or should I leave the shoes on but untied, and take the chance of tripping over the laces on the steps, thereby breaking my neck? By then the phone was on its third ring. *To hell with it*, thought; I kept my shoes on and ran down the stairs. I picked up the extension. "Hello?"

"Is that you, Jo? This is your dear friend Charity's brother."

I couldn't think of anything to say.

"Jo," he said, "are you there? I thought you might like to join us, Mama and me."

"My mother's with you? Let me talk to her."

"I'm sorry, she can't talk right now. But doesn't she look pretty today in her purple polka-dot blouse?"

He was right. That's what Mom had been wearing this morning when she left for work. "What do you want me to do?" I asked.

"All I need is your signature on a piece of paper. Then you can have Mama back, and I can have what you stole from me. What do you think about that? "

"No problem. I'm home. Come on over."

"I don't think so. *You* come over."

"Where?"

"Go to that park where you took the nice walk yesterday. Park in the same lot. If you bring someone with you or if police of any kind show up, the deal's off and you can say bye-bye to Mama."

After hanging up, I thought about calling the detective who'd phoned us Sunday morning, but I couldn't do it. I'd get Mom back and *then* I'd call.

I tied my shoes and rummaged through the stuff in my desk drawer until I found the small jackknife Weezie had given me two Christmases ago. It was the closest thing to a weapon I owned. Sticking it in my Levi's pocket, I threw on a sweatshirt, grabbed the car keys from the hook by the door, and took off.

There was a ton of traffic, so it took me the better part of five minutes to drive to the park. Before stopping, I cruised past the vehicles already in the lot: two compact cars, a pickup with a fiberglass cap, and a rusty old Chevy cargo van. I was looking for out-of-state license plates and familiar heads, but the plates were all New York and no heads were in sight, so I backed into a space and waited.

A Taurus wagon drove in and parked near me. A woman jumped out and sprang two kids from car seats. She put one in a stroller and held the other's hand tightly as they hurried across the sparse spring grass. A yellow school van drove in and laboriously unloaded four kids in wheelchairs. A man carrying a brown bag and thermos got out of a Saturn and headed for the picnic area.

I thought about Paul sitting here yesterday afternoon watching Mom, Rose, and me pile out of Mom's car and, later, pile in again. Had he followed us as we walked, eavesdropping on our conversation? How creepy is that?

I couldn't stand it one more minute. I got out of the car and leaned against it. The sun was out and it was a warmish day, but I was shivering from the inside out. In a couple of minutes the Chevy cargo van pulled out of its parking space and drew to a stop in front of me. Paul Redmun was driving, but I didn't see Mom. He got out, leaving the motor idling and the driver's door open, and approached me. His clothes were the oddest combination, an unbuttoned bush jacket over a tank top and Spandex bike shorts. He'd accessorized the outfit with a wide brown belt and latex surgical gloves.

"Empty your pockets," he told me.

"Where's my mother?" I demanded, sounding a lot braver than I felt.

"I'll tell you where your mother is after you empty your pockets."

I brought out my wallet and comb and Mom's keys, setting them on the hood of the car.

"Is that it?" Paul asked.

I shrugged.

"Then I guess you're glad to see me." He stuck his hand in and came up with the jackknife. He laughed. "You call this a knife? *This* is a knife." He pulled back his jacket and showed me a big hunting knife in a tooled-leather holster that hung from his wide brown belt.

After slipping my jackknife in one of his pockets, he patted me down with his latex-gloved hands. Anyone watching would have thought we were indulging in safe-sex foreplay. When he was satisfied I wasn't armed, he said, "Mama's in the backseat." He crossed to the passenger side of the van, opened the door, and climbed in.

I grabbed my stuff from the hood and put it back in my pockets as I ran to the driver's side and looked in. Mom was there all right, sitting in the center of a cracked vinyl bench mounted behind the two front buckets. There was a length of silver duct tape across her mouth, and the brown eyes above it were big and scared. "Geez, Mom," I said, and stuck my head in farther. Her ankles were taped together and her arms were pulled sharply back, presumably held there with more duct tape.

Behind her, in the rear of the van, a bicycle was bungeed to holes in the wall braces. *Bike shorts and now a bike. Hmmm.*

"Get in. You're driving," Paul told me.

There had been a poster on the wall in the Box Elder employee lounge. Among other things it said if a woman is accosted, she should never get in the accoster's vehicle, even if the guy is armed. Once she gets in his vehicle, she's a goner. "No," I said. "Give me your paper. I'll sign it here."

"Get in," he said again and took a large cell phone from another holster on his belt. He turned and pointed the aerial of the phone at Mom, who started squirming and whimpering. "It's a stun gun," he said.

"The phone's a gun?" I asked. Mom nodded vigorously.

Paul made a *tsk* sound. "She didn't care for it, poor thing. When I think of all the time I spent searching the Internet for an attractive model."

"You told Charity you didn't have a computer," I said.

"I told Charity a lot of things. Are you gonna get in or what?" He moved the phone/gun nearer Mom's shin.

Unfortunately, the poster in the employee lounge hadn't mentioned what to do if your mother is already in the vehicle and being threatened with severe pain. I got in and sat behind the wheel.

"Shut the door," he said.

I reluctantly did.

Paul turned forward but kept his left arm between the seats, pointing the stun gun at Mom. Consulting a hand-drawn map that was taped to the dash, he said, "Take Delaware Avenue north."

I put the van and my brain in gear and drove out of the parking lot. Should I run into a tree? No, if I didn't kill Paul or render him unconscious, he could still do us a lot of damage.

Should I drive to a police station and lay on the horn? No, same danger.

My best bet, I decided, was to lightly run into a police car. That would attract the policeman's immediate attention, and he could nab Paul on the spot. He might nab me too, in the process, but Mom would sort it out for them when they removed her duct tape. I knew there were cops on Delaware Avenue—I'd gotten my share of tickets there.

With his unarmed hand, Paul took a cigarette out of a pack of Marlboros and lit it, placing the box on the dash.

"Would you mind not smoking?" I said. "It makes me cough."

"Why would I care if you cough?" Smoke furled out of his mouth as he spoke. He flicked ashes on the floor with a white-latex finger.

"Fine," I said, rolling down the window.

He pointed the stun gun at Mom. "Close that!"

I rolled it back up. "How long should I stay on Delaware?" I asked.

He looked at his map again. "We don't make any turns until River Road, and then we take a right."

"That's the way to Niagara Falls."

"Bingo! Everybody should see Niagara Falls before they die, don't you think?" He chuckled. I didn't ask what was funny.

"Why don't we go across Grand Island?" I said. "It's faster." I figured if I didn't see a police car to run into, I could lightly run into the toll booth at the entrance to the bridge.

"Just stay on Delaware," he said.

Damn.

We hit green lights at Hertel and Kenmore, something that never happens when you want it to. I noticed the van was hard to steer. "The wheel keeps pulling to the right. Is the tire going flat?" I asked.

"I don't know what's causing that," Paul said. "I bought it the other day from a guy who seemed really eager to sell. That may be why."

"You bought this van just the other day? How'd you get plates already?"

"I borrowed them."

"Somebody lent you their license plates?"

"Sure, but they wouldn't part with their insurance papers, so drive carefully."

Duh, Jo, he stole them. Hoping some civic-minded driver would call the police and give them the plate number, I started driving in a manner that Deputy Conway might have called extreme wavering.

"What the hell?" Paul said.

"It's the steering. It's getting worse. I can hardly control it."

"Cut that out right now." The hand that was holding the stun gun had drifted to the front, but he stuck it between the seats again.

I stopped wavering and tried to get on his good side with friendly chatter. "Does that gun work as a cell phone too?"

"No," he said tersely but not unsociably, so I went on.

"You know, Paul, I'm surprised you've never been to Niagara Falls. Charity told me she went there with your folks a couple of years ago."

"Charity liked to spend time with our parents. I found them tedious."

I nodded. "Parents can be that way sometimes." There was a muffled *humph* from the backseat, so I added, "At least that's what I've heard."

Just ahead was the ramp to Highway 290. "Are you sure you don't want to take 290 across Grand Island?" I asked Paul. "I'll pay the toll."

"Yeah, I bet you will. Stay on Delaware."

"All right. But we'll want to go over to the Canadian side of the falls when we get there. They have some amazing gardens." *And I can lightly run into a customs booth.*

"The U.S. side will be fine," he said.

Double damn. As long as we were chatting, I figured I might as well ask him something I really wanted to know. "Tell me about Charity's marriage."

"Didn't she tell you?"

"She started to, but we got interrupted." I tried to see down the side streets by moving only my eyes. Where were the cops today?

"It was nothing, really," Paul said. "She met this guy Brad when she was a junior in college and married him. He was an artist, a pretty good one too, but he was lazy. After they were married and living on her income, he gave up painting and took up blackjack. My father had the marriage annulled."

Well, that was a lot less interesting than I'd hoped. "After your folks died, then, you were the only family Charity had left?"

"That's right. And now that she's dead, there's only me. Little Paul. Last of the rollicking Redmuns." He was downright cheerful.

"So did you kill her?" I asked. A strangled gasp came from the back. Mom was right, it was a brassy question. But it was a sure way to find out for sure if he was planning to do away with us after I signed his paper. If he answered truthfully, I'd know we were goners.

"Of course I did," he said.

Tears gathered in the corners of my eyes. *Bad time to cry, Jo. Keep talking.* "Tell me about it," I said. "So you got the gas station guy in Tucson to tell you where Charity and I were headed?"

"You know about that? The jerk couldn't stop talking about her. He had a giant crush."

"Why wouldn't he? She was a beautiful, smart woman. And she loved you a lot, Paul. She was going to set up a trust for you."

"A trust, big deal. I'm past the allowance stage. I've got expenses."

Like bankrolling a boot camp? "Then you drove to Big Bear Butte Spa to find us?"

"Yeah, but you weren't there. Which way did you go, through Utah? I'd just decided the guy at the gas station had screwed me when the ByVista drove in and you and Charity got out and skipped down the path to the pool."

"You were watching? Where were you?"

"Parked over by a vacant cabin."

"Cripes, why didn't we look around better?"

"You think it would have made any difference? I was going to get her one way or another."

When I heard that, an ocean of guilt rolled off my back. He was right. There was nothing in the world I could have done to keep Charity alive. Not a thing. Once he'd made up his mind, she was *fucking dead.* And now I knew who killed her, for all the good it would do. He was going to kill us too. What's that old saying? *Dead men tell no tales?* Sexist, but true.

"You know," he said, "that was a pretty nice pool they had at that spa. Too bad I didn't have time for a soak."

I had to ask. "Did you come down to the pool while we were in it?"

"Oh, yes. I was peeking over one of their pretty stone walls. And yes, I saw the kiss." He said it like it had capitals, "The Kiss." He looked back at Mom. "Hey, Mama, did you know your daughter's a flaming dyke?"

Mom grunted something that sounded like "Up yours."

Paul turned back to me. "After that, I went back to the campground, wondering how I was going to get Charity away from you long enough to kill her. But luckily would have it, she came back alone. I simply waited until she went in the motor home, then I paid her a little visit and took her out. Of course, if I'd known you'd talked her into leaving you the whole estate, I'd have hung around and taken you out too."

I started to defend myself about the will. Then I decided I didn't give a rat's ass what he thought. "Is that why you had your folks murdered, for the money?" I asked him.

"How do you know about that?"

"Why did you do it, Paul? Didn't you know they'd disinherited you?"

"You think they sent me an engraved notice?" he said. "They didn't even send a Christmas card. Fucking hypocrites. It was perfectly fine for my father to be morally corrupt, but let me get in a little trouble, and I'm dumped like a piece of garbage." He took another cigarette from the box and lit it.

"What do you mean? How was your father morally corrupt?"

"Do you know how many indigent people he displaced to build his upscale condos and hotels? Thousands. And his beloved art collection was 50 percent contraband, maybe more."

"Where did he keep it?" I asked.

"The art collection? What do you care? It's never going to be yours."

"I'm curious. You wouldn't exactly hang stolen paintings in your living room."

"Yeah, you would, if it was a living room nobody knew you had."

"It's in one of his buildings!"

"Smart girl! But he was smarter. You'd never find it."

Maybe I couldn't, but I was sure Interpol could, if by some miracle I lived to tell them. "Paul, did Charity deal in stolen art?"

"Miss Goody Two-shoes, are you kidding? She kept asking Dad to get rid of it, return it to where it belonged. The only way I could get her to sell any of it was to tell her I was in danger of being killed."

"Did her money go to the militia, then?"

"You've been doing some serious snooping into my affairs, haven't you? Of course that's where it went. We're going to be doing some real good there."

"What kind of good?"

"We're going to save America."

"From who?" I asked.

"The Mexicans. Don't you know what's happening? Mexico is trying to get back the land they lost in the Mexican-American War. They've already sent troops over."

I stared at him. "Troops?" It was just like Edwina had told me—he really believed it.

"Yes, troops. Keep your eyes on the road."

"So that's what the militia is training people for, the next Mexican-American War?"

"For that and for changing things that need to be changed. That's why I need my inheritance. Now shut up."

"Paul, I'll give you the inheritance. I *want* to give it to you. How about I pull over? You let my mother go, and I'll put my signature on whatever you want."

"I said shut up." He took the hunting knife from its holster and held it on his lap. The blade glinted in the sunlight.

We stopped at a red light, and a cement truck pulled up beside us. The guy in the passenger seat winked. I gave him a dirty look and turned away. *Wait a minute, Jo. He's sitting high enough to see the knife, and maybe even Mom!* I looked at the guy obliquely, hoping Paul wouldn't notice. "Help," I mouthed, shifting my eyeballs to the back a couple of times. The guy brightened and puckered up. "Help us," I mouthed. "Call the police!" I did the eye-shift thing again. He waved and blew me a kiss. The light turned green.

Once we hit River Road, it didn't take long to get to the town of Niagara Falls. Paul directed me to a street that paralleled the river. We ended up on a service road between two bridges to Goat Island, just above the falls. He told me to pull onto the grass by the first bridge and drive slowly to the edge of the bank, which was sharply slanted toward the river.

I stopped a couple of feet before the edge, but he made me inch up until the front of the van was even with the end of the grass. All I could see ahead of us was wildly thrashing water. With nothing before it but a sheer drop, the river was drunk with freedom. It gushed and churned, foamed and eddied. We were past the famous "point of no return." Anything entering the water here would be over the falls in seconds.

"Good," Paul said. "Now put it in park, pull the emergency brake, and turn off the engine." I hoped the emergency brake was in better shape than the steering mechanism.

Paul took a folded paper and a pen from a pocket and handed them to me. "Sign it," he said.

I unfolded the paper. It was a simple will, leaving everything I owned to "my dear friend Paul Redmun." Bracing the paper against the center of the steering wheel, I signed and dated it. "Do you want Mom to witness it?" I asked.

"I've got lots of witnesses." He grabbed the will from my hand and stuck it back in his pocket. "Now get out, go around back, and open the door."

"Let Mom out first," I said.

"No. Hurry up, get out."

I gripped the wheel. "I won't go without Mom."

Paul picked up the knife and stuck the point of it in the back of my right hand. He slowly rotated it a half turn. Bright red blood poured out. I heard Mom fighting sobs. I was afraid she might suffocate, so I said, "It's okay, Mom. It doesn't hurt."

I jumped out of the van and ran around back. As I opened the double doors, Paul turned in his seat and watched. "Take the bike over by the bridge, and be quick about it. Then come back." My hands were shaking, so it took me a while to get the bungee cords unhooked. "Get a move on!" he said angrily.

I finally got the bike out and wheeled it to the bridge, looking around for tourists, workers, anybody who might help. I saw a few people, but they were blocks away. If Mom hadn't been in the van, I would have screamed bloody murder. Actually, if Mom hadn't been in the van, I would have jumped on the bike and taken my chances. That's why Mom was in the van, of course. While positioning the kickstand, I made sure to bleed all over the frame for the CSI forces.

As I ran back I considered putting the van in neutral and releasing the emergency brake. Gravity would quickly pull us over the edge, but I'd be taking Paul with us. He wouldn't have time to roll out, as I was sure he was planning to do after disabling me in one way or another. By the time I climbed in the driver's seat, however, I'd rejected the idea. *If Mom and I have to die, let our deaths be at Paul's hand, not mine.*

At the moment, Paul's hand was busy propping open the passenger-side door. I saw an opportunity to buy time—I reached over and knocked his box of cigarettes off the dash. The cigarettes spilled out as they fell. "Fuck," he said when he saw them all over the floor. "How'd that happen?"

"I don't know," I said. "Here, let me help." I bent and reached for the nearest cigarette.

"Get up," he said. "Let's get this show on the road. Fasten your seat belt and start the engine, then put it in gear and take off the emergency brake." As I did those things, he started picking up cigarettes and putting them back in the pack.

I looked back to tell Mom I loved her and to apologize for getting her into this mess. To my amazement, she was sitting there wildly jerking her head. First I thought she'd flipped from stress, and then it occurred to me that she was trying to communicate. Unlike the Romeo in the cement truck, I snapped to attention.

It appeared the jerks were aimed at Paul. "What about him?" I mouthed. She narrowed her eyes, thrust her duct-taped legs a few inches in the air, and kicked. I nodded and turned back around.

Paul picked up the last cigarette and stuck it behind his ear. "Okay then," he said. "Push up your sleeve."

As I pushed my sweatshirt up to my elbow, I wondered what a stun gun hit felt like. Was it an electric shock, or more like a burn? If Mom's idea didn't work, I'd soon find out. Paul had the gun aimed at my forearm and was closing in. All that was keeping us from rolling over the cliff was the pressure of my foot on the brake, and that foot was about to go limp.

I looked up at the rearview mirror and said, "Where'd Mom go?"

Paul turned his head to look, and a pair of sensible heels shot between the seats and smashed him full in the face. I pushed him away, and at the same time pulled the steering wheel sharply to the left, taking my foot off the brake. The right front tire dropped partway over the edge and spun. We hung there for an instant, then the tire caught and the van jerked to the left. Paul rolled out of his gaping doorway and disappeared. I turned on to the street and the door slammed shut.

I pushed the accelerator to the floor and didn't slow down until I saw a crowd of people, at which point I squealed to a stop and laid on the horn. While I sobbed wildly, someone called 911 while someone else untaped Mom. An ambulance took us to the emergency room, where they dressed my hand and Mom's stunned arm, and we spent the rest of the day at the police station being debriefed.

When we got home I called Edwina in Tucson and told her what had happened, including what Paul told me about the hidden art. She said she'd pass the information on and that she was tremendously glad I was alive and kicking. I said I didn't know about kicking. Maybe I'd kick tomorrow.

Tuesday, Mom and I stayed home to rest and recuperate and ended up serving coffee to a couple dozen relatives and neighbors. They were impressed with what they'd read in the morning paper about my "heroism." Our next-door neighbor said she'd told her granddaughters she wanted them to grow up to be just like me. I said Mom was the one who had come up with the idea. "Still," she said.

My cousin Kimmy showed up with her mother and two sisters. She took me aside and apologized for not speaking to me after I saw her husband flirting in the Amherst restaurant. She said they were broken up again after he'd had an affair with a coworker last fall. I nodded solemnly and walked away. From now on Kimmy was on her own.

Mom still felt shaky on Wednesday, so she stayed home from work again, and so did Rose because she didn't want Mom to be alone while I took Great-aunt Concetta, who was really steamed that I hadn't shown up Monday to help her buy underwear.

When I got back home, Mom told me the police had called to say they'd fished Paul Redmun's body out of the Niagara River below the falls. I took my first deep breath in a long while. He was a dangerous man and I was glad he was dead.

"Just think, Jo," Mom said, "if he had gotten away with it, he would have inherited not only his sister's estate, but yours too."

"Yeah, I'm sure he wanted my DVDs."

"He would have gotten everything I've left to you in *my* will too, wouldn't he? Like my half of the house?"

"Oh, my God," Rose said, "he could have ended up being my housemate!"

"It would have served him right," Mom said.

Rose gave her a smack on her good arm. I told them to behave themselves, and that in any case, the will hadn't been legal. I'd signed it "Josefina Zucchini."

"Who's that?" Mom said.

"Exactly," I told her.

21

On Thursday morning I flew to Atlanta and caught a bus to Parsee. It dropped me off at a gas station next door to the Georgia's Best Motel. I asked the woman at the counter if there was a taxi in town.

"Yes," she said, "one and only one," which may have explained why it took 45 minutes for it to come get me. When I asked the driver to take me to Rip's Garage, he told me he was Rip's cousin.

"Small world," I said.

"Small town," he said.

My Toyota was out grazing in the back lot of the garage, keeping the two wrecked pickups company. The bill was more than $2,000, which I paid with Mom's credit card. Before leaving home, I'd called the bank about my Visa balance and was told it was only 50 bucks from being maxed out. Mom said since I had such great prospects I could use her card, and she'd only charge me 300% interest per day on the unpaid balance.

Rip didn't say much. Maybe he was still sore I'd spoiled his cross-country jaunt with Charity. After I paid, he brought my truck up front and said "Good luck." His tone made it sound more like "Good riddance."

I thought about stopping at the Parsee Home-Cook Diner for a burger, but the thought of seeing Charity's spot without Charity in it made me lose my appetite. *Oh, Charity, Charity!* I turned the Toyota's nose toward Tampa.

It felt great to be behind my own wheel again. Rip seemed to have done a fine job on the repair; I'd have to give him that. The engine just hummed along. Suddenly I realized in some uncertain future I'd have to choose between my little Toyota with a cracked grill and reconditioned engine and the late-model fire-engine-red tricked-out Ford Ranger Supercab. I worried about that for several miles before realizing I could probably afford to keep them both.

On the other hand, our driveway was already full of vehicles, and the spaces on the street were pretty much spoken for by the neighbors. So I spent the next several miles worrying about where I was going to park the two of them. It's a good thing I didn't want to keep the ByVista.

In the well behind the seat I found the bag with my maps and directions to Mrs. Phipps's house. It was in a suburb on the northeast side of Tampa, quite a ways from any substantial body of water. I was disappointed. I'd been on a trip to the beach for the better part of three weeks and had yet to see an actual beach.

Balmy Palm Court was a short street of neat little houses that were so white my Ray-Ban knockoffs couldn't handle it. I squinted at the house numbers, looking for 313. There were no people on the sidewalks, no bikes in the driveways, no toys on the lawns. The only sound I heard through my open window was the hum of air conditioners.

The houses on either side of 313 were already closed for the summer. Shutters of vinyl and corrugated metal were drawn across every orifice, converting them from homes into fortresses.

Mrs. Phipps's shutters were still open, but the Venetian blinds were firmly closed, giving it the same barricaded look.

I parked in front, walked down the sidewalk, and rang the bell. When no one answered, I went around to the carport, where a dark red LeSabre was parked. It was in marvelous shape for its age; back home, a car that old would have been half rust. For some reason it had been pulled so close to the house I had to sidle to the door.

I didn't see a doorbell by the frame, so I knocked. When there was no response, I yanked my arm back to give the door a great rap and smashed my funny bone on the LeSabre's window post. When Mrs. Phipps opened the door, I was madly massaging my elbow, my face contorted in pain.

"Jo Jacuzzo," she said. "I'd know you anywhere."

I wouldn't have known her at all. When I was a kid mowing her lawn, she'd been a tall stocky woman with iron-gray hair pulled back in a bun. She'd looked like the farmer's wife in my book of nursery rhymes, the one who was chasing the blind mice with a gigantic carving knife.

She looked better now. Her hair was still in a bun, but instead of iron-gray it was the soft blue of skim milk. Wispy strands had escaped, gently framing her face. Her features were further softened by legions of wrinkles, and she had shrunk— she didn't look to be much taller than I was. I wondered if she had mellowed.

"How are you, Mrs. Phipps?" I asked.

"I'd be a lot better if I didn't have to run around answering doors. By the way, there's one in back you missed."

"Sorry." *So much for mellowing.*

"Where've you been, anyway?" she said. "My plane ticket to Buffalo was for a week ago. I'll have to get Gerald to buy me another one. He's not going to be happy."

"I'll buy you another plane ticket, Mrs. Phipps."

"You will?" She smiled. It was the first time I'd ever seen her smile. "Come on in, then. I don't need to be cooling off the whole outdoors." She stood aside.

I stepped in, and that about was as far as I could go. I think I was in a kitchen, but it was hard to tell. Every surface was covered with boxes, bags, and stacks of newspapers. The floor was covered too, with a narrow path down the middle for walking.

"What's all this stuff?" I asked.

"What do you mean, 'stuff'? These are my things, and I don't want you touching them, hear? The guest bedroom's that way." She pointed down a hallway to our left.

Mincing like a tightrope walker, I took the path in that direction. On the way, I looked in the bathroom door. Like the kitchen, it had stuff—excuse me, *things*—on the floor, the back of the toilet, and around the sink. I stuck my head in farther— yep, the bathtub was full too.

I continued to a door at the end of the hall and opened it. The guest bedroom had not been spared. Stacks of newspapers, books, and magazines covered the tops of two dressers, the bedside stand, and the bed. I wouldn't want for something to read, anyway.

I cleared a space on the bed, sat down, and buried my face in my hands. Packing Mrs. Phipps was going to be a bigger job than I'd expected.